SETON RAX & COMPANY

A Chronicle of Umiat and Kenai

by

Elliot Symonds

authorHOUSE®

AuthorHouse™ UK Ltd.
500 Avebury Boulevard
Central Milton Keynes, MK9 2BE
www.authorhouse.co.uk
Phone: 08001974150

© 2008 Elliot Symonds. All rights reserved.

No part of this book may be reproduced, stored in a retrieval system, or transmitted by any means without the written permission of the author.

First published by AuthorHouse 10/20/2008

ISBN: 978-1-4389-1833-4 (sc)

Printed in the United States of America
Bloomington, Indiana

This book is printed on acid-free paper.

Also by Elliot Symonds
in 'The Chronicles of Umiat and Kenai'

'Tumbletick & Company'

Seton Rax & Company' is dedicated to my sons, Edward and William.

The work is also dedicated to Max Ray, maritime advisor, motivator and friend.

Your words of encouragement have come at crucial times and I thank you for them..I want to acknowledge Lemmy, Mikkey Dee and Philip Campbell. You are the soundtrack of Umiat and Kenai. Hammered, Track 11. Classic. Is-Is is a big fan too.

© Paul Beevis 2007

Chapter Zeroth

Seton Rax, hunkered down on his haunches and overlooked the fertile grasslands of the Noatak plains, his ancestral home. The barbarian felt happiness well up inside him as he took in the view. Descending from the Schwatka Mountains the air was beginning to warm as the sun, in the far northwest of Umiat, shone down. He chewed a large chunk of dried meat with a decorum rare in most barbarians. Although he used his hands and teeth to rip the preserved elk flesh, he did not open his mouth, that much, as he ate.

The crossing of the well trodden passes had not been too arduous. Seton Rax had ensured he was well equipped for his lone journey all the way from Rhyell. He was not going to make the same mistakes in kitting himself out as he had done on his recent sojourn to Kenai. Therefore the muscled barbarian was well wrapped in furs. He also still had the death black hooded cloak over his bulky frame. It was a trophy from his last adventure and a cause of remembrance, which he felt he would never discard.

Seton Rax still had a good four miles to walk before he would reach the flat grasslands and their migrating herds of elk. All around him was grey granite now, bulky boulders and lesser peaks. Behind him the towering menace of Noatak was obscured by mist and clouds. Seton laughed to himself quietly as he thought of his new friends who savoured the whiskey distilled on those heights by dedicated and obsessed monks, prepared to inhabit cold stone monasteries and craft the purest of liquids over the course of many years. The waters from the ice capped mountain were pure and fresh and ensured a constant supply for the art of distillation. The warrior promised himself that when he was settled again, in the city of Sitka, he would make a trip one day to the Rinkabar monastery and buy a case of whiskey for a couple of those friends, Tumbletick and Percy Fenton.

Seton stood up and shouldered his pack after his brief respite. He was looking forward to setting himself up in some form of business with the ten thousand gold pieces he carried with him. Fortunately, the money was currently in the form of promissory notes. All he had to do to free the money into coins was to visit an office of the recently passed Lord Jackson of En'Tuk and his clerks would do the conversions.

While part of him wanted to return to a nomadic life with his people on the plains, the dominating voice in his head was to start a career with his new wealth and look forward to the luxuries that city life could afford him. While some of his dearest friends liked to savour a good whiskey, Seton Rax wanted the pleasure of quality ales found in a superb local public house close to his own home. While he had spent his youth as the second son of a warlord on the plains, the yearning for horseback, grazing elk and fighting off raiders no longer truly appealed. Yes, he was decided, he must give city living and running a business a go. As to what business he had finally decided. He had money now and that had allowed him the privilege of choice. His real skills were fighting and courtesy, both delivered to those that deserved it with aplomb and that meant only a few career options were open to him.

As the barbarian strode along the tracks he pulled down the hood of his cloak and shook free his long, dark brown, hair. It felt good to be warming up and he knew that by the end of the day he would be able to pack away his furs and yomp through the tall flowing grasses of the plains with his torso bare to the wind.

The major burden he bore was the large double handed and double headed battleaxe that he carried across his back. The heavy weapon could be snatched from a tough leather strapping when needed but so far his journey had only necessitated the blade to be used for the cutting of wood for nightly fires.

Further along the track Seton saw that a ravine was created as a stretch of granite rose on both sides of the descent. Whether this had once been a mighty watercourse or had been ground down through the rocks by countless generations of travellers, Seton was unsure. It was however a notorious place for ambush by vagrant thugs or the Hill People of Schwatka, who were often in territorial dispute with the nomadic barbarians of the plains, which was odd as neither culture could carry on their traditional way of life in the others geographical area. Seton pulled at the handle of his battleaxe and shifted the weight of the weapon so he could easily carry it in front of him. He was a lone traveller and although he was exceptionally dangerous, any potential attackers might not know that he was and would probably hunt in packs, considering a single warrior easy enough prey.

Seton entered the first part of the ravine and adjusted his senses for any threat from above, ahead and behind. An ambush could come from any or all three directions. The rock was bare and little stones of scree lay at the foot of the steep inclines on both sides. The barbarian waited to hear any loose rocks falling against the sides of the gulley but nothing shifted, all was silent but for the breeze and the distant sounds of birds circling above. He continued to tread a little slower and found that he now approached the centre of the cut through the rock. If it was to come, now would have been the time he would have expected an attack. Nothing happened. No attack, no threat, just a lone barbarian warrior making his way back to his homeland and an uncertain but exciting future. Seton breathed a little easier and picked up his pace to something short of a trot and made his way out of the ravine.

He shook his head free of the warrior's natural paranoia. He was now fundamentally in the foothills and tangibly close to the fertile plain. Plants had a hold here, trees fought with scraggy bushes for life in the loose soil. Above the ravine all was bare. Here hardy animals and flora ventured, not just man. Seton swung his battleaxe to his side. His massively strong arms were easily able to handle the weight individually. His thoughts turned to another old friend who had died defending his party of adventurers in Ende. Y'Bor Kaz had been so strong he could actually fight with two double handed warhammers, one to each hand. Seton wondered whether he could develop the skills to fight with two battleaxes at a time. That could make him famous and at least fearsomely formidable. All warriors really wanted a legend he mused and a barbarian who could take down his foes in that manner would be well remembered.

Seton heard a distant incongruous noise. He stood still and focused all his senses on listening. This was different to the slight rustle of wind in a bush or a falling stone behind him in the steep gully. Hooves, shod with metal, hitting the rock higher on the mountain. The barbarian heaved the battleaxe into both hands and awaited the approaching horse through the ravine.

The beast was chestnut brown and labouring heavily as it ran. White sweat lathered down its flanks and the rider was hunched over the neck. The shaft of an arrow was deep in the thigh of the man riding the horse, he wore a weather beaten broad brimmed hat, long coat of leather and was clutching at a peculiar looking rectangular case.

Seton Rax having taken in the sight felt the threat was not a great one.

"Woah," he shouted in an effort to rouse the rider and halt the horse.

The man straightened his back in the saddle and looked upon the barbarian blocking his path. He reined in the steed with a jerking tug on the reins and looked Seton Rax in the eye as the horse vehemently pranced and then presented its flank to the barbarian.

"I am on official business, do not block my path," the man scolded.

"I offer no threat to you sir," Seton replied. "It is just that you are injured and galloping to the plains. Perhaps I can offer help?"

"Just let me pass unhindered," the man said. "And if the brigands are still chasing me I would suggest that you distance yourself from me quickly."

"Brigands?"

"Yes. A pack of about six ambushed me a while back thinking I probably carry items of value. They only caught me with this arrow. I should be fine and will seek aid in Sitka. My delivery will be made."

"Do you think they are still chasing you then?" Seton asked.

"Probably," the man replied. "It is a sad state of affairs that such people are wandering the lands more and more these days. As I left Rhyell the people were celebrating the return of the Umiat Stone. It protects us from the attack of foreign enemies it is said. What or who will protect us from the filth that exists within our own midst?"

With that the man sharply kicked the side of his horse, it skitted around the barbarian and charged off, down towards the plains. Seton watched the rider depart briefly then turned his attention up towards the ravine and listened for the approach of any chasing thugs.

Seton did not have to wait long for the noise of approaching brigands. An uncouth raucous rampage came from above the ravine and Seton soon saw a group of a half dozen scabby looking individuals scrambling down the rocky slopes. They looked poorly fed and desperate. Armour was mismatched and patchy, the spoils of previous attacks handed out around the band of robbers.

'Enthusiastic bunch,' thought Seton Rax to himself. 'Thinking they can catch up with a man on horseback.'

Seton stood his ground and adjusted the battleaxe as the first of the wretches saw the lone barbarian and came to a skidding halt. The others soon responded too. They stopped their descent and bunched into a group, briefly conversed in whispers about the single warrior ahead of them and then charged.

They were only armed with a few clubs and a couple of swords and they obviously felt they could rush and overwhelm Seton Rax as a mugging band. The barbarian narrowed his eyes and took in the threat. They had probably chosen the correct method to assault him. If they had spread out as individuals he would have had no problem in despatching them. There was little time now, they were nearly upon the barbarian. Seton thought to himself how happy the brigands would be if they did defeat him and then found the notes worth ten thousand gold pieces in his pack. This encounter was not looking too promising. Seton decided that to run further down the hill and attempt to make it to a copse of trees would be beneficial. Here he might be able to break up their attack a little, with the trunks acting as restrictive barriers. As he turned and started to sprint down the slopes towards the trees he heard the attackers yell in rage and derision.

'Don't worry boys,' he thought. 'You'll have your chance to test your prowess.'

Seton made it to the tree line and swerved a couple of times as he ran to get into the depths of the small wood. He turned and awaited the band to make it to the copse as well. His plan worked and as soon as the enemy reached the trees in their tight knot they immediately took differing directions to make it around the trunks and were quickly dispersed into individual attackers. Seton smiled, they probably expected him to continue to run or attempt to hide in a scrubby little bush, a terrified lone traveller against their mighty horde.

The barbarian heaved the battleaxe into the air, directly above his head and stepped forward and to the right around a tree, carefully avoiding the low hanging branches he suddenly charged at a surprised brigand and brought the blade of the axe heavily down and into the skull of his foe. The eyes of the brigand were a staring, bulging delight as he died. Seton briefly wondered if they would fully explode forth from their sockets as the blow he had delivered was so vast. There was no time to examine the niceties of battle though, Seton lifted the axe and released it from being embedded in bone and brain and immediately looked for the next threat.

To his right a thug was approaching with a roughly hewn club, more of a dug out stump than a shaped weapon. The man went to jab Seton in the face with the wooden weapon. Seton stepped back and as the enemy over balanced, swung his axe in an underarm motion as if batting away a thrown ball rather than attacking a man. The axe's blade caught the foe right between his legs and bit deeply into his lower abdomen. It was a move favoured by the barbarian and he relished in the death throes of the man as the weight of the attack and the strength in Seton's arms meant the brigand was lifted from the floor and visibly began to split before him. There was no time to try and un-seam him completely though, so Seton shifted the axe blade a quarter turn and watched the body peel off it and slump to the mulch strewn ground of the copse.

Four men remained, having just seen two of their number nearly split in half in differing directions, they hesitated in their run. This was obviously not a lone and weary traveller with little skill or stomach to defend himself. Seton turned to their ranks and smiled at them through the sparse trunks, the light dappled on his superb physique and he began to walk towards the quartet of brigands.

"I think that perhaps you should give up thieving like your two friends," Seton said. "Laying in wait for an innocent traveller is one thing but to attack those on official business is really not on."

"Shut up you crack of nothing," the boldest spat back.

His companions did not look as sure of themselves and began to saunter away from the insulting bandit. The one with venom on his tongue and confidence in his mind held a sword that he had killed many men with before. He felt certain he could best a slow and clumsy barbarian with a battleaxe. So he charged at Seton Rax and was left alone by his fellows who were already now fully turned with their fleeing heels leaving clumps of loose earth scattering behind them.

With a knowing eye Seton noticed that the wretch looked under nourished and was very thin around the waist, so Seton heaved the battleaxe into a horizontal position. The brigand was yelling maniacally and waving his sword in the air. Seton Rax shook his head in despair at the clumsy nature of the assault. The muscled barbarian stood still looking as if he was to receive the charge and then with lightning speed sprang towards his foe when they were about two yards apart. As the enemy's sword began to sweep down, Seton struck with his battleaxe in an awesome flat arc, his body turned to the left and the blade of the brigand's sword slashed harmlessly behind Seton's head and down the length of his back as the blade of the axe thwacked into the stomach of the swordsman. Metal sliced through poor leather armour and into skin, it neatly separated muscle and guts and chopped through the spine beneath the lowest rib. Seton need not give any final tug to rid the blade of the body, the sweep from his arms and weight of the blade sliced the crafted axe head through the entire torso. The axe being double headed was efficient when hacking in either direction and in an attack like this not only did the blade that first hit do damage but the reverse of the other blade, being crescent shaped and sharp on the inside curve, acted like a cutting edge with the sweep of the blow. Seton was facing away from the man as the yelling war cry ceased. The barbarian listened for the differing sounds of body parts hitting the copse floor. The thumping torso, arms and head and the previously running legs and lower trunk of body made a slumping sound. The barbarian looked with professional interest at the final positions the two lumps of dead flesh took on the ground. He was impressed that he had made such a clean separation but was disappointed that the remains ended up about a foot apart, their bloodily oozing ends still connected by a thin strip of skin and muscle that had once been the flank of the brigand, just above his hips. Seton had hoped that he would achieve a completely clean brigand bisection.

With three dead bodies in the copse and the living brigands racing back to the mountains Seton Rax walked calmly from the tree line and turned to head down towards the plains of the extreme northwest of Umiat. He knew that the hewn corpses were unlikely to be found by anyone who would particularly care. He doubted that the cowards that had left their companions would return to bury them. These fresh kills were to be unexpected feasts for the carrion hunting beasts of the Schwatka Mountains.

Seton whistled a victory song to himself, an ancient and well known hymn of his nomadic tribe. Maintaining the elk may not have been his chosen career but he still held certain of the customs of his people dear. There was still about seventy miles of walking ahead of him when he reached the level grasslands. He would then follow the Noatak River all the way to the city of Sitka where he planned to set himself up in business. That being done he looked forward to finding a good local pub and making half hearted complaints over a pint of ale that the wilder parts of the land were no longer safe for travellers as he knew of where at least three had found their death in the wilderness recently.

Chorus Zeroth

Sitka sprawled before Seton Rax in wooden agonies of architecture. Steep peaked roofs spiking toward a cloudy, coastal sky. The city built by crab fishing, cod harvests and the trading of elk flesh. The city built by the tough immigrants who trawled the seas. The city built by the merchants who bartered with the nomadic barbarians and their migrating herds of elk. The city was rough and remote and its buildings reflected the sturdiness and realities of the men who had created it over the eons.

Sitka sat looking like a clotted scab of bumped and ruffled brown, hulking within its palisades. The spiked and wooden racking stretching off to the east and west for the drying of elk steaks and salted cod, took on an appearance of stitches, linking the land and the sea with the wound of Sitka in between.

Seton loved the city now that had haunted his dreams as a child. To travel there with his tribe once a year for the great market to the southwest of the palisades that surrounded Sitka meant crowds of people. Sitka meant meeting with other tribes. Sitka meant money from merchants. Sitka meant girls with new faces and blonder pigtails than the common faced wenches of his family tribe. Sitka meant ritualistic combat to strengthen the arms, hone the skills and attract the eye of discerning fathers looking to marry off daughters to the finest warriors.

Sitka was larger now than the city of Seton's youth. The perimeter wooden walls that enveloped it with spiked, rough hewn logs now nearly reached the vast elk market, empty for eleven months of the year. To the northwest the barricades touched the end of the sprawling racks of wooden frames, forty foot tall, laced with filleted cod drying in the ruthless, ravaging sea salt gales that buffeted the coast.

The walls had been expanded over the centuries in pulses of defensive pride. Inside the boundaries the buildings had a distinctively foreign feel, not the stone style of Umiat or Rampart. It was always wood for Sitka, always the steep roof and beams and small windows to protect the city folk from the constant storms and rains blowing in off the Sea of Umiat. Seton wondered what villainy and pleasures lay beneath those roofs and within the structures of Sitka and began to walk towards the city of his memories and dreams.

Chapter One

Seton Rax stood in the main atrium of the solitary stone building of Sitka. Lord Jackson of En'Tuk First National Banking Corporation was a mouthful of maniacal monumentalism but it was the only bank in this outpost of humanity and Seton had at least met the recently deceased owner, if only briefly. He had relished the sensation of skipping up the few stone steps and through the open main doors, passing a couple of armoured guards to the vast bank. This was a moment he had long been waiting for. Having so much money that he had to deposit it in a vault was a circumstance long yearned for. The bank was on the main square of Sitka and it hunkered with imposing might among the terraced four storey wooden structures on the other sides of the piazza. This was the glamorous heart of the city and the solitary area of any real grace. These buildings with their beams and diagonally latticed windows had the feeling of homely pleasures, of real ale in the finer pubs of town, of antiques shops and interesting afternoons browsing for gifts.

As he slowed to a saunter and entered the venerable institution, Seton looked around at the columns at the edge of the marble floor, the dark mahogany counters, carved with the images of trade, the domed ceiling of moulded concrete. To his barbarian sensibilities he understood that the stone walls made protecting the vaults easier but he wondered if using architecture as a negotiation statement really worked. He knew that as a customer with ten thousand gold pieces in promissory notes the visage of power and threat would quickly melt into obsequiousness and fawning. Still he could at least try and enjoy the process he was about to go through, the condemning eyes of underestimation of the clerk at the counter, his revealing of the money, the change in the tone of voice of the bank staff, the offers of drinks and a comfy chair in a private office as a more senior manager was summoned for the 'man of means' with the bare torso, muscles and furs.

It transpired exactly as Seton Rax had envisioned. The attractive female clerk changed her demeanour immediately upon the barbarian revealing the promissory notes and asking to open a new account with them, with this amount of money as only an initial deposit. Seton found himself quickly bustled and hustled out of the public areas of the bank, manicured hands were placed attentively on the small of his back as he was guided along corridors and through doors until he found that he was sitting in front of a very large wooden desk, with a green leather surface and gold studs around the edge. The man on the other side of the impressive looking piece of office furniture was anything but. He was quickly wiping away the remains of a lunch from his greasy mouth and short cropped moustache with a crumpled napkin. He proffered a food stained hand to the barbarian opposite him and only the demands of etiquette meant that Seton took it. The bank controller, for so the sign on the door had declared, had been eating a ground up piece of elk steak, mashed together with egg and onion, shaped into a squat disc and then quickly heated on extremely hot stones. He had placed it between two pieces of bread to make it easier to eat with his hands as he had not been expecting anyone to disturb his meal, otherwise he may have opted for some cutlery.

"The name's Abron Bose. I'm pleased to meet you Mr...?" the corpulent rounded man leered a smile towards the barbarian as the clerk who had guided Seton to this inner sanctum whispered in the bank controller's ear. "Ah, Mr. Rax. Yes, I'm very pleased to meet you. How can we be of assistance here at Lord Jackson of En'Tuk First National Banking Corporation?"

"I just wish to open an account and make a deposit before starting a new business in town," Seton replied.

"Ah a new business. With this amount of money you really could set up something very new and interesting. Yes, I've got a few ideas that you might find beneficial. Here at Jackson's we offer a very strong personal client relationship for the discerning businessman."

Seton then had to endure a half hour rant of insane ramblings from a man working for an organisation that felt it could advise others on the course they should take with their own investment. Abron Bose seemed particularly passionate about a concept he had devised himself and that was a florist and off license combined. Perfect for either women or men so they could purchase goods for themselves as well as their partners.

Seton found himself drifting off, surprised by the quality of the advice he was receiving. He had visions of the florist and off licence boarded up and letters being sent, signed Mr. Bose, expressing disappointment in recent business performance and that the company would have to be closed. Seton turned his focus back on to the whining man in front of him and wondered if Lord Jackson had known that such mediocrity existed within his organisation. At the extremes of the continent of Umiat it was obvious that the hierarchy of the bank did not pay that much attention to personnel matters and that any level of detritus could float to a high rank if given enough time.

Seton however was still a barbarian of breeding and he maintained his composure of polite attentiveness until he had opportunity to speak to the rotund Abron Bose.

"No. I'm afraid I will be going into a business where I feel I can have some chance of success. I already know who my partner will be. I just need the account to ensure that I can purchase some property and be able to pay some wages until the cash flow begins in earnest."

"And what line of business is that Mr. Rax?" asked Abron Bose.

"Bounty Hunting," replied Seton. "From what I can understand there is a big demand for it and my talents can be well applied in its execution. Play to your strengths. Do not develop you weaknesses."

"It is a highly risky undertaking though Mr. Rax," Abron Bose said.

"Less risky than the career I have been following recently though I'm sure."

"Well we here at Lord Jackson of En'Tuk First National Banking Corporation will be happy to see to your affairs."

"Glad to hear it," Seton said. "Now if we can get the formalities over with and the money safely in the vaults, I've got to find premises with a nice apartment above them and a hostelry of superior quality nearby. I'm looking forward to putting down a few roots and helping to tidy up the lawlessness which seems to be growing and making a tidy profit in the process."

"Certainly sir. It will be our pleasure to assist you, from helping you search for property to paying you nought point five percent on your investments."

With that a few documents were signed and Seton left relieved to be out of the awful little man's presence. He set off into the streets of Sitka and started to seek out one of his oldest and most capable adventuring companions from his past, Pavor.

Chorus One

Pavor was an ex-military man and an adventurer. He was older than Seton Rax by fifteen years and had enjoyed some reasonably successful times on foolhardy quests for gold and adventure with the barbarian. Now he supplemented his income by working as a bodyguard for merchants when they negotiated on the price of elk flesh with the nomadic tribes but that only paid well for one month of the year. For the other eleven he found himself doing weekend door work in the rough pubs and bars of Sitka's port.

Pavor's past had left him lean and wiry, strong and resilient. He was like a wall of gristle, tough meat that you never wanted to come up against in one on one combat. While he was still dangerous and fast and could have continued to turn a well skilled hand in weaponry to a further life of questing he now felt a longing to stay in Sitka. A place to rest each night that he could call home and a set of friends down his local ale house seemed so much more appealing than cold nights in the mountains or damp days down dungeons. He had done quite well during his adventuring days and had enough gold stashed away in Jackson's to ensure he could afford the rent on his lodgings and a few ales each day.

Pavor was just over six foot tall. His face was pock marked from an adolescent disease and his body was covered in scars from being a retired adventurer, the encounters with monsters or the blades of enemies leaving their record on his skin. He had also done well in the

Umiat Army and had risen to the rank of veteran seeing action during one of the Ahrioch Wars.

He had grey facial hair, neatly cropped into a moustache and goatee beard, joining together to frame his thin lips which hinted at grimness and occasional laughter. He shaved the rest of his skull except for a long ponytail which protruded from the back of his head and was bound by thin black leather straps. It was this hairstyle which marked him out as having some barbarian heritage and it was this barbarian heritage that had led to him knowing Seton Rax. His favourite weapons in his current line of work were large iron knuckle dusters worn on both hands, thickly wrapping around his fingers into metal fists. They caused pounding pain to anyone assailed by them.

Seton Rax walked into the bar where he knew Pavor would be drinking. The hugely muscled Seton hugged the thinner warrior with the bear like affection of old friends.

"How come you ain't dead yet?" chided Seton with a grin as he indicated to the landlord that more beers were needed.

"Just never came up against anyone better than me," Pavor replied.

Chapter Two

"Well what do you think?" asked Seton. His hands were on his hips as he gazed up as an artisan on a low scaffold was painting a final 'S' in neat white letters nine inches tall. The black wood background to the shop front clearly stated what services could be found within.

"Seton Rax & Company: Bounty Hunters," read Pavor. "I think you've found the perfect business. What did that crack at the bank recommend again?"

"A joint florist and off license," Seton replied with a twitch of his lips that hinted at a smile of contempt.

"When do we start?" Pavor asked after stifling a laugh.

"You and I? Immediately. We just need to round up a couple of others. I think four is the perfect number for this type of enterprise. We need to be able to be a squad. A perfectly balanced bunch of troopers. Able to move fast and deal with the kind of scum we are going to be going after quickly and without attention being drawn."

"So you provide muscle, bulk, strength and axe work," stated Pavor.

"And you provide speed, unarmed combat, experience and intelligence," replied Seton. "But let's not kiss each others egos too much. We know we've worked well together in the past. I know we'll work together well at this as well."

"Well, well," said Pavor. "What can I say?"

The artisan had finished the final details of the final letter and he started to dismantle the scaffolding immediately. Seton and Pavor stood in silence for a while and watched the final bits of wet paint dry. They were in the street of a rough part of Sitka. Situated in the southwest of the city, about a hundred yards from the docks, the buildings here were constructed of the ubiquitous wood and most were a couple of stories tall, then topped with steep peaky roofs. Around them were many ale houses and lower quality eateries offering quick and easy bowls of meat and potatoes for the dock workers on their way home. A few other shops crowded the frontage, two tailors and a barber were nearby but there were no other bounty hunters. There were no other bounty hunters set up in this way in the whole city. Pavor looked to his left and right and picked out one of the white 'Wanted' posters stuck to the wooden pillars of door frames of the shops. The authorities of Sitka had plenty of people they wanted rounding up or removing.

"Why the need for a shop though Seton?" Pavor asked. "Most bounty hunters do quite well working out of the pub they prefer."

"We are not going to be 'most' bounty hunters, Pavor. We are going to be the best. We are going to change how bounty hunters are perceived. We are going to have business come to us rather than just picking up posters."

"Private bits of work as well as sanctioned jobs by Sitka?"

"Exactly. Lucrative private contracts," Seton replied.

"So we've got offices at the front, what's in the back room and upstairs?"

"A staffroom at the back and upstairs and in the eaves of the roof there is an apartment with three bedrooms, a living room, water closet and a space to prepare food."

"A water closet!" Pavor gasped. "Where did you get enough cash to get a place like this?"

"Finally did a quest that paid very, very well Pavor my friend. But now I want you to share in a new adventure as a bounty hunter. Will you move in here as well as be my business partner?"

"Absolutely Seton. Absolutely. Let's build the best bounty hunting business there's been," Pavor extended his hand to Seton who instantly grasped it and the two friends vigorously shook.

"Shall we?" said Seton unclasping his hand and sweeping his arm with open palm towards the door of the offices.

The two warriors walked from their vantage point and the larger barbarian and proprietor pushed open the black framed door so Pavor could cross the threshold first.

Pavor looked around the room that would welcome potential customers and was interested to see that Seton had selected a range of plush leather sofas that had been placed around a low wooden table. Towards the back of the room there were a couple of desks, with armchairs behind them, plus a long bench where any captured convicts could be sat while they were processed. On the walls Seton had had mirrors hung with carved wooden frames. Pavor wondered whether it was to create an illusion of space or so that the barbarian could catch a view of his sculptured bulk from almost anywhere in the room. There was also a large blackboard behind one of the desks. Pavor noted how Seton had arranged a range of coloured chalks neatly on the little rack that ran along the base of it.

They went through to the back room. A plaque on the door stated 'Staff Only'. A set of stairs, on their left, led steeply up to the floor above. In the far corner there was a cell constructed by close metal bars reaching from the floor to the ceiling. A single window was set high in the wall, it was small and also barred for extra security. Otherwise the room was bare at the moment. Seton picked up on Pavor's observation.

"I was thinking of just lots of cushions," the barbarian said.

"What? Some sort of subdued memory of nomadic life?"

"No. Just comfortable. Figure we might want somewhere to crash out at the end of the day. Plus it will really annoy any brigand we've got held in the cell. No cushions for them!"

"Let's have a look upstairs then," said Pavor.

The two men clambered up the steep stairs, hands on the steps above to stabilise the climb. The rooms were exactly as Seton Rax had described. Three bedrooms, a living area with space attached for the preparation of food and an indoor water closet hanging over the alley at the back of the building and the gutter beneath. The third bedroom was up a couple of steps and filled a third of the eaves. The living area and two other bedrooms had a peaked ceiling as the roof had never been filled in a way that could have created an additional loft area. Beams of dark wood were everywhere in the structure and Pavor looked around in awe at the space created compared to his own humble lodgings. In each bedroom there was a large double bed with a wool filled mattress, stuffed feather pillows and blankets neatly folded in a square pile. A set of wooden drawers also provided storage in each room. The living area was strewn with extremely large, oversized pillows and cushions, some cylindrical, some puffy squares. Seton fell backwards and onto a pile of the pillows under the leaded latticed window letting in the early evening sun. The barbarian smiled broadly as he watched his wiry friend look through the doors and into rooms with interest. Pavor thought to himself that Seton had great taste in furnishings for a barbarian but was maybe limited in his seating solutions.

"And I get to live here while I am in your employ?" asked Pavor.

"I wouldn't have it any other way my friend," Seton replied, hands behind his head, hedonistically relishing in the comfort of the collection of cushions.

"Can I have the third bedroom all to myself?" Pavor asked. "I like the little steps up to it. Kind of separates it away from the rest of the rooms."

"Certainly," Seton replied. "That leaves two bedrooms for the rest of the company. I would envision that one of us will always be awake and keeping an eye on the shop downstairs or lounging around in here."

"So we're definitely going to recruit another couple of bounty hunters then?" asked Pavor standing in the doorway of his chosen room at the top of the little flight of stairs looking down on his reclining friend.

"Yep. Four is the perfect number for this enterprise. I think we need a sword expert, as well as someone good at intelligence gathering and communication."

Pavor gazed at the huge double handed battleaxe that Seton had stashed in the corner earlier in the day.

"You provide the heavy weaponry, so a swordsman skilled with swift slashing blades would be good yeah?"

"Yep," Seton replied. "You got someone in mind?"

"As a matter of fact I do. For both positions. A'Lastor for the swordsman and Eris for our fourth."

"A'Lastor? Yeah I've heard something of him before I set out on my last quest. He's a good guy yeah? What's the name of those swords he fights with again?"

"Xyele. Short, slightly curved and only edged on one side. He's cracking good in close combat with them," Pavor replied. "Plus the fact he is bounty hunting already as a free lance individual. He is also an expert tracker and therefore a perfect partner for us."

Seton Rax sat up from his luxuriating recline.

"And who is Eris? Sounds like a girl's name," he said.

"It is," replied Pavor striding down the steps towards his friend and gazing out of the window as the setting sun dropped below the Sitka skyline of jagged roofs.

"Go on," Seton urged.

"Eris is an absolute goddess. She works at one of the clubs I do door work for."

"Any special skills that would qualify her as a bounty hunter?"

"The ability to calm angry men down. To attract the eye while others bundle off the quarry to the authorities. To move freely in the underworld because a beautiful woman is always welcome everywhere. Oh and she's also a sassy assassin, extremely effective with any type of weapon you care to mention and she's my friend."

"I like her already," said Seton. "But do you think it is right just to select a couple of associates? Shouldn't we do some sort of interview?"

"What possible benefit could a long drawn out interview process bring us?" said Pavor bluntly. "People say a lot of things at interview which might well be elaborated. And if we set up trials of combat they might just be on a good day. No Seton, I think a warrior that we both know who would jump at this opportunity and my recommendation of Eris will go down very well indeed, I'm sure."

"Pavor. I trust you completely. That's why I wanted you as my right hand man. How long do you reckon it will take us to get A'Lastor and Eris?"

"We can talk to Eris tonight. I know she'll like this change of career. A'Lastor might be a bit harder to track down but he'll be about somewhere. We'll get the word out that we are looking for him but the last I heard he was hunting someone down in the Schwatka Mountains."

"Let's go see Eris then," said Seton standing up and grabbing his axe.

"Excellent, but you won't be able to take that where were going. We'll find her at 'Demons'."

Chorus Two

'Demons' was the second most expensive lap dancing and strip joint in a city with two such establishments. Seton Rax followed Pavor through an arch just wide enough for the barbarian to pass through. It was set slightly back from a row of shops that were on a gradual incline in the centre of Sitka. The alleyway leading from the arch was dark and enclosed but it soon opened up into an irregular shaped courtyard. In one wall of this area a thick wooden door with black square nails studded into it suddenly swung open and a group of young men poured out in a pack. They were giggling and red faced and upon seeing Pavor and Seton they quickly broke ranks and melted around the duo and slipped into single file as they strode down the alleyway in search of other pleasures in Sitka. With the group of men a heavy drumbeat also emerged in a pulsing, gut thumping rhythm. Seton broke into a broad smile and followed the sauntering Pavor over the doorstep and into 'Demons'.

"Hi Pavor," said a slinky brunette in black lace underwear, sitting behind a small counter on a tall stool. Two huge men also smiled at the wiry warrior as they blocked the way into the rest of the club.

"Good evening my darling. Lads. I'm a customer tonight," replied Pavor pulling out a few coins from his pocket and neatly stacking them in the girl's outstretched hand. "Keep the change!"

"Thanks Pavor. If there is anything else I can do for you, or your friend tonight, then just let me know," the girl said smiling, eyeing Seton's muscles.

Pavor twitched her a wink and turned to his left and headed straight up a set of stairs. Seton followed at a bounding pace as Pavor seemed keen to get to the upper level. The stairs turned sharply to the right and came to a small landing with another large and grim faced man guarding a door. Upon seeing Pavor though the visage broke from granite to sunshine and the door was pushed fully open for both bounty hunters to enter into a wonderfully plush room of leather sofas, a well stocked bar and a sectioned off area of dancing delights. The room was filled with an atmosphere of temptation. Several men lounged in sofas, well dressed and affluent, several less well dressed ladies, sidled up to the gentlemen and entered into easy conversations about the level of eagerness to have a dance. There was a small raised stage area in a corner upon which a lithe young girl writhed in semi nakedness to the continual beating of the drums.

"The drinks are double the price up here Seton but the quality of the dancing is increased as well," said Pavor looking around the room. "Let's get an ale and wait for Eris. I can't see her at the moment. She must be performing."

Seton and Pavor stood at the bar and ordered a couple of extremely expensive ales from a coiffured bar steward wearing a black shirt and pink cravat. The man smiled apologetically to Pavor for the price as he placed the pints on the bar. The beer was a little warm, probably as a result of the sultry temperature in the establishment and being on the second floor the beer had a long draw through the pipes all the way up from the cellar in the basement. However, the glass was clean enough and the pint retained a good head. They took a big gulp each then holding their tankards turned and leaned so the bar pressed into the smalls of their backs. They surveyed the scene of dancers and denizens of 'Demons' plying their trade and the desire to purchase. Many moments elapsed as lap dancers stroked cheeks and played with their hair to encourage the more reticent of reclining rogues to part with their money. Seton was essentially a shy barbarian when it came to establishments like this. He knew several of his ilk who would relish spending their money here but would find it hard to face the brigands in single combat as he had done in the Schwatka Mountains. Seton found it slightly degrading that men would enjoy this kind of pastime. Women should be attracted by acts of physical bravery and prowess in battle, not by the amount of coin held out in a lecherous hand. The barbarian noted in disdain some of the uglier and weaker men in the room, ravaged by age and lessened by lives spent behind desks. He noted with derision that it was this type that attracted the more nubile, the more beautifully curved wenches dressed in exotic and revealing underwear. Seton felt his distaste beginning to turn to rage as he focussed on one oily individual whispering into an ear of a stunning blonde girl, hair down over her shoulders and white stockinged legs draped over his lap.

"Tut tut", shouted Pavor suddenly into Seton's ear above the noise of the continuing drums. "I've seen that look before Seton. Keep it calm here please my friend. Remember we are to steal Eris away from this line of employment. Let's not cause any other issues with the owners and the doormen by upsetting their customers too."

"Yep, sorry Pavor," Seton replied back loudly. "Still at least the beer is passable. Where is this Eris?"

"Probably been paid to do a series of dances rather than just the normal single. Patience Seton, patience."

The men waited, Pavor smiling broadly and Seton chewing his bottom lip to help with the suppression of his thoughts. Then it was obvious that patience was no longer necessary. Into the main room, from the enclosed and hidden area, strode one of the most beautiful women Seton had ever seen. She was tall and lithe, long perfect legs accentuated by black boots with high heels and tight leather clinging to the curves of her calves. Her thighs were fully on display and Seton marvelled at their length, shape and the purity of her smooth white skin. She swayed and moved in perfect time with the music, attracting attention and causing Seton's blood to pump a lot harder. She continued the black motif of her boots with underwear that revealed her curves enough to draw nearly every eye in the room in either desire or jealousy. Seton noticed the muscle definition in the flatness of her waist that spoke of strength and dedication to her dancer's craft. Then there was her face, framed by a neat brunette bob of luxuriant hair. Her dark eyes glinted back around the crowd as she playfully pursed her full painted lips into coquettish smiles of pleasure to all. Seton however was perhaps most drawn by the beauty of her nose. Without a perfect nose all beauty formed in a face would be tainted. Eris' was straight at the bridge and cutely flared at the nostrils when she gave her kittenish grins.

The loud and thumping drums that had become background pulses of noise suddenly ceased and Pavor clicked his fingers in front of Seton's eyes and moved off towards the vision of desire just as another couple of men made the same decision. Eris saw Pavor approach with the massively muscled long haired barbarian behind him. She greeted Pavor with a kiss on each cheek and a gently placed hand on his hip.

"Evening Pavor. Good to see you here on your night off," she said in an even and silky voice, tempting and with a purring depth.

"Oi! We're next!" came an angry bark from one of the other two men who had set off at the same time as Pavor and Seton. They were short and stocky with shaved heads and angry faces of bulging eyes and spittle stained lips, sneering in aggression at Pavor and his bulky companion. "We've been waiting for her for ages. There's no cracking way you're cutting in!"

Eris turned calmly and with grace, still with her hand on Pavor, she looked at the two seething customers. They instantly stopped talking and gazed at her serene smile. Pavor could not hear what Eris said to them as she leaned slightly forward between their bald heads and whispered to them in sultry tones. After about ten seconds of such words hanging in the air the two thuggish men turned to face each other and immediately started throwing punches at their erstwhile companion. Pavor knew what would happen next as he and Eris turned away from the brawl but Seton watched in interest as four hard looking men emerged from the shadowy corners of the club and grabbed the two combatants and dragged them to the exit and then out of sight, down the two flights of stairs to be ejected into the street.

Seton found that his hand had been taken and he looked back around from the efficiently handled ejection to see that Eris was smiling at him and gently pulling him to a sofa where she indicated he should sit. Pavor was already relaxing with a broad grin and both his arms out along the back of the long brown leather seat. He soon had to move to the end though as Eris made it clear that she wanted to sit between the barbarian and warrior by pulling Seton to sit on her left with a slinky tug of his hand.

"Now what can I do for you two boys tonight?" she purred as the thumping drums begun again.

With the music starting afresh a new girl took to the little stage to begin her well practised dance routine. Pavor turned to the beautiful woman between him and Seton Rax and made a proposition to her that made Eris smile more broadly than any man had made her smile before.

Chapter Three

Seton awoke in the apartment above the bounty hunting offices with the nervous feeling of what his head and stomach were about to do to him. He knew it had been a late night, dawn had not been too far off and he also knew that he had switched to drinking wine in the early hours at 'Demons' in celebration of Eris' agreement to join with them in the bounty hunting venture. Seton groaned as pain cut around his eyebrows and round to the back of his head in a thumping lump of hung-over agony. At least he could try to get back to sleep for a while, Eris wasn't officially due to join with 'Seton Rax & Company' until midday. The barbarian turned his attention to how his stomach was treating him and found that it was being merciful in its repercussions of the alcoholic assault Seton had imposed on it the night before. He turned over to shield his face from the rays of light that had woken him through the window and sought the solace of sleep again. He heard his door open with a slight creak and he groaned at the disturbing enquiry from Pavor.

"Hey Seton! You awake yet?" the wiry warrior wondered.

"Sought of Pavor. Why?" Seton replied from his recumbent position.

"I've fried up some ham, eggs and beans. Fancy some?"

Seton realised that showing any sign of frailty would be a mistake and briefly thought about how Pavor could be sounding so perky when the much smaller man had drunk as much as him in the club.

"Sounds good buddy. Dish it up, I'll be straight out," said Seton.

Pavor retreated and Seton could hear the clattering of plates and pans as the breakfast was laid out. The smell reached him a little after the noise and the barbarian gauged that he was actually famished and the desire for food became stronger than the need for sleep.

He swayed a little as he made his way from the bed to the door of his room but a deep breath and a resolution of strength helped him as he made it to the table.

"I'm really looking forward to Eris joining us," said Pavor.

"Me too," Seton replied pulling out a chair and placing himself in front of the fried meat, eggs and legumes swimming in hot elk fat. "Me too. We just need to ensure we get A'Lastor as well."

"Oh we'll get him," Pavor replied. "All we have to do is track the tracker down. Like I said yesterday I've heard he is up in the Schwatka Mountains working freelance already."

Seton scooped up some of the pig flesh and dripping yolk from a briefly fried egg and placed it tentatively into his mouth in a final test of his stomach's constitution with such a hangover. He didn't instantly retch so he chewed and swallowed it down with a shrug of resignation for his famished frame.

Seton continued to eat finding that Pavor's culinary expertise with hot fat was actually just what his body did need and very soon he was beginning to feel all barbarian again and looking forward to the rest of the day. He scooped the remaining bit of pig gristle, a couple of beans and the detritus of a broken egg up with his broad wooden spoon, curving it in the contours of the bowl. Slurping it down his throat he wiped his lips with the back of his hand, spoon still held and leaned back, letting out a bellowing belch of satisfaction.

"That hit the spot!" he shouted to Pavor who was scrubbing clean the remains of the breakfast preparation.

"Cheers fella" Pavor called back over his shoulder.

As the barbarian reclined in satiated joy and considered that his headache was nothing of any major concern, both warriors heard a rapping at the door on the floor below. Pavor took the very few steps necessary to cross to the window which overlooked the front of the shop if one opened it and stared down. He lifted the latch that kept the neat windows with diamond shaped lines of lead shut and peered down upon the early morning visitor. He smiled, Seton noted, as he saw a brown bob of hair and an elegant and lithe young lady attired in tight black leather trousers and an even tighter laced bodice which accentuated her curves. Blades were lashed around her personage, darkly sheathed in scabbards.

"Let me in," shouted up Eris to Pavor.

"You're early," he replied back down.

"Got our first bit of business," she called back up and then waved a sheet of paper towards the wiry old warrior.

On hearing Eris' voice Seton was soon up and pounding down the stairs, through the staff room and into the reception area and unlocking the front door.

"Morning," he smiled broadly along with the greeting to his new associate.

"Morning Seton," she replied, stepping into the establishment and giving the barbarian a slightly too long kiss of welcome on his cheek. "I'm looking forward to this Mr. Rax."

Pavor upon closing the window again had now joined them in the front room of the bounty hunting emporium.

"What have you got for us then Eris?" Pavor asked, scratching an irritation in the beard of his goatee.

"Well I know you said last night that we are to become bounty hunters of elegance, class and distinction. I just couldn't resist picking up this wanted poster on my way over here. I figure we have got to gain a reputation for success before we start getting sought out for job offers," she reasoned.

"Fair point," said Seton. "What have you got there then?"

Eris handed him the sheet of paper, torn from a wall where four large nails had impaled it at each corner. The authorities of Sitka would post such desires of legislative vengeance in places known by the public and bounty hunters as a way of reducing the general level of villainy in the remote city and surrounding areas. The figure at the bottom of the communications was what instantly drew most eyes upon perusal. A couple of gold coins for a trouble maker who needed rounding up by the mob might be most common but when the numbers got into triple figures and the description of the miscreant became a rant of misdemeanours which terrified the mob, then the bounty hunters would take note. Seton looked at the parchment and the picture of the wanted man, imagined by some bureaucratic artist of the authorities from descriptions given by their victims. He scanned to the bottom of the communiqué and saw the reward of two hundred and fifty gold coins.

"If you would Pavor," he said handing the poster to his intrigued colleague. "You have a better reading voice than I."

Pavor took the sheet, gave it a brief scan to be prepared and then standing a little taller and puffing out his chest began to read.

"Wanted for 'Highway Murder and Villainy Most Foul'," Pavor extolled in a mocking baritone often used by theatrical types. "Sciron the Bandit. The beast of the coastal road. Sciron is known to have robbed, raped and murdered at least six local traders along the coastal road to Sagwon. More disturbing is his method of murder upon the poor merchants. After divesting them of goods, coin, clothes and dignity he is known to have his victims wash his feet on the edge of a cliff. Upon completion of such a demeaning act, Sciron kicks his naked victims over the towering edifices to their doom. As such the Merchant's Guild will pay two hundred and fifty gold coins for his capture alive."

Pavor paused in his reading and then passed comment.

"No good bringing this one in dead. I guess they want to execute him themselves," he observed.

"Decent enough first mission for us?" Eris enquired.

"Absolutely," Seton replied. "The coastal road will take us close by the Schwatka Mountains as well. We have to secure A'Lastor to complete our quartet and the rumours are that he his hunting down some other murderers in the mountains."

"That's correct," confirmed Pavor. "Going to 'Demons' last night also gave me an opportunity to have a little chat with one of the best sources of information in the city and they told me that A'Lastor is tracking down the killers of some lighthouse keeper. Turns out this guy was in a bit of trouble with some local adventurous types, owed money or something, anyway, he was tricked into climbing down an old well, dried up and useless, by two hitmen hired to take him out. They told him that a great treasure was buried at the bottom of this well and when he climbed to the bottom they just stoned him to death by dropping large rocks on him. Poor old crack couldn't get out of the way and was just crushed to death. Any how, the hitmen got drunk, started boasting about how elegant and inventive they'd been in carrying out the contract in a swanky tavern in town. In that bar were some local government types who take a dim view on professional hitmen, a row broke out, some noses were broken in a scuffle and now descriptions are out for their arrest and trial, or death. Not for the murder of the lighthouse keeper, you understand, but for the brawl which hurt the feelings of and rearranged the faces of the bureaucrats."

"And A'Lastor is after them?" Eris enquired.

"Yep," replied Pavor. "Two hundred gee pees each. Dead or alive."

"Right then," said Seton. "We head up the coastal road on our first mission to capture this Sciron and we hunt for A'Lastor at the same time. Guess if we don't find him on his own quest he's going to come back to Sitka one way or another."

"Either with his quarry in tow or back to resupply," said Eris readjusting a secreted simple blade that nestled between the pressures of her cleavage.

"Correct," replied Pavor. "But me thinks he'll be successful. The word is that his prey are laying low in a desolated and ruined old mountain town."

"My word your contact at the club had loads of information didn't they!" exclaimed Seton. "You'll have to introduce me next time as I am sure they must be able to help us in the future if they had this much info on the two A'Lastor is after."

"Shouldn't really reveal my professional sources to anyone. Not even to you. I might be replaced," Pavor joked back.

"When do we leave then?" asked Eris, checking her hair in one of the many mirrors of the reception room of the bounty hunting offices.

"This afternoon," said Seton. "We'll pack lightly. Weapons, food, restraining equipment and a bivouac."

"Plus fire lighting accoutrements, compass and a map. A good length of a solid rope, extra clothes and some coinage for information transactions plus any other goods we might need to purchase whilst out in the field. Like good quality cloaks to protect against unexpectedly foul weather," said Pavor.

Seton shot him a quizzical look and wondered if his old friend was either trying to impress Eris with his loquacious list or if he had picked up on random comments about Seton's last expedition that might have been made in an earlier casual conversation around the apartment.

"Oh I don't travel anywhere anymore without an extra cloak," the barbarian said and Pavor responded with a quick wink that Seton was sure was aimed in his direction and not towards the luscious brunette frame of Eris who stood with her curves and a minxy expression of interest.

The warriors now busied themselves around the building in the acquisition of the supplies they needed. Seton had had the premises well stocked with the items bounty hunters required to ply their trade. Naturally each had they own favourite weapons with them. Seton with his vast double handed double headed battle axe, Eris with daggers and knives strapped over her body and limbs. Pavor was a weapon in himself, lithe, quick and with a disturbing strength in his body, he still carried with him his knuckle dusters, the fists of iron pain, so useful against foes for a swift knocking into unconsciousness.

Within an hour Seton was locking up the shop and thinking how he would need to hire some other staff, eventually, to man it while he was away on missions. Success in claiming some rewards was sure to take his business to the next level of private assignments and he would need some reliable individuals back at base, as well as beside him, in the battling for bounties. As a pale northern sun reached the zenith of its track the trio strode through the streets of Sitka with barely a soul noticing their transit.

Chorus Three

Seton and Pavor crouched behind a large granite boulder on the slopes of a coastal mountain. The wind pushed rolling clouds laced with rain off the Sea of Umiat as the twilight of evening wrapped itself around the rocky northern limits of the continent. The two warriors squinted with interest as Eris ambled with a seductive slink towards the just lit bonfire in the middle of the transitory camp of Sciron and his handful of men.

It had taken only three days to make their way to the east and with the skills of Pavor and Eris at questioning other travellers and reading the clues of the crimes that Sciron had committed, they had soon tracked him down. If there had have been an effective law enforcement body in the northern lands of Umiat they would have had little issue in rounding up this bandit of the wilderness as well. Sitka authorities however felt that the setting of bounties and allowing freelance individual to take the risk of capturing criminals was a far more effective solution to a full time employed force. Effective in terms of success rates, at eradicating crime and also more efficient in terms of overall cost. Seeking such a cost now, as a reward, was 'Seton Rax and Company'. Eris, though, had been selected to apply her talents against Sciron and his thugs.

Seton turned to Pavor as they crouched behind the grey lump of rock.

"We'll consider this her real audition for the role of bounty hunter," the barbarian whispered to his friend.

"She'll do just fine Seton. They are only level one thugs. No skill. No panache. Just bullying brigands who mug others among the boulders of the coastal roads," Pavor replied. "Just watch her go to work."

They could see six men hunched up around the fire, anticipating a cold night in the northern foothills. A couple of cloth tents provided a little more shelter from the winds, grey and triangular they began to merge into the backgrounds as the night languidly seduced the mountains. One of the men jerked in surprise and stood up sharply as he caught sight of the solitary figure walking towards them out of the murk beneath the dark clouds of night.

"Who the crack are you?" the thug shouted bringing his fellows to a rousing response. Weapons were snatched from scabbards and grabbed from atop the bedrock by the bonfire.

"Just a lone female traveller seeking warmth and companionship against the cold," Eris replied walking straight up to the men, not stalling in her stride for a second. She lifted her arm and placed an open hand on the waist of the man who had hailed her so insultingly.

One of the men, the largest, with a vest of black chain mail over a dark leather doublet, nodded with vigour towards the dark and two other ruffians skirted off between the rocks to scout around to see if the woman was indeed as alone as she had claimed.

"Idiots," said Pavor to Seton. "Dividing their forces so easily."

"If they come this way you take them down silently," replied Seton.

Back in the robber's camp Eris found that the remaining four brigands were crowded around her rubbing their stubbled chins and appraising their good fortune at such a beauty coming across their path. The large man, had dark hair, shaved at the side but long on top. It was greased back with animal fat to hang swinging towards the middle of his shoulders. He reached out and grabbed Eris at the top of her thighs and heaved her towards him.

"Take her into the tent Sciron!" enthused a loudmouth.

"Umm. That's what I wanted to hear," moaned Eris, moving her cheek to the side of Sciron's ear but murmuring in her own mind, 'It's just too, too easy.'

Eris turned around within the hands of Sciron, her thighs firm within their leather. She began a snaking dance, lifting her arms and running her fingers through her short bob of hair, seduction and eroticism enhanced by months of routines at 'Demons'.

"She's a live one!" growled one of the watching men.

"Probably a travelling whore searching for a bit of coin," said another.

"I'm having her after you Sciron," informed the third lasciviously.

Eris continued in her controlled writhing and watched as the trio of thugs started jostling each other for a better view of her form. Sciron standing behind her moved his hands over her flanks and reached towards her curvaceous chest. Then she made another move. She lifted her right leg, dragging the boot up the calf of her new admirer. Eris sighed amorously and smiled as she heard Sciron let loose a lusting moan and felt him thrust against her. She then placed the heel of her boot just below his knee cap, felt Sciron move his hand against the taut muscle of her bended leg and readied herself for the first capture working for 'Seton Rax and Company'.

Within the heels of her boots were placed dense lumps of squared off metal. Not only did this help make a pleasing sound as she walked but with the toughened encasing of leather surrounding the base of her boot it became an effective weapon if used well. Sciron roared in pain as Eris shoved down her foot with all the force she could muster, his shin was brutally scraped and his foot smashed as Eris suddenly stood erect. The trio of remaining brigands snapped out of their revelry as their leader collapsed in pain grabbing at his mashed right foot and rolled away from the firelight in agony.

Eris had no interest in capturing any of Sciron's men and she launched herself against the aghast warriors. Athletically the brunette took a couple of running sudden steps and leapt into the air between two of the adversaries catching each in the solar plexus with a well placed knee.

Seton Rax nodded to Pavor with a down turned grimace of respect for Eris' first couple of attacks. Three were down, one remained and two were prowling the darkness looking for any potential threat, while Eris was taking down their companions.

The female bounty hunter turned on the remaining man as he scrambled to draw his sword and retaliate to the unexpected threat in their midst.

"You cracking slut. You'll pay for that!" he spat at Eris.

"Uncalled for derisory drivel," she replied pulling the hidden blade from between her bosom and with the four inch knife she casually walked towards the warrior with his yard of brandished steel.

"You ain't gonna' take me by surprise bitch!" shouted the thug slashing his blade in the air in front of him.

Eris judged the man's grip and handling of the sword and found that he was an inadequate foe as he held the sword too tightly and too far down the hilt. Plus he had the blade in a vertical position. When attacking a human opponent having the blade horizontal was the mark of a skilled warrior as it could slip in more easily between the ribs, hack through vertebra or lop off an appendage.

She gave a little sniff and instead of engaging the last man she took a couple of steps away from him and kicked hard at the head of one of the winded men who fell into an agony and then a quick unconsciousness with a second stamp from her boot. The violence of her action brought on a frenzied run from the sword wielder in an attempt to bring some defence to his associates. Screaming in rage it was the last sound to ever utter forth from his throat, except for the bubbling of vomit and bloody froth as Eris skipped around his assaulting run, dodged his blade and stabbed deeply into the side of his throat with her dagger. Leaving the blade stuck in his neck she then reached round the man in a mocking hug of affection, prised the sword from his dying hand and tugged her smaller dagger back out from the gristle of the man's windpipe with her left hand. Letting him drop she then walked towards the knocked out victim and simply shoved the longer steel blade under his sternum sending him from one black void to another. Sciron and the other winded man remained. Both tried to roll and crawl away from the unexpected vision of death that Eris presented. Sciron was not the main target at the moment and Eris pulling the sword back out from one dead man's gut soon had the blade in the back of the other and bisected a kidney. She marvelled in the extreme agonies of a human with a vital organ butchered, incapable now of anything but bleeding and pain she left him to die in the shadows of the night.

Eris turned her attention to Sciron who was slumped on the rocky ground, clutching his broken foot with his knee pressed closely to his chest. She stalked smartly towards the bandit who started gibbering, spittle falling from his mouth.

"Who are you?" he whined in fear.

"Put your hands behind your back. Now!" Eris ordered in response. She was pleased to see Sciron do so immediately. The bounty hunter then swiftly walked behind her quarry. She dropped her dagger and acquired sword to the ground and with practised speed pulled some leather lashings from a pocket and brightly bound his wrists together, tight and secure.

"I think your remaining two men have probably fled Sciron," she whispered into the ear of the captured man. "Probably watched me butcher their chums from the shadows and decided to run away. Either that or the rest of my team have already dealt with them in the dark."

"Are you going to take me to Sitka?" Sciron asked.

"Yes. Plus you are going to walk all of the way. Every step in pain and fear. Like the pain and fear you caused your victims."

The large robber bowed his head in resignation. His frame covered in the black chain mail slumped as he realised he had been captured and his brief reign of terror had been concluded with now only his own execution to look forward to.

Pavor turned to Seton Rax and indicated with a gesture of his head that they should now walk down and join with Eris by the fire and ensure that the two wandering brigands did not return. As they were about to move off they head a loud and rhythmic clapping from behind them.

Seton turned with the reflexes of a professional warrior but was still slower than Pavor who was already prepared for a fight. No fight came though as both men stared at a previously silent shadow that sat cross legged on a flat outcrop of rock. The shadow was still clapping.

"A'Lastor!" Pavor gasped. "How long have you been there?"

"Long enough. Long enough," the shadow replied in a soft voice with a hint of an alien accent. He was completely swathed in black. Black cloth trousers, black high felt boots with soft leather soles, a back baggy top and tight ninja style headgear covering all his face apart from a slit for his eyes to stare through.

"We've been looking for you," said Pavor walking towards A'Lastor.

"Thought so," replied the lone bounty hunter silently jumping down from the rock pulling a bag and a pack along with him. "Doubt you could have found me though. Unless I wanted you to. So I thought I'd seek out the new competition I'd heard about. Looks like you've got a good team around you Pavor. I've had my eye on Eris for a while and the muscle power of Seton Rax is well known in these parts."

Pavor and A'Lastor quickly shook hands and gave a swift embrace then all three bounty hunters turned and made their way down towards the summoning light of the camp fire and the victorious vignette of Eris standing over her capture, arms crossed and foot tapping as she waited for her companions. The look on her face, shadowed by the fire was an exquisite piece of inquisitiveness as a trio emerged from the night rather than the pair she had expected.

"You needn't worry about the other two Eris," said A'Lastor calmly. "I mean Sciron's pals rather than these couple of reprobates. Sciron is the sole survivor of his thuggish operation."

The black garbed assassin opened the bag he carried and poured out the contents. Four heads tumbled and rolled around on the rocks, some ending face up, others down but which ever way they ended up looking with their dead expressions the decapitations inspired interest in Eris, Pavor and Seton. Sciron looked briefly at the heads and then turned away as he recognised that all five of his gang were now dead.

"Four A'Lastor?" asked Pavor. "Been busy have we?"

"We'll let's stoke up the fire and I'll tell you what I've been up to for the last couple of days and the last couple of minutes."

Chapter four

A'Lastor looked again at the piece of parchment which described his mission so simply. 'The capture dead or alive of the two killers of Pallomedes'. The wind in the mountains rose a bit and tugged at the corner of the paper making it flap in cracking ripples. The bounty hunter ripped it up and simply released the pieces to the coastal breeze. He looked down upon the ruins of some old mountain village, probably once the home of the worst kind of hill peasant. Walls of cottages with no roofs and ghostly vacant windows sat by a crumbled church with crashed tower. The victim of a storm in the distant past. Completely wrapped in black he pulled the xyele out of their sheaths that were strapped across his back. The swords were slightly curved and only bladed on one side. A'Lastor had always found them a perfect sword for his slight and fast frame. The curve of the metal aided to cutting deeply as he slashed with speed rather than the hacking power used by other warriors with other weapons. Another weapon he had liked was the khopesh blade which was used many miles to the south by the black warriors of the deserts close to the equator. However that elongated question mark shaped blade, while excellent for hooking other swords and cutting flesh was difficult to sheath properly and to secrete for a silent killer like A'Lastor.

He smiled to himself beneath the black headgear. It had been ridiculously easy to track the two killers of Pallomedes. Sniffing out the rumours in coastal towns, watching in local markets for the frowned faces of farmers not recognising the men buying goods to supplement the poor hunting in the northwest mountains of Umiat. A few extra coins for the landlords of the rare public houses and inns of the one main road around the Schwatka Mountains, plus other innate senses of the tracker and A'Lastor had soon found his prey. As he looked down on the two men hiding out in the ruined village, huddled around a meagre fire, he put one of the xyele down beside him and in a seditious desire reached into a trouser pocket and gently fingered a heavily engraved metal tube. It was thin, hollow, nine inches long and had eight small triangular blades spiking out of one end. This favoured device made his mouth water, he licked at his lips and teeth and fought the need to use it immediately only as a way to heighten his addiction. He breathed deeply as he watched the men. They had relished in the murder of Pallomedes as they stoned him to death at the bottom of the well that they had tricked him into descending. Now, unaware, a killer with more hits than them was scintillating in the moment just before he was about to add two to his own impressive tally. He reached down, picked up his xyele again, twirled both swords and strode in the twilight towards the ruins. Wrapped in his ninja black, confident the two men would not see his approach, he knew his silent footfall would not attract them either. As he got close to the outskirts of the desolated hovels, A'Lastor checked his bearings and headed for the cottage he had to get to. Now only one was inhabited. His soft heeled boots and his ability to move in the darker shadows now paid dividends. He crouched a little and skirted chunks of remaining wall, always moving towards the decayed residence of dead peasants that was now a den to murderers. The wind whipped and slipped by crumbling stones and A'Lastor skipped onto an old track of the village. There was perhaps a hint of a rolling shard of rock, skittering among the reclaiming bits of scrub that sprouted within the ancient path, but it was no alarm.

The bounty hunter strode straight into the ruined cottage, no pause, no ceremony, no comment and with his xyele held precisely decapitated first one man and then the other. Both heads landed and rolled to the stone walls, the bodies, sitting moments before, slumped and spurted hewing gobs of blood by the fire. A'Lastor sheathed his swords simultaneously upon his back in their 'x' shaped strapping and luxuriously reached into his pocket as he regarded the dead men. His job was so much easier when the subjects of his missions were designated wanted 'dead or alive'. He pulled out the metal tube and looked at the patterned engraving and exquisite images of demonic figures within the crossed raised diagonals of dark grey metal. The work woven upon it was of an ancient skill, lost now to the men and beasts of this world. Looking at the corpses, slowly flooding blood onto the broken floor of the cottage, A'Lastor squinted in the darkness. What he searched for was difficult enough to see in any light but his kind were sensitive to such things and the flames of the fire glowed strongly enough.

A'Lastor waited, searching in the cutting cold air of night. The bodies beside him had ceased their seeping now and with the blood beginning to congeal in the dirt the bounty hunter saw the wispy warped air raise from the severed necks. That was what he was searching for and craved. Stepping towards the two floating threads of nothingness he waved the metallic pipe through the ruined room and the rising strands. The eight triangular blades at the end of the pipe hooked about the very slightly sticky substance as it tried to ascend in thin shimmering ribbons towards the heavens. A'Lastor smiled beneath his headgear and twisted the tube in his fingers. Tightening the fleeing strings of haze around the blades still further. He lowered the cloth over his mouth, revealing his perfect lips, slightly pushed out by prominent incisors and between finger and thumb kissed the end of the device. He inhaled deeply, pleasurably, filling his lungs fully with the horrors of the night and death.

Having satiated himself with the welcome bi-product of his profession, A'Lastor placed the pipe back in his pocket, grabbed a suitable bag from his backpack for the transportation of proof of a completed quest and picked up the two heads. There was nothing else of interest to him in the makeshift camp. A'Lastor swung the bag over his shoulder, exited the ruins through the gap that had once been framed and held a door and headed back west out of the valley and into the mountains.

A'Lastor brought himself back to the present and the recently fed fire. Beside him his old friend Pavor sat with the barbarian Seton Rax and the lethal Eris. Sciron had been well trussed up, gagged and thrown into a tent while the bounty hunters enjoyed the warmth of the fire, ignoring the scattered corpses and heads. A'Lastor went to pick up the two prizes he needed and popped them back in his bag. He had just related the tale of his hunting of the murderers of Pallomedes so felt it was time to reclaim the heads as a final testimony to his prowess. He had just told the entire story exactly as it had happened, apart from anything to do with the metal pipe in his pocket and the sucking in of souls.

"Then as I was heading back to Sitka I heard you guys tramping through the foothills making a colossal amount of noise as you were hunting down Sciron," A'Lastor continued. "I wasn't really all that interested in capturing him, as he is only worth money alive but I thought I'd follow your enterprise and see how you worked. Eris you appear to be a very promising young bounty hunter."

"Thank you A'Lastor," Eris replied with a smile. "And thank you for taking care of Sciron's scouts."

"That was my pleasure. Extremely easy piece of work. They came out into the dark to look for threats and couldn't even see the dark shadows and fears that they should have been looking for," A'Lastor answered.

"The ones that move and wield blades," Pavor said.

"Exactly. Easy kills but I enjoyed them," A'Lastor, unbeknown in the dark and hidden by the black cloth that swathed his face, ran his tongue between his lips in memory of another couple of decapitations.

They sat in silence for a while, looking at the flames, observing little licks of light bursting out from logs where hidden pockets of sticky tar bubbled forth flammable gases. They listened to the cracks of burning, braking wood, smaller blackened twigs falling to the charred base of the fire.

"A'Lastor," said Seton breaking the silence. "No doubt a man of your skills and knowledge already knows that I have set up a bounty hunting business in Sitka."

"Yes," A'Lastor replied. "An interesting concept for people who ply a trade such as ours. Having a base where you can be found by those requiring our services. Or a target for those seeking retribution for the capture of their family, friends or colleagues."

"I hadn't thought about your second point," Seton admitted.

"Then you need to ensure that you are surrounded by those who are best suited to deal with either occurrence," A'Lastor observed. "Personally I have always found that picking up quests I wanted has worked best. However, you do of course have superb support with Pavor being in your employ. And young Eris is likely to be an excellent acquisition."

Again Eris smiled and nodded her thanks for the compliment. Seton looked deeper into the flames, his barbarian mind considering the point that his name above the door meant many people could find him easily. Pavor turned his shaven head, the long tightly tied ponytail swaying in the dark. He saw his friend's usually cheerful face fall into pensiveness, heavy shadows caused by firelight accentuating the rare visage of sullen thought.

"In regards to your second point A'Lastor," the thin bounty hunter said in support of Seton. "You are absolutely right that we need 'the best'. We had thought to come and find you in the wilderness or failing that tracking you down to 'The Gardener's Arms' where you are often known to frequent. We want you as our final fourth."

"I'm honoured but I have worked alone for such a long time that I fear it has become a habit. Plus I have affectations that perhaps make a solitary nature the best course of action," the ninja garbed tracker replied in a considered voice.

"I've known you a long time my friend and I've yet to see anything that would make you an inconsiderate or undesired colleague," retorted Pavor. "I made it clear to Seton Rax that as we required a swordsman you would be who we wanted as our first choice. He had heard of your reputation with a blade plus we all know of your skill as a scout and a hunter of men."

"You honour me again Pavor," A'Lastor replied. "But how can you want a man in your party with whom you have never shared a meal or ever seen his face unveiled?"

Pavor laughed. Seton became inquisitive and Eris lightly chewed on a thumbnail.

"By seeing a man's face? I have made many mistakes in trusting those who have smiled at me," Pavor stated. "Your particular choice of clothing has never disparaged your words or actions. They demonstrate your true intentions my friend. As for never sharing a meal with you it is not a vital part of my cultural heritage to share food or judge a man by his skill and etiquette with a knife and fork. Your ability with a sword and a history of coming good on promises made is far more important. The fact I've never had a beer with you is perhaps worrying though. Especially as you are so often down 'The Gardener's Arms' when you are in Sitka."

"I use it as a place to sleep and to gather intelligence," A'Lastor replied stoically. "The landlord is not just a purveyor of ale but of beds as well. He doesn't mind me sitting in the common room listening and talking with other guests of an evening."

"In fact, come to think of it, I've never actually seen you ever eat or drink," Pavor frowned a little with his observation.

"Oh I eat and drink. I just prefer to do it in private. It's part of my cultural background not to reveal such things in public. My kind considers it an obscene act. The chewing of food and swallowing of liquid when others are there to see it."

"Really?" Pavor probed.

"Yes. We keep such things sacred to ourselves," A'Lastor paused for a while bowing his head. He picked up a stick from the supplies stacked next to him, previously gathered by Sciron's men and threw it into the heart of the fire. "On rare occasions we might eat with an especially favoured friend or a mate, but never in public. However, I'm sure a man of your sensibilities would not hold such a cultural imposition against me, would you?"

"Not I," said Seton, interjecting. "I'm with Pavor on this. Your reputation has been built by your actions and your skill with a blade. Not your ability to quaff ale. You probably find my heritage and its habits disgusting. Ripping roast meat with my teeth and sinking a gallon of good beer in an evening. Awful really if you think about it."

"Well, I wouldn't hold it against you," replied A'Lastor.

"I don't particularly like eating like a barbarian either," said Eris. "But I do enjoy a night in a restaurant with a pint of wine."

The group laughed a little at Eris' comment and fell into silence again. Seton looked to Pavor to make the request again.

"Well A'Lastor, you know we want the best, we have no prejudice versus any groups dietary habits plus we offer free accommodation. So your takings from quests do not have to go to the landlord of 'The Gardener's Arms'. Also we want your companionship. Will you join us?" Pavor asked intently.

"I'll need three things as conditions," A'Lastor replied.

"What would they be?" Pavor responded.

"Twenty five percent. A room to myself at the shop. Privacy when I want it."

"Done," said Pavor holding out his hand.

A'Lastor reached out to shake with the ponytailed, pockmarked faced bounty hunter and wondered to himself why Pavor could conclude the deal but Seton Rax had his name in the title of the company.

"I appreciate you equitable demand of the takings," Pavor continued. "The room is easily done but I fear with Eris in our ranks I will have to give up the room I had picked."

"I don't mind sharing," said Eris with a grin.

"Plus I'm sure we will be able to give you all the privacy you want," Pavor said with a hint of hope in his heart that Eris meant sharing with him. "So welcome aboard."

"Exceptionally pleased to have you," added Seton.

"Well let's get back to Sitka tomorrow and seal our new arrangement by sharing the bounties on Sciron and the killers of Pallomedes," A'Lastor said throwing another branch onto the fire.

"Seems slightly unfair on you," said Pavor. "You had one third of the kills from this mission, we had no hand in yours and you say you want to split it all twenty five percent."

"Consider it an investment from me in the company," A'Lastor replied calmly. "And not an indication of my inability to negotiate a contract."

The quartet of warriors, satisfied, sunk into a night of conversation and hopes of a successful future.

Chorus four

It was now four weeks since the formation of the four out in the mountains. The bounties had been collected and shared and then saved or spent as each individual saw fit. Other missions had followed and their reputation began to build within the criminal as well as judicial fraternity. Those with money on their heads had even, in the last week, begun turning up at the offices of 'Seton Rax & Company' and simply presenting themselves for capture rather than risk an encounter with the crew. Interestingly, the only criminals to surrender were those who were wanted alive.

In terms of the sleeping arrangements in the living quarters of the office, A'Lastor had taken the second bedroom, Pavor kept the third with the little steps leading up to it which he had liked so much, leaving Eris with the largest room. Seton hadn't minded at all not having a designated space to himself. After years of barbaric nomadism and adventuring he was more concerned with the contentment of his crew than where it came to him sleeping. Seton also found that a corner festooned with cushions in the backroom, downstairs, was more fitting to his needs and somehow it increased his feeling of security, being on the ground floor, next to the shop front and any criminals they had in the lockup overnight.

A'Lastor had proven his need for privacy and would often saunter to the seclusion of his room in an evening. He was never rude about it and would also often talk long into the night with the others when they took their meals. He would just sit cross legged, nearly fully in a corner, with two walls to his flanks and contribute to the conversation or provide an insight on how a capture had been conducted earlier that day.

Eris was always perfectly charming and lit the room with her wit. The men had now grown very accustomed to her other charms and her physical attractions now played only lightly upon their minds. It was totally her skill at arms and disarming others with her presence that won her so much admiration with the other warriors. The fact that she was brilliantly quick with her intellect and so pleasant to look upon was purely a bonus.

Pavor had never felt so happy. He got to spend time cooking for Eris and Seton and the work was ultimately so much more rewarding than the recent doorman duties he had had to perform. The money was building up for the first time in a long time and he was absolutely treated as an equal by the others. There was no poxy junior management structure where some limited gimp gave him orders on how to control the door and who was allowed access that evening. If anything he felt that it was he who actually held the unit together. One because he knew everyone else before they had become a team and two because his own ex-military experience was often drawn upon as they worked together as a specialised squad.

Seton himself was in a constant state of joy. Not only did he get to fight regularly but he also had a place to really call home and a tavern round the corner where they already knew him by name and the ale was better than to be expected in this outpost of humanity. He was extremely pleased by the way Pavor had developed his leadership abilities and the way Eris and A'Lastor had been the ideal additions to the company.

So far they had still been able to pick up work from the posters placed around town by the authorities. The recent addition to the coffers by crooks giving themselves up was welcome but Seton still wanted the lucrative business of private contracts to come his way. He was disappointed that the local judges who paid the bounties could not be corrupted into giving the odd piece of information about who was up for capture next. Seton and the others therefore still had to look out for new posters going up and had to risk the fact that any of Sitka's other bounty hunters could go for the same kill or capture. However, if he was honest with himself, during the last month he and his team had only lost out twice to other individuals or outfits, so results were going well really.

Seton was laying in the back room early one morning lounging on his large cushions, pondering on how his business was performing and remembering other cases. One capture in particular came to mind as he relaxed. It was the case of Kerkyon the Wrestler. The band of bounty hunters had found that a local ruffian was wanted again for incarceration as he was staging illegal fights in a tavern nearby. Kerkyon would encourage drunken men in the pub to wrestle with him for a stake of ten copper pieces. If they could throw him down and pin him for ten seconds then he would give them one hundred gold pieces. Gambling of this nature was outlawed in Sitka as it was not seen as a game of chance but of prowess. Kerkyon was a renowned professional fighter who, in his dotage, was now ripping off drunks and taking their savings with ease. He probably also had a deal with the landlord who gained a large customer base from the activity and provided the bravado needed by the combatants through strong ale.

Seton, Pavor, Eris and A'Lastor had all decided that his capture could be entertaining. The reward was only a hundred gold pieces but as Kerkyon was currently plying his criminal trade in a hostelry round the corner, by the name of 'The Greyhound', it should be an easy night's work. Plus the pub served magnificent meat sandwiches and a good range of ales.

The bounty hunters had arrived at the tavern quite early in the evening and had a very pleasant time all eating and drinking, except for A'Lastor, and waiting the expected arrival of Kerkyon. The pub was packed. This was known as good entertainment. Kerkyon had been in every night for the last fortnight and had not been beaten yet. An area was already cleared in the centre of the large common room. Wooden trestle tables were covered in tankards of brown ale and empty plates, the detritus from where, the only item on the menu, 'elk steaks in a loaf', had been consumed. The crowd was in a jolly mood and pipe smoke thickened the atmosphere with a bluish haze and a gorgeous aroma.

The front door of the pub opened and in walked the well known frame of Kerkyon. The famous wrestler had made a name for himself in the Court of Rhyell where he would represent the royal family against champions of visiting states in staged bouts. He was bald, stripped to the waist, powerfully built but maybe turning a little to fat. He sported a massive moustache that drooped and then curled up and stopped in well oiled points near to his ears.

The crowd in the pub roared their approval at the arrival. Kerkyon rubbed his hands and walked to the centre of the room and took his position. The routine had been played out now for many nights. Several potential combatants were already stretching and limbering up. Kerkyon stood with his hands on his hips and slowly turned to survey the crowd.

"Who will challenge me?" he called. "Kerkyon the Great! Kerkyon the Undefeated! Win yourself a bag of gold simply by pinning me. Ten copper pieces to win yourself a hundred gold? The odds have never been better. Step up!"

A few willing bravos held up small purses or fists clutching the stake money. It appeared that Kerkyon had an assistant as a hunched and wrinkled old servant man, in brown robes, started to collect money and take names.

The bouts began in the order the money had been received. People stood on benches and tables. The pub took on the feeling of an arena as the banks of spectators, thickened, curved and rose around the space given over to wrestling. Kerkyon was impressively strong and well skilled in his art. He toyed with some adversaries and threw others down swiftly. He clapped his hands above his head and struck poses to display his might. The crowd loved him and cheered and roared in approval. His defeated foes left the ring with broad smiles and with a large pat on the back from the wrestler. They would have a story to tell now, bruises to display with pride and they were only a mere ten copper pieces worse off for the privilege.

"Seems like we have to apprehend a bit of a hero," Pavor whispered to Seton as they sat in the audience watching the martial skills of Kerkyon.

"Yes. But apprehend we must," said Seton in reply. "Come on. We've had enough fun watching and we won't be ruining an entire evening's entertainment."

With those words, Seton stood and followed by Pavor, the luscious Eris and black swathed A'Lastor they approached Kerkyon who had just dispatched another hopeful.

"Ah!" shouted the massive wrestler. "I suspected as much. My dear audience. It appears that I am about to be arrested by bounty hunters!"

A chorus of disapproval rang out as the four stood around the warrior, exposed by the space of the ring.

"My fans!" Kerkyon called. "Do not be harsh on them! 'Tis but an occupational hazard of my trade. For we gamble illegally here tonight!"

A few laughs rang out knowingly from the crowd, along with others with a more nervous tinge. Most however booed in disappointment that the night was to end.

"I will be released from the cells in a week!" Kerkyon shouted. "With the landlord's permission we can resume our entertainment then."

The landlord from behind the bar of his thronged pub shouted an enthusiastic agreement and the crowd clapped and cheered. Kerkyon took the opportunity of the noise to talk with Seton.

"Don't worry. I'll come quietly. You're not the usual bunch of bounty hunters who come and collect me though. Guess they must be busy elsewhere, hey? The deal is still the same yeah? We split the bounty fifty fifty. I drop the judge a small bribe. I get back out plying my profession. This is how the real money is made. Okay?"

"Oh I see," said Seton. "Sorry, no. We're not in on any scam. So we just take you in and collect all one hundred."

"Ah," sighed Kerkyon. "Fair enough. The posters have brought in freelancers rather than the gang approved collectors. Okay. I'll still come quietly but what say you and I, Master Barbarian, have a little wrestle? Just to give the crowd one last theatrical turn. Same stake from you though. If I don't get to earn my usual out of the bounty I'll have to scrape together a few more coppers."

"Yeah alright," replied Seton. "I fancy making two hundred out of the total deal. Take a seat guys. This should be fun."

A'Lastor, Eris and Pavor returned to the crowd and an excited hubbub instantly frothed around the throng of spectators.

"Gentlemen," called Kerkyon as Seton Rax began a few stretches. "We have a final piece of combat for your delectation. Before I am cruelly carried off to incarceration, these noble bounty hunters have agreed to allow one last fight. Betwixt I, Kerkyon the Undefeated, and a magnificently muscled barbarian of the plains. What's your name son?"

"Seton Rax," came the quick reply. The barbarian was almost prepared as he already had a bare torso and was now tying his hair into a loose pigtail.

"Seton Rax!" shouted Kerkyon. The crowd cheered. Eris clapped her hands together enthusiastically. Pavor took on the look of an expert appraiser of wrestling. A'Lastor, under his gear, was alert to any possible subterfuge.

Kerkyon and Seton circled each other, throwing out quick grasping hands, trying to gain a grip on their adversary. It happened eventually, with the backdrop of a cheering crowd urging them on, that both men grappled, grasped and gained a grip. Seton was surprised by the immense strength of Kerkyon, his iron hold and smiling face. Kerkyon did not seem bothered at all that the man he was wrestling with was also extremely strong and probably a good two stone heavier. All of it muscle.

Seton tried to lift his opponent but found that as he did so Kerkyon moved his own grip in swift reply. Kerkyon shoved an arm between Seton's armpit and rounded his shoulders. Then by straightening the limb it unbalanced the barbarian and he was reduced to clinging to Kerkyon again looking for a better grip and readjusting his stance.

"I'm playing with you boy," Kerkyon whispered at one point in their struggle. "A warrior you might be with that great axe of yours that I saw slung across your back in the crowd but there are other skills to fighting rather than just hacking about with a big bladed stick."

With that Kerkyon swept a leg and took out both of Seton's. The barbarian fell and was then heavily winded by the large wrestler who landed on top of him. Kerkyon did not go for a pin. He stood and raised his hands to the audience, to enjoy the adulation. He then grasped one of Seton's wrists and hauled him back up to fight again.

Kerkyon threw Seton three more times to the delight of the crowd. Once from a half nelson, Seton collapsed to his knees in immense pain caused by the classic combined head and arm lock. Another time Kerkyon ducked a charge and lifted Seton into the air with a raising flick of his shoulder. Seton was sent skidding on his side, on the rough wood floor into the feet of the front row. Shaking his head and standing again Seton realised the skill of the warrior in front of him as the audience both jeered and cheered. He was the baddy. Seton Rax was the unpopular one. Here he was come to collect a legitimate criminal and they turned against him. A criminal in name perhaps only because an authority had declared his behaviour as wrong. The final throw followed a gesture from Seton. The barbarian offered his hand to shake, a sign of defeat. Kerkyon took it, pulled Seton forward and turned. Pulling his extended arm, Kerkyon had Seton onto and over his back to land with a thud on the floor. Kerkyon fell instantly upon him and slithered quickly into a lock with his arms and legs around the limbs and head of the barbarian. Kerkyon claimed a final victory for the night and did indeed live up to his promise in giving himself up. However, he did not go quietly, as a crowd of devoted fans cheered and sang all the way behind him through the streets of Sitka as the bounty hunters took him to their offices to be locked up for the night.

Kerkyon had taught Seton a good lesson. He was better than the barbarian in his chosen field and had been a gentleman about it too. The bounty had been a small one but the teaching was invaluable.

'Never underestimate anybody,' Seton mused. 'Everyone that you meet is better than you. At something.'

Seton came back to reality after his reminiscing. He was still lying on his pillows in the back office. He started to think about the future and was wondering whether it would seem strange if he started setting monthly targets for income derived from captures. Then he could create a graphical representation of performance versus his set budgets and talk about them to his team at regular meetings, perhaps every Monday morning. He was just beginning to think where these strange thoughts were coming from when he heard someone coming lightly down the stairs.

Swathed in his customary black, A'Lastor tread confidently on the steep steps, the only noise coming from the creaking of wood under the weight of the assassin.

"Morning A'Lastor," said Seton raising himself to a seated position and shaking his head of the disturbing thoughts of different coloured lines of targets and results against time.

"It is indeed as you say 'morning'," A'Lastor replied, his veiled head nodding with the response as well.

The warrior looked through to the front room and then back up the stairs as if to check curiously for other company. Then assured they were alone the ninja garbed A'Lastor swiftly lowered himself in a graceful move to his cross legged repose, back straight and masked head looking directly at the bare torso and shaggy mane of the barbarian before him.

"I have had a dream Seton. A vision. Within the month you will be closing the front door for a long time. We will all follow you though," and with that A'Lastor rose without the use of his hands to steady himself and headed off to look for new posters, for it was his turn. Seton blinked and shook his head again. A'Lastor had never spoken of dreams before and he was a little shocked by the terseness of the delivery, however, if A'Lastor was right, there was now very little point in setting a target for this month's earnings anyway.

Chapter Five

A'Lastor swung open the door to 'Seton Rax & Company: Bounty Hunters' setting the little warning bell into a twinkling frenzy on its metal spring. He clutched in his black gloved hand a parchment, ripped from its place of posting so all four corners were tattered remains, rents slashed from the nails that had once held it.

"We've finally got a tough one!" A'Lastor shouted, his original accent filtering through a little in his unusual outburst of arousing attention.

Seton was first through to the main office, running footsteps above and then a clattering descent on the stairs brought Pavor and Eris swiftly into the room. Seton leapt over the back of one of the opulent sofas, landing neatly on his rump with both arms spread broadly along the back of the firm leather couch. Eris went and stood behind him and casually started to massage the barbarian's neck.

"Go on then," said Pavor cracking his knuckles. "Who have they posted?"

A'Lastor threw the parchment with a little flick so that it flew flat, spinning and landed on a displaced minor cushion of air, flush in front of Seton and Eris who looked down at the two main words of the title.

"'Wanted Dead'," said Eris in tones which could hardly disguise her interest.

"A demand for assassination without trial," Pavor mused. "That is only ever issued for crimes which are, how shall we put it? Interesting."

"Who is it for then A'Lastor?" asked Seton unable to make out the small print and unwilling to leave the constant firm caress of Eris who still squeezed away at his neck and shoulders.

"Areithous!" A'Lastor replied with venom in his voice.

"The 'Club Swinger'," said Pavor, turning away from his colleagues in shock.

"Never heard of him," said Seton sinking into the sofa and seduction a little further. Pavor paced the room as A'Lastor entered into an unusually long monologue.

"Areithous is a gang land boss in the docks of Sitka. Usually left alone by the authorities to manage his territory as best he sees fit. Running the whore houses, gambling dens, taking his cut of produce bought and sold, he's a traditional leader of a traditional gang and obviously until recently he wasn't doing anything that warranted any unusual interest. He is a man who is well known to my own people and I have been looking forward for a long time to test my skill against him," A'Lastor paused for a brief moment and took a seat on the sofa opposite to Seton. The black garbed bounty hunter leant forward and turned the parchment on the highly polished table so that it faced him. He caressed the lines of the text with a pointed index finger. Luxuriantly reading the words of permission to kill, silently, to himself. He looked up again into the eyes of Seton, ignoring the pacing of Pavor.

"Areithous is a terrible man who has done terrible things. Ah, yes, like all good bosses of the criminal cartels he must have murdered and tortured to get to where he wanted to be. But, Areithous did other things not notable for those of a usual criminal disposition. He sacrificed to the dark gods. He vehemently proclaimed his loyalty to the demon kings. He has inscribed his body with runic texts talking of his abhorrence of the true faith and his lust to lie in sodomitic ecstasy with succubi from the depths of Hell. He wants to raise himself above the ranks of mortal men and take on the mantle of an everlasting demon."

"You seem to know a lot about him," said Seton a little more engaged now by the strange passions in A'Lastor's tones.

"All of my kind knows a lot about his ilk. He is why I do what I do. I will take great pleasure in cutting him down," A'Lastor replied.

"What exactly is your kind?" Seton asked in an attempt to dive deeper into A'Lastor's background.

"The same as you. A bounty hunter. A tracker. One who wishes to rid the world of villainy for profit. For sanctioned profit," A'Lastor coolly retorted.

Seton might not have been the most educated in the room but he could still read the number of four thousand gold pieces at the bottom of the page, even though it was now upside down.

"Four thousand gold pieces! How long does it usually take for a 'demand for assassination without trial', as Pavor put it, until the requested victim is brought in by someone?" Seton asked finally pulling away from the touch of Eris in interest at the huge sum indicated at on the table.

"About four hours, in most cases, by someone who knows them," replied Pavor. "Though I suspect those around Areithous are so loyal that an offer even that large could not hope to persuade them to change their allegiance."

"Why?" asked Seton Rax.

"For the exact reasons A'Lastor has been alluding to," Pavor replied.

"What? Are they worshippers of Ahrioch?" enquired Seton.

"No, no, no," A'Lastor said quickly. "No doubt followers of Ahrioch are dark, dark believers indeed. Areithous believes in a different strain, a different code of demonology. Maybe more dangerous, maybe not. But quicker, much quicker to give power and influence. Less subtle than Ahrioch and that's not saying much. Areithous will have had to have sacrificed human young himself to get to where he is now and I guess the 'authorities' have decided that it is best to rid him from this world now. I want, I need, to be the one who ends his life. Now that it is sanctioned."

Seton raised an eyebrow at the strange enthusiasm of A'Lastor. He turned to look at Pavor who was still pacing around the sofas and desks of the office.

"Pavor, you called this Areithous the 'Club Swinger'," said Seton. "What's that all about? It's pretty stupid sounding. What is it, some sort of nickname?"

"Yeah and a pretty blunt one," replied Pavor ceasing his striding. "It's his name in the underworld of Sitka. He fights with a very large iron mace. It's at least six foot long with a massive black metal head to it. He's got to be twice as strong and you and I combined Seton. He's an absolute beast of a man."

"Really?" said Eris.

"I don't even think your charms would work well with him Eris," Pavor replied coming to take the seat next to A'Lastor. "I can't really believe there is a four thousand gold piece bounty set. That's just huge."

"Probably due to recent activities in the south. Ahriman and the Ahrioch Horde rising for a while in Kenai, atrocities at the Court of Rhyell, the treason of Vixen," said Seton. "I would surmise that perhaps royal influence from Rhyell may well be influencing the local judiciary here. Both on reeling him in and in setting the level of bait. Four thousand should bring in some tough types from beyond the boundaries of Sitka. So we better act quickly and take out this demon worshipping, piece of scum, crime boss they call the 'Club Swinger'."

"What ever happens," interjected A'Lastor. "I get to make the final kill."

"We'll try and plan it that way," said Seton. "You seem quite determined in this case my friend."

"He is a name I have wanted to see on the lists for a long time," the black clad hunter of men replied in a steady tone. "But we had better act fast as you say Seton."

"Agreed," said Pavor. "But this isn't going to be a quick hit and run. Areithous will be too well protected. He is going to have to be lured, tricked, out witted and all this when he knows that there is a very big price on his head."

"Hardly our strong point," said Seton. "Yet we can all work on development especially when there's such a large reward at stake."

"I think perhaps rather than a lure, as Pavor puts it, we should not be fearful but actually hunt him down," said Eris sitting on the back of the sofa now that contained Seton's bulk. "When one is hunting certain animal prey, and you said he was a beast, then one employs beaters to thrash the quarry out of hiding."

"Yes," said Pavor in support. "Or the use of smoke and raging fires to drive the animals into waiting nets."

"And when hunting fish the use of tighter and tighter closing nets to push a shoal into such a dense pack that it is impossible not to be able to spear one," Eris concluded.

The door opened briefly, the bell tinkling and the local postman stepped in and handed a couple of letters to Seton who stood up to take the proffered envelopes. The postal worker then left the offices without passing the time of day or offering a curt greeting and continued on his rounds.

"I think Pavor has a good point and I may be able to offer a suggestion which would be a variance on a technique I saw work well on a recent adventure I was partaking in, in the dread city of Ende," said Seton Rax rubbing his chin, still standing and casually glancing at the envelopes. He put them down on a table, retook his seat and continued to speak. "It was a diversionary assault with burning fear and terror mixed in with greed and addiction. No matter how hard this Areithous is he is unlikely to be immune from the effects of smoke and flames."

"Yes I think we can all see where you are going with this," said Pavor unsure if Seton was going to give the credit fully for his earlier point.

"First though we had better send Eris on a reconnoitre to suss out if Areithous is at his usual hangout. If he is, we buy some barrels of olive oil, roll them down to the front door, set them on fire and wait by the exits for Areithous and his thugs to come spluttering out into the street."

"You don't think it's too subtle?" asked A'Lastor. "You don't think that people are going to notice us rolling up a load of barrels to the outside of a notorious gangster's den and setting fire to them?"

"It's about results," replied Seton. "Set fire to the building he's in and he's bound to come running out or die burning inside. If we get the second result there may be some issue in proving the charred remains to be his for the purposes of claiming the bounty though. If he comes barging out then we rely on our skill to beat him and his bodyguards."

"I thought we had already identified that Areithous is a pretty tough customer with that mace of his," said Eris. "I think that A'Lastor is right. Perhaps some more subtlety is needed here. A different kind of lure. Into a place where perhaps his proficiency with his large weapon might not come into play. Men are pretty easy to trap and honey is sometimes better than vinegar to catch a cockroach. As my mother used to say."

"You did do good work with Sciron and his men," said Pavor. "But you won't catch Areithous in the middle of the wilderness where women are hard to come by. No offence, you're far more desirable than most as you know but I don't think even your ample charms will work with this one. I think his true tastes might lie in other areas than the pleasures you could offer him."

"Oh, that's a shame. I was going to attempt to seduce him down some alleyway and then when he was, vulnerable, let A'Lastor step up for the coup de grace," replied Eris.

"Hang on," interjected Seton. "You may be on to something there as well. If he fights with such a large weapon we ought to get him into a confined space, like an alleyway. On my last adventure in Kenai I had a little difficulty wielding my battleaxe in a corridor against some zombies. If we can trap this Areithous somewhere where he can't 'swing his club' so freely then we take away some of the prowess from the 'Club Swinger'."

"And a well swung xyele could separate his head from his torso," added A'Lastor. "All we have to do is get him into this restricted area. Perhaps we go back to the plan then of smoking him out. That could work well but not necessarily with some very obvious and large barrels of oil stacked outside his base."

"I have it!" shouted Pavor. "All we have to do is become invisible, lock the front door as we enter and then set a fire in the basement with some very smoky substance that sends him and all of his men into a panic. We know exactly where they are and the network of alleys behind is narrow enough for Areithous to be unable to use his mace if we can lure him into them."

"And just how are we going to do all of that?" said Seton, a tinge of frustration entering his voice. He continued to muse out loud. "Perhaps a full frontal attack with another gang would be a good idea. We could share the bounty. There would have to be some casualties on all sides, so the money would go a bit further. Although obviously I don't want to lose any of you."

"No, Pavor's idea is a good one," A'Lastor enthused. "I think I've just thought of a way to gain entry unnoticed, be able to gain access to the cellar with a large bundle of elk fat saturated rags and then smoke the cracker out!"

"Even with your levels of stealth A'Lastor I've yet to see anyone who is able to become truly invisible," said Seton.

"Really?" said A'Lastor. "How many of us have been in this room during this conversation?"

"Well the four of us A'Lastor," replied Seton.

"Hmm, interesting," pondered the ninja out loud. "And how did you manage to get today's post? Did anyone notice when the postman came in? Could anyone remember what he looked like? Seton is an incredibly dangerous fellow and yet he allowed access to his home turf, took two envelopes without question and just let the guy leave."

"Crack in Hell!" swore Seton. "You're right! Who has access to every home and establishment in Sitka? The Umiat Postal Service. To interfere with them is not only against the law but also taboo. Everyone wants to get their parcels and letters unmolested. But to impersonate an Officer of the Service is punishable by death. Pavor, do you reckon your contacts could get you a uniform within the day? Or are your sewing skills up to scratch enough to whip up a fair costume?"

"Consider it done," said a smiling Pavor. He quickly left the offices and was off into the back streets of Sitka to a destination held within his own mind and not revealed to the others.

"Eris, if you could go and purchase some elk fat and some reams of old cloth, along with a large bag, A'Lastor and I will remain here and sharpen our blades," instructed Seton. "Take some copper coins from the petty cash and be back here within the hour."

"Yes sir, Mr Rax!" replied Eris with a cocky tone and then going to a desk she unlocked a draw to dip her hand into a pile of low denomination coins sitting on a shallow silver salver. She then also disappeared into the streets and towards the nearest market for the desired supplies.

"Right," said Seton. "Blade sharpening time A'Lastor. I'll deal with any of his cronies that we smoke out, you get the prize prize as requested."

"Excellent," beamed the hidden face of A'Lastor from behind his black hooding. "Let's just hope it works."

"Why wouldn't it?" replied Seton. "It's about the best plan I've ever come up with or been involved in. It can't fail."

Both bounty hunters went to care for their weapons, slipping whetstones rhythmically and repetitively over the blades, eradicating little nicks and chips of metal leaving only a lethal cutting edge. Sitting in silence apart from the comforting rasping of their work, stone on metal drawn with professional care, they waited for Pavor and Eris to complete their tasks as they thought of their plan and the killing to come.

Pavor pounded his way, running along side streets to the house with the cellar and the seamstress he knew who could whip up a postman's uniform that would fit his frame. Pavor felt that his wiry body would be the most convincing for the role. He looked like he walked the streets all day and with his noticeable long lock of hair tied up and hidden beneath a postal service cap he would complete the masquerade. He arrived in the tight little street and slipped up to the door that opened at the top of a narrow flight of grey stone stairs, down to the basement beneath the three storey wooden terrace house that was so similar to those around it. The sign above the door was unassuming and let those passing by, who did manage to notice it, know that a 'Master Tailor' resided within. Pavor took the stairs three at a time and turning to his right at their base he entered into an incredibly cluttered shop. Clothes were hung everywhere, mannequins emerged from between cloaks as they swayed in the draft caused by Pavor's opening of the door. Boxed wooden shelving set on top of massive drawers displayed stacks of differing coloured shirts. The warrior sidestepped his way to the counter, its glass top showing hundreds of differing buttons beneath. A grey haired tiny crone, thick bristles bursting from many moles on her worn face, wearing thick lenses, three pins held in her lips, looked up at her solitary customer.

"Hi mum." Said Pavor. "I need you to make me a uniform."

Eris found the local market less crowded than the shop Pavor was in and it took her slightly less time to gather the items on her list than it took Pavor's mother to make his uniform. Elk fat was plentiful and although there was a quizzical look on the face of the costermonger who sold the large amount that Eris purchased, he was pleased to make the transaction with such a beautiful customer. It took her hardly anytime to find the right colour of grey sack to add to the costume's authenticity, they were a ubiquitous form of simple luggage in Umiat. Eris bought several of these bags thinking that all but one could be ripped up and soaked in fat they would become the fuel for the smoky flames they planned to create in the effort to catch Areithous.

Chorus Five

Phineas Bunch cursed as another lashing sheet of rain whipped out of the perpetual downpour and seemed to drench him further than he already was. A pirate of his years was used to bad weather, especially around the coasts of Kenai, but he wasn't at sea now. He was perched in the grey wet rocky crags of some unnamed mount on one of the God forgotten islands off the coast of the Tanana Strait. This was a lookout duty with little chance of rest, no crow's nest to curl up in against the battering wind, just the aged rocks and a backpack stuffed with dry fish for sustenance. The posting was for a month, part of Percy Fenton's string of lookouts, staked around the wilds of the world hoping for some sign of the traitor Raven Hill, otherwise known as Vixen. Fenton was High Captain of the Pirate League, a king of the underworld, regular attendee at the Court of Rhyell and unofficially the Admiral of Umiat. Phineas swore again and tried brushing some of the rain out of his foot long white beard.

'I'm, too old for this,' he thought. 'This ain't real pirating. But what Fenton wants, Fenton gets. Damn this rain! Will it never cease?"

Of his thirty day stretch of scanning the island from his lofty perch, Phineas had only been watching for anything unusual for ten. He pulled his longshoreman oiled jacket around him a little tighter and thought how his little shelter would be getting flooded in this perpetual rain. The previous watchman had staked out a bivouac over a cleft in a thick slab of granite. Underneath, the crack widened a little enough for a small fire and a rocky wall to lean against to sleep in the dark of night. From that tiny den of uncomfortable retreat however, you couldn't scan the plains below so each pirate who took his turn had to climb a little higher and then wait and watch. This island had been selected as one to be observed as deep in its ancient past it had been a location of Ahrioch worship. Dilapidated, weather worn and collapsed stone circles jutted from the lower lands. Boulders had been dragged, shaped and erected by the early demonologists and then placed into diabolical designs for their own, old forgotten purposes. Vixen, now known to be a lead follower of those ancient and reoccurring ways, may well bring new acolytes to one of the abandoned places of sacrifice as it had been reported how pockets of unholiness were cropping up again.

Phineas scanned the sky to the east, judging the weather. The black of the storm above with curling dark talons twisting towards earth at the edges of the clouds was swamping the heavens and moving westwards. He saw how a lighter coloured sky followed behind, dragged to fill the void left by the power of the storm. A bolt of lightning cracked and flashed its way through the air and made the old pirate jerk in shock. He had been anticipating the promise of calm from the sky behind the tempest and a quieter evening as he finished one third of this stint of duty. Phineas listened to the thunder that closely followed the bolt of bright light. He closed his eyes feeling thick drops released from his lashes as the sky loudly grumbled its antagonism in response to the stark excitement of the lightning.

'Ah the dejection,' thought Phineas. He had been young and vital once. A writer who had published works on the coastal waters of this region. He knew every cove and every rip tide. He had killed a score of men and plundered boats and villages with the best of his pirate kind. Yet here he was in the remains of a storm, eyes closed and reminiscing about his past, lost youth and the knowledge that very few had actually read the words he had lovingly put to paper in his work on piloting watercraft, "Sea Sense: A Pilot's Guide."

Phineas lifted his lids and looked down on to the plains beneath as the shadows from the storm left the largest of the megalithic constructions to the evil of Ahrioch. From this height he could see old tracks, worn deep in the land that followers had traipsed in their ancient processional devotions. He reflected on how these paths spiralled around the circle rather than just approaching in a straight line. Perhaps the new theory of sunlight appearing between certain stones on certain days was not applicable to the ways of the ancients and that they had interacted with their temples in a different way. Walking round and round the stones, the old ceremonies would have replicated the shape of the moulded boulders, and walkers would have seen the sun or moon glint between the gaps many times. Then with the constant pulsing of sun or moon light influencing their minds hypnotically the worshippers would enter into the sacred confines of the circle itself, to practice their darker acts of devotion and prayer.

Phineas shook his head and brought himself back to reality and away from such anthropological perusals. He needed to focus on his task. He blinked firmly and stared at the flat valley. He watched as the storm continued to move, dragging its final curtain of dark rain behind it and towards his lookout. Phineas strained to see through that final barrier of precipitation and at the plain and was certain that he saw figures rising from the grass, ghosting from beneath grey cloaks that they had had draped upon them. He rubbed his eyes with his fists and struggled to make out what he felt must be an illusion caused by his dreams of the ancients. He knew he hadn't been drinking and was now certain that there were men down on the island. He quickly counter, ten, twenty, no at least a hundred. Men dressed in grey, standing from the shadowed land and shaking the rain from their cloaks. How had he missed them before? Day dreaming during a storm, cursing his luck at his posting. He reached down for his telescope and swiftly rubbed at the end with the driest bit of his coat.

"Damn this rain," he said out loud as droplets hit the lens and merged into larger tears as he tried to focus in on the band of men beneath him. He twisted the tube to bring the image closer, bringing out the details as he scanned the group. They were amassing after the storm which must have hit the valley harder than it hit the hills. Phineas felt his stomach tighten and his heart begin the race and pound. These were strange and uncertain tidings. He moved the telescope quickly from man to man, grim face to grim face. These were tough men, warriors all. Then a sight that lurched into his mind was vividly different. He paused as he took in the image, shot into his mind by the dark confines of the telescope. There in the circle of the lens was a stunning woman, in tight black leather, with a face that cut into the hearts of men with lascivious desire and burned like her flame red hair. Her mouth was moving fast, obviously with loud instructive words. Phineas had found and confirmed the presence of Vixen.

He grabbed only his backpack and stuffed the collapsible viewing tube into a pocket. Phineas started to run down tiny tracks and flowing slopes of scree, down the back of the mountain and towards a hidden cove and his tied up dinghy. Although old and at the end of his pirating career, Phineas was still fit from years of deck work and fighting but he soon found himself panting as he pounded down the steep sides of the mountain, the rain still lashing around him and the ground running with myriads of tiny streams.

Finally, after an hour of running, stumbling and slipping, a couple of falls and long rolls on the rocks, finding himself bruised and panicked with the news he carried, Phineas threw his backpack into the dinghy, untied it from around a useful rock and pushed it out and into the sea. He rowed and rowed, chest bursting with effort, using the currents he knew to take him further out into the depths found between the Sea of Kaltag and the Circle Sea.

Phineas laboured in his efforts to speed his craft along. The waters of the Tanana Strait vomited great voluminous swells out into the wider seas and it aided his speed but Phineas was still impatient with haste. His back hunched then straight, his muscles yearning for relief, he continued to pull on the wooden oars against the unforgiving waters beneath. He knew that with evening the winds were likely to change and he would be able to raise the small sail to aid the vessel's progress but for now it was his knotted strength that propelled him.

It would have to be dark and as far out to sea as he could possibly get before he could hope to be seen.

Fenton's fleet was large and observant but Phineas needed to be picked up quickly. The sun set and still he rowed, the value of his knowledge continuing to guide and the urgency of the information on Vixen spurring him on. The moon now lit his way, following the storm its light was bright and blanched the crests of water around him with its pale beauty. Phineas judged his position. He was close to the regular routes of the patrols. The stars were in their right settings and with the lunar illumination he could just see the towering form of Rampart to the northwest. The horizon gave him fifteen miles of sight in all directions and he could see no ship lanterns. Phineas was taking a risk, all alone at sea, in the dark, but he had his orders. He reached down to a small chest beneath his bench and pulled out a single signal flare. He felt certain that this technology could be used for other things than just decorative explosions and alerting associates with its glory painted on the black backdrop of the heavens. He held the tube firmly and aimed towards the sky, one firm tug on the string was all that was needed. Phineas pulled tightly and the compounds of powders ignited. With a satisfying sound of gas at high pressure escaping the flare shot towards the dome of heaven. Its speed was such that nearly within the briefness of a blink a huge firework had burst with orange falling flames five hundred feet above and drew all the eyes of those that were looking for such a signal on the swelling sea.

Chapter Six

Pavor took a deep, chest expanding, breath, held it for a while and then set off at a postman's pace, rounded the corner of a warehouse in the roughest part of Sitka's docks and headed for the solid green door of his destination. Pavor looked the part in his perfect postal replica, created by his mother. The cap had had to be purchased from a ragamuffin who was paid to steal one and it now sat neatly on top of Pavor's head hiding his ponytail which was coiled within it. With the sack swung over his shoulder, the undercover bounty hunter held a large yellow envelope in his hands as he approached the heavily guarded main entrance of 'The Reeking Rat'. Two large, shaven headed, bent nosed thugs, stood either side of the door even at this early part of the day. Pavor walked with the pretend purpose of a man who knew the value and importance of his job, not making eye contact but heading straight to the entrance, brandishing his envelope. His plan was to tell the guards that the mail he handled had to be signed for by the intended recipient and the name of Areithous was emblazoned at the top of the address. The letter contained only one piece of paper, the wanted poster, the demand for execution without trial. As he made it closer to the front door of 'The Reeking Rat' Pavor was only slightly surprised when one of the guards, with the grace and politeness of a professional doorman, reached out a thickly muscled arm and pushed open the door for the approaching postman.

"Thank you," remarked Pavor casually as he stepped over the threshold and into the main corridor of the hostelry. There were two doors on the left, one on the right, with a kitchen at the end and a flight of stairs that led both up and down to offices above and the cellars below. Pavor picked up movement in the kitchen, its double swing doors were held open on hooks and a couple of servants were preparing fires in the ovens. He suspected that Areithous would be upstairs at the current time of day with his lackeys. The common room, snug and dining room were likely to be empty behind the remaining doors from this corridor. Pavor moved swiftly towards the stairs and swung lightly around the post at the top of the banisters before sneaking down to the cellar. This was not a fine wine type of establishment and the bounty hunter was not surprised to find the cellar in a poor state of maintenance and cleanliness. One half was dank and slimy, swimming with filth and rotten food that had fallen into puddles of seepage from the sewers and broken bottles of beer. The other half was drier but only, Pavor suspected, because there was a noticeable slope to the floor. Ten barrels were well looked after though and were neatly racked on a stilted platform, keeping the beer away from any slurry on the cellar floor. Light made its way through a slit of a slight grimy window which would have been at pavement level. Pavor suspected they weren't securely sealed and although they were far too small for anyone to break in through, the street excrement and rain water could easily slop in to add to the stinking fetid pools which formed throughout the lower part of the room. The bounty hunter was pleased to see that there was plenty of broken crates and general rubbish in the drier half of the cellar which would probably burn well when the sack of rags caught alight and would begin to fall, flaming all around the site of the fire he was about to light. He slung the sack off his shoulder and selected a complete crate to act as a suitable base to rest the bags of prepared rags on. He opened the neck of the bag and looked upon the mess of fat, ripped up cloth and scrunched up bits of paper soaked in olive oil. There were also some large lumps of dried moss that was often used as kindling for fires in most households. He reached into a pocket and selected a small fire lighting kit. Holding a flint and rectangular piece of metal over the incendiary device he began to flick with the stone at the sparking stick. Constant movement with his fist drove the flint and metal together and sparks began to rain down into the bag. They cascaded and glowed quickly and then a few caught in the moss and began to smoulder. A quick blow and the orange glows burgeoned into licking flames which then burst forth to lap at the oiled paper and fat gorged rags. Pavor waited as long as he dared, ensuring that the flames would burn well. As soon as he saw the expected oily smoke begin to rise from the bag, Pavor knocked it over, spilling burning rags over a wide area to catch and burn the broken pieces of crate in the room or continue to churn out dark clouds from the burning piles of rags. Satisfied, Pavor began to execute the second stage of the plan. Stampeding up the stairs, he ran to the closed front door and slammed shut the bolts which could withstand any expected raids from other gangs. Then he turned and ran straight for the kitchens and the back door to the filth strewn alleys behind.

"Fire! Fire!" he shouted as he shot a look back at the top of the cellar stairs, certain that the choking smoke was billowing up the flights of steps that formed a natural chimney, channelling the smoke to the rest of the building.

Pushing by the kitchen servants he slammed the envelope down onto a table, if it was to be found and opened then the message would be clear that Areithous was being sought by bounty hunters. The postman then screamed again as loud as he could that a conflagration was consuming the building before leaving 'The Reeking Rat'.

Pavor emerged into the rubbish strewn alleyway behind the building. Kitchen waste combined with churning heaps of rats and the bounty hunter wondered if these particular denizens of the town had influenced the naming of the tavern. He turned in time to see the kitchen hands running to escape as the thick black clouds of smoke began to fill the tavern and then tumble out of the open rear door and plummet upwards, pouring into the sky.

Pavor looked for Seton and A'Lastor, they stood either side of the thin passageway that led from the backyard area of the pub. This one exit was the crux of their plan. As the kitchen staff fled by the peculiar postman and the two shadowy warriors in the alley, Pavor reached into his pockets and placed his favoured knuckle dusters onto his fists. He then took up a predetermined position behind the barbarian and the ninja, who both heavily armed would face the expected resistance first. Eris was concealed, observing the front of the building, in case the option of taking the front door was taken by fumbling hands looking to release the shut bolts in the dark and choking smoke, rather than just sprinting for the easier and open exit in the kitchen. Her orders were to follow any attempted escape via the front door and to effect an execution, if she felt it was plausible. Failing that she was to report back to the office on where Areithous had escaped to. That was not the expected outcome though and the three men waiting in the alleyway were grim faced and ready as a bunch of six large and choking gangsters stumbled into the courtyard.

One of the smoke choked men stood at least a foot taller than the largest of the others, vastly wide as well, he clutched a massive mace. It was thickly shafted, shod with steel and had a head of solid black metal. He had a shaved head, a broad nose that had been broken many times and as he recovered in the cleaner air of the alley he started to bark orders at the other men to get back into the tavern and find the source of the fire. In the shadows of the narrow passageway A'Lastor saw that they had an opportunity to attack if Areithous had fewer men around him, for the moment though they remained hidden. The ninja turned and saw that the hesitation in the group was compounded by Seton who was gawping at the size of and the threat that the gangland boss posed. Areithous did indeed look twice as strong as the barbarian and Pavor combined. His arms were as thick as most men's chests and his own torso was at least the size of a hogshead barrel.

"Some say his mother was raped by a troll," A'Lastor whispered to Seton, slightly mocking in the fear that was registering on the face of the warrior.

"I can well believe it," Seton replied. Called back to the purpose at hand by the words of his colleague the barbarian steadied his nerve. "Half troll or not we have got to take him down. Think we can do it?"

"Absolutely," A'Lastor replied without hesitation. "Let's do it quickly though and now. Look there goes three of his bravest bravos to fight the fire, rather than us."

The trio of bounty hunters watched with interest as three of Areithous' men pulled cloaks up over their mouths and noses and re-entered 'The Reeking Rat' unaware that the copious amounts of black clouds pouring out of the pub was only caused by one large sack of fat soaked rags and some burning broken crates.

"Let's do it now then," said Seton heaving his battle axe into a favoured pre-battle stance. Then he shouted. "Oi, Areithous! Time to settle up."

A'Lastor sighed at the crass arousal of the target, then his teeth suddenly set tight together as they all saw the enormous man turn and face the raised voice from the darkened alleyway.

"Who the crack in Hell are you?" Areithous bellowed as he frowned towards the bounty hunters.

"Debt collectors," said Seton stepping forward into the light. He shook his head to loosen his hair a little and struck a gallant pose that he felt the scenario deserved. Tensing his chest muscles and flexing his biceps the barbarian found glory in the moment.

"Oh dear God," gasped Pavor in surprise at Seton's sudden inability to take this case forward in the correct manner. He could only surmise that the chance of such a large reward was playing on Seton's mind and that he wanted some sort of legend associated with the fight as well, rather than just a straight forward back street execution and claim. Dressed in his postal outfit, with only the slightest hint of timidity in his posture, Pavor strode forward to take a position at Seton's side.

Areithous sneered and indicated to his two remaining men that they should intercept this peculiar threat of a barbarian and a postman shouting from outside his burning establishment. They drew swords and casually approached, confident in their ability to dispatch the duo to an ignoble death amongst the garbage of the courtyard of 'The Reeking Rat'. They had stabbed and hacked their way through scores of men before, in battles of territory, disputes over bar bills and sometimes just for pleasure. As such they had become captains in Areithous' empire, his confidants and his bodyguards. To them a loud mouth 'pretty boy' barbarian and a postman were nothing to be concerned with. They had though failed to see the ninja who backed them up. As they raised their swords to make a quick kill they were astonished to see a genuinely battle hardened response from the barbarian, as he held his axe with a well shaped warrior stance and the scrawny postal worker showed no fear in their approach. The feeling of astonishment was only slightly less bemusing than the confusion they felt as a swiftly moving, black dressed tumbling jester of death came spinning towards them. A'Lastor ran, did a couple of flips on his hands then taking a forward roll perfectly he drew his xyele, arriving slightly ahead of Seton and Pavor, with one knee firmly placed beside a balancing flat foot of his other leg, he stabbed a sword into each of the gangster's guts in an exaltation of his martial ability. As the thugs both roared in the agonies caused by steel slicing through their stomachs, they offered no resistance to Seton as he heaved the blade of his axe into the face of one, cleaving the skull in half horizontally, ending the raging note of the man's scream instantly. Pavor punched the other in the temple with his iron clad fist, mercifully taking his opponent to dark unconsciousness and away from the blinding pain of his current intestinal issues, before delivering him up to the land of permanent night.

Areithous roared in anger as he watched two of his finest henchmen murdered with such efficiency by the trio of warriors. He had expected hunters to come for him but had perhaps thought they might have been a little less upfront in their approach. The poison dart from a silent blowpipe, a hail of crossbow bolts in an ambush, an attack from another gang. These he had expected but an attack like this seemed petty and unlikely to succeed. Still, now it was up to him to deal with the threat. He could call for his other men in the building but he felt no fear now, just anger at the fact that the barbarian, postman and ninja were not only responsible for the death of two of his men but were likely the cause of the fire as well. He heaved up his massive mace and started swinging it around his head. He ran towards the three men as his own stalwart companions lay dead on the courtyard floor.

Seton, Pavor and A'Lastor knew what they had to do against such an expected attack and they quickly backed away from the threat of the gigantic gangster and retreated back into the narrow passage behind them.

Areithous was enraged, his jagged teeth bespoke of not a totally human background or of some nifty filing work to enhance his already fearsome demeanour. His heavy weapon cleaved the air as he advanced but the retreat of his enemies into the thinly wedged confines of the alley meant no room for the six foot shaft and black heavy head of iron. As the trio of bounty hunters made it back to the relative protection of the passage Areithous made a last attempt at an attack with the mace. Wielding it with a powerful stroke it caught the corner of a wall and exploded brick and mortar, leaving a craterous mark where the metal had mauled it and added a large cloud of dust to the fetid smelling air.

"You think I need this to beat you?" Areithous roared, holding up the fathom long bludgeon. "I'll rip you to bits with my hands and teeth."

Saying that the gangster launched the metal cudgel like a harpoon, head first, with a quick punching throw towards Seton Rax. The lumpy head of cast iron smashed into the barbarian's chest, the alleyway not only preventing broad sweeping attacks but also swift evasive manoeuvres. Seton grunted and stumbled back before falling to the floor, landing clumsily, obviously knocked out from the strike and the sudden expulsion of all the breath from his lungs. The light of his mind vanished, the barbarian lay still while the beast that was Areithous followed up his missile attack with a charging run.

Surprised by the swiftness in the depletion of their own ranks and intimidated by the enraged bull like man bearing down upon them A'Lastor and Pavor bravely stood their ground. Pavor held his fists pugilistically, with just his knuckle dusters, he felt suddenly inadequate. A'Lastor, with both xyele glinting in the mainly dark passage, shifted his stance in order to receive the charge. Areithous pounded towards them, emerging though the explosion of mortar and brick dust, his massive weight stomping the floor through thick soled and hobnailed boots.

Pavor boldly moved to engage first, thinking that a quick leap and a crack to the side of the head maybe enough to bring the ogre like thug to the ground. The bounty hunter found his mind racing with the thought of a bank of crossbowmen aiming nine bolts at Areithous.

That was what they needed at the end of the alley, rather than a comatose barbarian, a ninja and a knuckleduster wearing doorman who had turned his skills to this line of trade. Pavor leapt and struck with a straight punch towards the gangster just as Areithous swept back with his fist balled to the size of an average man's skull. The reach of the bigger man connected with Pavor first, smashing against a shoulder and half his chest. The leaping postman changed directions instantly from the force of the strike, one moment a flying punch, the next crashing against the brick lined passage way and peeling off the wall into an ungainly lump on the floor. His cap dislodged in the attack, rolled and tilted away to slump like its master. A'Lastor watched as Pavor's curled up ponytail unravelled and limply lay, soaking up filth from the shallow gutter.

"You're next ninja!" bellowed Areithous, continuing his run, eyes bulging from his shorn skull and jagged teeth dripping spit and aggression.

"I surrender," A'Lastor calmly replied, throwing down his xyele with a metallic clatter.

"No surrender you black crack," taunted Areithous, now striding towards his foe who tried to back away from the gargantuan threat. "You came here to collect your bounty and all you are going to claim is death."

Areithous again demonstrated his prolific ability to strike and lunged forward with startling speed and grabbed A'Lastor round the throat. Too fast even for his reflexes, A'Lastor found the massive hand of his enemy almost encircling his neck. The gangster, bended slightly and then thrust his arm up, turned and held A'Lastor against the wall, bringing their eyes to the same level. A'Lastor's shoes dangled a good two foot from the floor. Areithous leered and leaned closer, their heads almost touching. A'Lastor could smell a rancid combination of salted cod and stale ale on the breath of the beast, he could see the pores of his nose filled with blackheads and pus, feel the heat from his sweaty head but it was the eyes that attracted most attention. A'Lastor breathed calmly, he was unconcerned. He looked deep into the eyes of Areithous and judged their content. He was looking for the slight change in shape of the pupils, the additional thin veins that would increase their imaging capacity over that of a normal man. A'Lastor saw what he expected and maintained his gaze.

Areithous was naturally brawny and strong and tougher than most of the demonic creatures he had encountered in his apprenticeship and rise through the dark arts. Now though he was beyond human. He was beyond the strength meant for man and his muscles burned with the promises of the underworld. Areithous hoped to gain high levels of influence within the very inner circles of Hell. The coven he had joined had provided excellent learning so far. He was intelligent, aware and talented in the dark arts. His over burly frame and vast size had meant people had unwittingly thought him a fool in his youth. He would not be underestimated again. He was going to be a High Master and an overlord in Umiat. He only had to share his body with a minor demon and give it the nourishment it desired. It wasn't much of a payment or an imposition. Areithous looked back into the eyes of his captured enemy, looking for the fear he had seen many times in his victims, this time, however, there was none. A flicker of bewilderment twitched through his heavy brow. The shape of the pupils of the man he was about to crush were wrong. He had to look close but they were not circles. They were perfect octagons, even in this alley and the dank light it provided, demons had to enlarge their ocular orifices in order to be able to see better.

"You've come for me?" Areithous' question was intent and incredulous towards the bounty hunter he held. He began to squeeze his mighty fist in rage and fear. "Why now?"

A'Lastor was unable to respond, his throat beginning to tighten. Held against the wall and firmly pinned by his back, the bricks and the thrusting grip of his target, he gently reached a free hand into his pocket and grasped the metal pipe he always carried. A'Lastor stayed calm and turning the tube prepared to strike. Areithous, thinking his assailant was now unarmed, did not suspect that the demon he held would reach and find a device more deadly than he had ever encountered in his years of villainy and dalliances with the blackest of magic. He continued to squeeze, intent on killing the creature that had come to claim his life.

A'Lastor stabbed the spiked end of the pipe directly into the throat of Areithous. Metal speared flesh, cartilage and vital veins to emerge into the windpipe. The assault did cause pain and shock but beyond all of the physical sensation was the fear. Terror and horror of all that he knew combined and swelled in his mind, Areithous knew he was destined for worse than Hell. Not dropping the creature he held, Areithous ripped away the cloth covering its head and confirmed his deepest fears. The face smiling back was flawless, perfectly smooth skin, devoid of stubble or scars. The cheekbones were high and there was a perfect and delicate chin. It was the epitome of idealised beauty from an older age, yet the fangs which protruded beyond the blood red and pursed lips represented an agony of despair and terror to the tracked man. Areithous recognised the face from the books of arcane lore which he would browse in his own study. A face of the real underworld. He tried to speak, to plead for forgiveness but only managed to gargle a frothy combination of saliva, phlegm and blood which bubbled in his throat. The liquids pooled and began to drip from the guttering end of the pipe, like an animated gargoyle in a bloodbath.

A'Lastor grabbed the wrist which still pinned him to the wall and bracing himself by raising his legs to the wounded warrior's chest, he shoved hard, his back firmly against the brick passageway giving him the leverage he needed. The fight in Areithous was dissipating and he slumped away and fell to his knees. A'Lastor landed lightly, swathed his face, pinched fingers holding the cloth tight as he bound his head in long, practised, circular movements. All the time he stood, watching his quarry suffering, hunched on the filthy floor. Then, redressed, A'Lastor took the couple of steps needed to reclaim his xyele from where they lay.

The much sought after bounty bled and struggled for breath. His huge fingers reached for the pipe and he bravely attempted to tug it free from his throat. The metal spikes, deep within his neck acted as barbs as well as a piercing weapon, shaped beautifully they caused an exquisite yet solid pain as they caught against the bloody walls of his windpipe and grabbed firmly.

A'Lastor now standing above the defeated man raised his sword to the defined stance of a decapitating executioner.

"It is uncharacteristic of me to comment before I make a kill Areithous," the demon's voice was clear. "You said that I have come to claim a bounty but I have come to claim far more than just that. And as to why now? Well now it is sanctioned. You over stepped the mark in your aspirations and now I can claim your soul."

The demon's arm fell and the xyele parted head from torso neatly below the rougher incision of the metal pipe. A'Lastor walked to the rolling orb of the head, steadied it with a foot and cut away a slight amount of excess flesh from the remains of the giant's now bloodied stump of a neck. He reached in through the bottom of throat and with delicate fingers, grasped the spiked end of the tube. A'Lastor pulled the device neatly through the rent remains and out of the bisected windpipe so that the barbs did not catch. He removed most of the gore that had collected within the tube with a couple of flicks of his wrist. He didn't mind the taste of blood in his mouth but the device had to be clear of any major lumps of flesh so that A'Lastor could cleanly suck through it. He then stood and waited, watching for the expected swirling, rising, strands of soul that he so relished.

Seton Rax awoke in a world of groggy pain and confusion. He shook his shaggy mane of hair to clear his head and collect his thoughts but with the pain that shot through his body he remembered the attack and instantly feared that his sternum must have been broken by its connection with the mace which still lay beside him. A broken chest bone was almost impossible to mend, so he was relieved when a gentle fingering gingerly suggested that he would only suffer a massive bruise. His muscled bulk had cushioned a lot of the blow. He turned his head, as he lay on his back, to see Pavor still unconscious beside him. He wondered how they could both still be alive after the assault. Realising that A'Lastor must have somehow succeeded in the mission, he reached for his dropped axe. He quickly sat up, winced at the pain that wracked his torso and turned round to surprisingly see A'Lastor, hunched and swaying in the shadows. He was moving as if he was performing a dance to no earthly heard tune and miming the music on some metallic piccolo, over the corpse of Areithous. Seton Rax blinked and passed out again, slumping to the alley floor. The pain was too great after sitting up and the hallucination of A'Lastor acting so strangely was far too much for his mind to cope with at this moment.

Chorus Six

Vixen marched at the head of a band of warrior worshippers who had managed to congregate after the devastating assault on their temple at Beth Col. That was over half a year ago now and the new leader of the Ahrioch Horde had summoned the devout to quest in revenge for the death of Ahriman. She intended to convert and subjugate others on her path, but for now it was her intention to amass with a secondary force and then strike out for an attack against the monastery of Aklavik in the far northeast of Umiat, situated on an island near the Porcupine Gulf.

The reason for currently being on such a forsaken isle off the mainland of Kenai was simple. Vixen had to get her shock troops to a boat and boats were often intercepted by the Pirate League if you travelled the main sea lanes between Umiat and Kenai. The Pirate League was led by her erstwhile companion Percy Fenton and his dread protector, Mr. Battfin. The Pirate League was the unofficial navy of Umiat, paid by the slut queen of Umiat, Annabella Blaise, to patrol and protect the seas between the two continents. Vixen knew that Fenton would have all his vessels out looking for her and her followers. She cursed his name and that of his bodyguard. She could not contain her anger at how the black first mate had protected Fenton against the undead guards and mercenaries that had been hired to defend Beth Col. However, they had survived, just as she had survived the carnage that had ensued when her leader had been murdered in the rescue of the despised Tumbletick and the Umiat Stone. She had fled through a window, climbed rather than jumped as suspected, and then watched from the rooftop of the temple as those that she had once travelled with escaped. She listed their reviled names, Percy Fenton, Mr. Battfin, Is-Is, Egremont, Seton Rax, Tumbletick and that crack, Campbell the Weasel. She had seen them as they had battled their way through the riot and fled back to Rhyell, her only consolation being that Beran and Y'Bor Kaz were both proficiently cut down by a knot of Landsknecht mercenaries.

She thought to herself how much she would enjoy meeting with Campbell again, to finish the knife fight that was left unconcluded in the inner sanctum of Ahriman's personal quarters. Since his death she was stronger. She was now the head of the Ahrioch Horde. She had taken control when he had translocated his evil guiding spirit to her with his last breaths. Vixen was stronger than the vessel that last contained the original spirit of Ahriman though. It couldn't control her so completely. Couldn't reshape features and corrupt her voice and thoughts. Although she was truly devout to the cause, retaining nearly all of her original characteristics, savvy and skills meant she was more apt for the challenges of the real world and the tasks that lay ahead. Possession was fine as long as it was a symbiotic relationship and Ahriman was behaving himself nicely within the contours of her body and the depths of her mind. With Ahriman being so compliant, Vixen could concentrate on trudging to the rendezvous, meeting with the rest of her cohorts and then exact a revenge atrocity on the people of Umiat.

The last assault had been against the heart of Umiat by stealing the precious talisman that mythically guarded the island. This time it would be a vengeance against their religious soul and the Aklavik monastery was a fine and secluded target for a damaging raid.

After several weeks of forced marching the sight of the meeting place, filled with another hundred loyal warriors and the fabled black ship, anchored in the shallows, was most welcome. The cove was well sheltered and revered by the faithful as an old landing place for pilgrimages to the sacred stone circles. Vixen struck out with renewed vigour to get to the camp. All looked in order, all looked ready, her captain had done well. Her men too felt their morale and hopes rise. Both groups, those who had marched across Kenai and then braved the Tanana Strait, ferried by exorbitant merchants, and those who had risked the seas in the black ship, cheered as their numbers doubled within the cove. Praise roared into the sky to the Dark Lords of Hell for bringing the faithful together. The coteries rushed together to meet in a crashing tide of friendship, hands were clasped, backs slapped and loyalties sealed. The campfires were stoked and fed extra driftwood so that the sacrifices could be roasted after having their throats slit. The blood offering would flow thick from where it fell, gurgle through the stony beach and out into the sea tonight. Two hundred worshippers of Ahrioch would need to be well fed after their travels and with Vixen as High Priestess performing the ceremony of adoration, the twenty slaves selected for the rite could feel honoured as their pitiful lives were offered up to Ahrioch and their bodies butchered, cooked and consumed by the faithful.

Vixen dodged her way between the embracing groups and sought out her captain. Hoarfrost was a good and loyal servant of Ahrioch and a great leader of men. Vixen felt sure he could make it to the inner circle, in time, especially if he performed well in the impending assault versus Aklavik. Hoarfrost would have been easy to spot if he was standing with the rest of the men, Vixen thought, so he must be attending to strategy, logistics or the ritual purifications needed of the sacrificial slaves. She headed to one of the larger tents that had been pitched at this staging post. Pulling back the grey canvass flap, Vixen peered inside and looked upon the dark cloaked man, hunched over a large, elongated trestle table. Nearby a collapsible field chair was unfolded as the officer chose to stand, not sit, in his deliberations. He was pouring over a map of the eastern portions of Umiat, details of the sea depth and known currents in the Porcupine Gulf engrossed him. He knew the black ship at their command could out run anything at the Pirate League's disposal but it could not outwit the shallow seas of the infamous gulf if it became stranded on a shoal or sandbank. If that happened and the pirates of Umiat caught them at a low tide it could well mean a boarding party and that was a fight they did not want. Monks and local militia were one thing, facing a band of heavily armed and experienced pirates with daggers twixt their teeth, swinging aboard via swiftly spliced ropes, was another. The tactics that had worked best against Umiat were unexpected hit and runs, assaults that were bloody and terror inducing against the weak and undefended, not versus other fighters.

Hoarfrost sensed the presence behind him and knew that Vixen was with him again. His muse and inspiration. His converter. She who had taken him from a life of professional fighting and given him a purpose, other than that of mercenary gold. A warm smile swelled in his lips as he remained contemplating the charts. Would she speak first or would he have to turn to her? Obsequious gestures and grovelling postulations were not needed between them, despite her high rank. 'Highest of all ranks now,' he thought quickly. She was powerful and cunning before, now she was everything. He heard the tent flaps muffle together as the cords that would hold them were laced shut. He then sensed that she had removed her cloak and thrown it to the floor. He stood slowly, his massive height and girth swamping the space of the tent.

"Raven Hill. My mistress," his voice was sonorously deep and edged with a rasping growl. At a fathom and a foot tall he turned slowly to face her. The last time they had been together was after the disaster at Beth Col. He looked down at the exquisite beauty and form of his red headed leader.

"You call me by my real name. I am glad to hear it from you," Vixen replied. She took in the ruggedness of his visage. His massive jaw, with a rough black stubble beard and a white scar, jagged on his right from ear to chin. His broad nose, flaring nostrils as his lungs swallowed vast slugs of air. She looked into his dark soulless eyes. Almost black, no discernable pupil. The eyes, set deep in his shaven skull, of a killer and devout believer in the faith. Vixen relished in the muscles of his shoulders and chest which curved his cloak magnificently. 'Yes', she thought. Here was the captain that would help her in cutting bloody swathes of retribution against her foes. She had never met his equal in combat. He should have been at Beth Col with her when Tumbletick and the Umiat Stone had been taken. No marauding band of adventures would have been able to resist his martial skills. She felt certain that Hoarfrost could deal with Mr. Battfin and could even be a match for the terrifying Is-Is, should they ever encounter each other.

"We leave at dawn?" she asked reaching for the top clasp of her black leather corset which served as a top.

"Yes mistress. Once the men have feasted and slept."

"We have to process some sacrifices then?"

"Yes mistress. They have been cleansed already. They only require to be relieved of their souls. By your revered hand and a blade dedicated to Ahrioch. The Dark Lord of Hell will drink deeply this night and the men will be well fed."

"We have a little time before the setting of the sun," Vixen replied, reaching to the next clasp and unhooking it.

Hoarfrost's eyes blinked away from her face and down to her appearing cleavage. Her well remembered bust was smooth and pale, the releasing grip of her corset revealing a lithe and lusty frame.

"Yes mistress," Hoarfrost replied in the confident tone of an ex-lover.

"Good. Then you can help me get into my ceremonial robes," said Vixen. She playfully bit her bottom lip as she advanced and let the corset fall to the floor.

Chapter Seven

Boiling black clouds, nature's raging torment, slowly circled across the north-western skies. The people of Sitka pulled closed and bolted their doors and where they didn't have shutters for their windows they nailed on boards for extra security. The old folk had talked of large storms from off the Sea of Umiat before but few were still alive who could remember what seemed like a wall of pitch slowly rolling towards them in such a threatening way. Prayers were offered up, fears gnawed at stomachs and children cried as they were huddled together in cellars by parents hoping the wooden structures of the town could hold out.

Relentlessly, the power pushed towards the coast. The seas swelled under its pressure and waves sent by its still distant force were precursors of its savagery. Around the protected harbour, great peaks of sea chopped and broke against the rocky shore, bursting and spitting in great slashes of spray onto the town. The winds began to pick up, light faded to an eye straining grey and jagged spikes of lightning struck down at the ocean and then sent forth the ominous harbinger of thunder to all the fearful ears of Sitka.

The streets of the exposed town were empty but for the buffeted pieces of litter and detritus that were whipped into corners by the bullying breeze which whispered of its paternal storm to follow.

Rounding the headland, tucking into the coast and racing the storm, a three masted ship, sails straining and curved, chased by the gods of storms and violent seas, headed for the harbour. The bow burst asunder the white topped waves and spoke of the ship's speed. On board, ravaged sailors responded to the raucous commands of a large, bald, black man with a ritually scarred face. His arms, thicker than most men's thighs, bulged as he held the wheel firmly on course. Captain Battfin had won his title by dint of deed and a common consensus from his men. All respected him and the two sabres which were sheathed safely at his sides could earn respect from any that did not shortly before they died. He wore high leather booths, black trousers and a black sleeveless jerkin. The only colour that graced his frame was a deeply purple sash, tied with a buccaneer's flair around his waist. Captain Battfin had captained 'The Brazen Manticore' for a while but that was too small a vessel and not nearly befitting enough a command for a pirate of his renown. When he had found an enemy ship to his liking he had taken it as his own and now the pirate stood proud, unfeeling against the storm, just committed on getting his three passengers, crew and ship safely to Sitka and a long hoped for rendezvous.

'The Peppercorn' creaked and strained ahead of the storm. To be caught fully in its power meant being slammed into the rocky coast and like the waves, to be broken, crushed and splintered. Captain Battfin, however, knew that would not be the case. Let the less confident pirates pray under their breath as he ordered a brace of men up the rigging to unfurl a top gallant and add a couple of extra knots to their pace. The sailors feared Captain Battfin more than any storm or drowning. A punishment from him would hurt far more than any watery grave.

The top gallant caught at a slicing cut of air fathoms above the deck of 'The Peppercorn'. Captain Battfin allowed a twinge of a smile to twitch but for an instant. He had known the gust was there and the ship lurched well in response. He had considered renaming the vessel that he now captained but had found that it had a ring to it which worked well when you muttered it a few times. It had been traditional to have a vessel named after a fearsome beast or a creature of legend but 'The Peppercorn' was a good name he felt and it was sometimes unwise to rename a lady to your own liking. She was fast, yet sturdy, a spice ship built for speed, to turn a profit rather than heads. Technically she was a barquetine, a three masted vessel with more speed than a barque or a schooner. However, some sailors felt that the barquetines lost some of their handling due to square rigging on the foremast and fore-an-aft rigging on the main and mission masts. Yet Captain Battfin found himself loving his command more and more with each league that had slipped by in the months since he had taken her as his prize and there wasn't a sailor in the fleet who would dare to say that Captain Battfin lost some handling in the name of speed.

The pirate berated himself a little for slipping off into thoughts of his ship's name and appropriateness for the task. The storm was at her stern and the harbour was now in line with the bow. Every now and then the port was hidden by the spinnaker leading the way as it pulled hard on the foremast and the barquetine pitched and yawed with the waves. Timing would be everything as the swelling seas lifted 'The Peppercorn' and then tipped her forward. The waves would be gentler in the harbour but the zephyrs would still claw and lick at her sails. Captain Battfin roared to his crew, all hands took position around the deck. He had enough for the task ahead. Of his three passengers only one would be useful in the rigging but let him rest now in the cabin and exercise his tongue with the other two, not his frame out on a yard arm, frantically furling rugged sailcloth, set to a storm sail plan of Captain Battfin's devising.

The rains hit the railings at the stern just as 'The Peppercorn' passed by the two wooden lighthouse beacons at the entrance to the harbour. The winds had already blown out the bonfires, heating them with gusty blasts, the fuel had been consumed too fast and no man was brave enough to restock them. 'The Peppercorn' wallowed and sat a little in the relatively sluggish waters of the port, then the winds grabbed the sails again to spur her on to the docks. Captain Battfin barked his command and pirates rapidly climbed, perched and untied knots and slickly redressed the ship to a barren set of sticks and rigging. Skeletal she looked after the blossoming bloom of sails before. The rain lashed down as the last sail was lashed up, squalling around the crew in rapid patterns of intensity. Captain Battfin blinked away some rain and tasted the salt of the sea as the storm's tears fell to his lips. He savoured the briny quality he loved so much. Then with great piloting skill he brought 'The Peppercorn' alongside a straining wooden jetty with her remaining momentum as bobbing fishing boats pulled at their fixings on the other side of the dock.

Captain Battfin's first mate came running up, saluted a respectful swipe in awe of his captain's sailing ability and then wiped away a combination of precipitation and sweat from his forehead.

"Briggs, secure her well," shouted Captain Battfin above the encroaching storm. "Me and the passengers won't be long. We leave after the storm does. If she remains intact."

The fearsome black pirate showed a momentary sense of affection in front of his first mate and stroked the wheel of the ship.

"She will sir. She will. She's a fine old spice clipper. Been through worse than this down south I'm sure sir," Briggs replied back loudly through the increasing winds and rampant rain. He then cantered off calling down some of the stronger boys from the rigging to lash 'The Peppercorn' in the correct fashion, to the rickety dock.

Captain Battfin strode towards the door to the cabins and was not surprised to see the handle turn and a vast chain mailed hare stoop through and under the lintel to emerge and stand with his ears erect in the rain. All eight feet of Is-Is was an impressive sight. With kukris and daggers strapped around his body, arms and legs and slung over his back his double handed sword, he looked like the monumental legend that he was. Is-Is sniffed the air and bit his bottom lip with his one remaining and protruding buck tooth. His gold rings glinted in the half light and the rain. Memories of past battles and encounters, inserted into old wounds in his unprotected towering ears.

Captain Battfin smiled at the giant hare. A broad, all giving smile of love and respect. As Captain Battfin's teeth gleamed also in the murk, Is-Is' ears began shaking tremulously under the pounding of the wind and rain, setting them to a rapid, vibrating and swaying. The storm's fury was now very close.

Following Is-Is, Campbell the Weasel scampered quickly out onto deck. His pointy nose also sniffing the air above a pathetic growth of facial hair which sprouted forth, the result of a full week at sea. He pulled his customary dark cloak around him and lifted the hood for a little protection from the slicing rains.

Then, the High Captain of the Pirate League emerged. The devastatingly handsome and always immaculately dressed, Percy Fenton, stepped out on deck. His high leather boots drumming a resonant beat from the heels. No man could pull off the ensemble of a three quarter black leather jacket, bright mustard waistcoat and a pink cravat swathed around the neck quite like Percy Fenton. With a coquettish grin to the elements engulfing him, Fenton now took the lead and strode to the railings to starboard and leapt over them and down to the dock. His coat flapped around him due to his falling momentum and the storm's venting fury. He landed solidly, on both feet, causing a hollow boom on the planked jetty that drummed out louder than the elemental rage around him. Buttoning his coat he turned to see Campbell lightly spring overboard as well, followed by Captain Battfin's vault and the graceful bound of Is-Is. Is-Is some how successfully landed with more grace and panache than any of the quartet, despite his bulk, armour and attached weaponry.

"Right then Campbell," Fenton shouted above the swirling maelstrom. "Lead on. Let's get to Seton's before the storm makes land. You sure you know the way?"

"Oh please!" Campbell called back, tucking himself further into his already drenched cloak. "If the information is correct and the information is always correct, I know the way. The Thieves Guild is not one for making mistakes in its communications on matters such as this. Follow me, it's not far."

Seton Rax & Company

If any of the inhabitants of Sitka had been peeking through the slats of their shutters they would have just been able to make out a lean and wiry man slinking through the shadows and gloom, his head bowed against the downpour. Following him was a terrifying black warrior, with cutlasses, scarred and awesome, a man to be feared. Dressed in black he whispered through the rain like a memory, half seen, an unrecalled nightmare playing at the back of the mind. Next came flamboyance and colour, striking boots, long leather coat, a yellow jerkin and a shock of pink by the throat. All of that combined with a face that beamed despite the torrents and drew you in with its beauty and confidence. Then flowing him, bringing up the rear, the tall grey lethal hare, shimmering full chain mail curving around his lithe yet muscular frame. Daggers, knives and kukris ready to be drawn to deal out slicing death. He had a vast sword strapped to his back and his short cropped fur of his face was beginning to clump up revealing scars and cuts on that ravaged visage. He alone walked like he was ignoring the rain. His thoughts steadfast on their mission.

It was not far to the offices of 'Seton Rax and Company', about a hundred yards and Campbell led Captain Battfin, Percy Fenton and Is-Is swiftly there. There were few cities and towns in Umiat that Campbell did not know well. His adventures and roles within the Thieves Guild had taken him on wide journeys and it was his business to know the ways in, out and around. Upon arriving at the door to the establishment, Campbell quickly surveyed the rest of the street for any signs of watchers, wet in the rain and spying. The winds were strong now and shop front shutters rattled, signage swung on metal arms, the creaks of rusty joints ominously loud above the howling gale.

Campbell, sure that no-one was about, reached inside his cloak and pulled forth a favoured pick, ready for a discrete entry. If the door was bolted then they would have to knock but Campbell's profession allowed him a swifter escape from the rain than waiting for an inhabitant to respond to a pounding unexpected guest. No bolts were drawn however and the lock clicked easily allowing the thief to open the door. The storm was blowing so strongly now that he could only just hear the shimmering tinkle of sound made by the petite bell set to life on its metal spring. The four adventurers slipped into the offices, shut the door and started shaking off the rain.

"You Hoo! Seton, are you in?" Fenton called effeminately. The memory of the barbarian in a too short top and a cerise wrap out in the wilds of Kenai on their last adventure together was still fresh enough to summon up a mocking invite to come down and see his old companions.

"Who's there?" came a shout from the upper floor, followed by rapid footsteps on the ceiling and then climbing down the steep stairs to the back room.

"Just some old friends," called back Percy, searching the office for a location to strike a pose upon their re-acquaintance. Fenton selected to sprawl in one of the leather sofas, his arms spread wide across its back.

Campbell and Captain Battfin gave each other a look that spoke of their bond and a common understanding of Fenton's ways. Is-Is remained by the front door, water dripping from his ears and pooling around him. His thoughts were of rust and armour and weapon maintenance. All of their packs were back on 'The Peppercorn' but he felt certain that Seton would have some of the essential oils and cloths needed to care for the large amount of metal upon Is-Is' person.

Seton entered the room, battleaxe in hand against any potential threat. One didn't expect visitors or customers during a storm such as the one that battered the town now. He was backed up by Pavor, A'Lastor and Eris.

"Hmm," the barbarian quickly said as he looked around the room. "I should have known that a lock would have been little use if Master Campbell was in town. We should have bolted the door and placed a large barricade behind it. Then set a cohort of guards to secure the door. Yet I suspect you still would have got in. Hey guys, how you doin'?"

The barbarian put down his axe and rushed to embrace his old friends. The storm outside was well on land now and it rattled and tugged the window shutters and door of the building as the erstwhile adventures hugged and clasped hands. Seton quickly introduced Eris, A'Lastor and Pavor. Campbell the Weasel was all charm and manners, kissing Eris' hand and politely responding to the salutations. Is-Is nodded to each in turn still standing as if he guarded against the gale which continued to ravage the wooden city. Percy conjured up his most practiced smile for the buxom Eris and flourished a bow for the mysteriously clad A'Lastor and well worn Pavor. Captain Battfin remained silent, stern and brooding.

"Well guys, now that you all know each other, why are you here?" asked Seton. "Sheltering from the storm?"

"Creating one probably," replied Campbell. "It's Vixen. We've found her. Or rather found where she was about a fortnight ago. And, we've come to collect you and the rest of your company to aid us in her apprehension. We at the Thieves Guild and the Pirate League knew you had set yourself up as a bounty hunter and what with questing with you before we thought you might be interested in a lucrative private contract which has been offered by Princess Annabella Blaise herself."

"Vixen!" spat Seton after he had recovered from the impact of Campbell's tirade. "If I knew where she was I'd hunt her down for free!"

Eris, Pavor and A'Lastor became more alert and attentive as well. You didn't have to work with Seton directly to have heard the stories of the former Head of Umiat's Secret Service and her betrayal to the realm. Traitor to her country, faith and friends, Vixen was infamous.

"Well it isn't going to be for free," Campbell replied. "The reward is one hundred thousand gold pieces and the bestowal of titles and lands too. But, but, my dear barbarian friend, she has to be returned alive for trial and public execution. The princess was quite specific and adamant on that point when we last spoke. It's not being offered out to anyone else either. Well not at the moment. Not unless we fail. And how could we possibly fail when we've got Captain Battfin and a handpicked crew on board his new ship 'The Peppercorn'? He can take us, a hardcore bunch of warriors, villains and reprobates, under the command of the Crown to catch one of the worst offenders of loyalty, betrayers of men and downright despicable damsels this world has ever seen. I will ask you again. How could we fail?"

"When do we leave?" asked A'Lastor. "I have waited long for a sanction to hunt such a foe."

"Yes. We know about your particular needs Master A'Lastor," said Campbell with a wry rise of an eyebrow. "The Guild has long considered approaching you with formal offers of employment. For is it not so that bounty hunting really is a discipline that falls under the remit of my organisation? Stealing away life and liberty from those who may well deserve it but would resist your attempts."

A'Lastor bowed his covered head in response, an agreement at the observation.

"I appreciate the Guild's interest," he replied. "Now that the task has been ordered by a high authority, I am keen to be part of the mission."

"Good. Very good," said Campbell. He turned to look at Eris and Pavor. "I trust that the two of you would wish to partake as well. Both of you have more than adequate skills and are building a reputation for success."

Eris blushed a little and Pavor merely shrugged modestly.

"I'd love to be part of it," said Eris.

"Honoured to be so," stated Pavor.

"Then in answer to A'Lastor's earlier question, we leave as soon as this storm has blown itself clear of the docks," said Campbell. "We'll explain where we are going when we are on board 'The Peppercorn' but you had better pack what you would want for about three months away from home in some pretty remote environments. You got any food about Seton? The only thing we haven't got on board ship is a decent cook. I've been eating nothing but biscuits for a week!"

Chorus Seven

Vixen stood on the deck of the black ship having conducted an inspection with the behemoth, Hoarfrost, who now stood beside her. She had never been on board the boat before and was filled with admiration for its ingenuity and design. She had of course known that it moved without oars, or sails and that its technology enabled it to strike and retreat far quicker than any other vessel of the age. The shipwright who had taken the leap of imagination needed well deserved the reward that Ahriman had bestowed upon him with its commission. A guaranteed seat to the left of the throne of one of the mightier Lords of Hell, Fraz-Urb'luu.

She recalled the slaves and horses beneath deck, on their treadmills and positioned at cranks, that, when exercised into motion by encouraging whips, turned the paddled wheels that ran the length of ship on both the port and starboard side. Hidden from view by the water's surface and great covering planks of pitch painted wood. The realisation that water turning wheels to provide power through a rotating beam could be reversed so that the wheel could propel the sea and therefore move a boat was genius. The constant application of many blades from the wheels would thrust the boat onwards and it was hers to command.

Hoarfrost gently touched the small of her back, rousing her from the joy she felt with such a valuable device at her whim. Her whim to reek the havoc of death, terror and revenge against her former state. Hoarfrost's great hand caressed her again and she turned to look at close to two hundred warriors on the beach. The dawn sun cast long shadows from the hills to her left that protected the bay. They were to take to the ship after they had heard their mistress and leader address them and to a man they waited in silence. Devout zealots, they were eager to follow the flame haired beauty Vixen into carnage and revenge. Vixen turned her gaze to take in a broad swathe of upturned, loyal faces. She grasped the rail at the bow of the deck and her impassioned voice struck clearly above the lapping waves across the myriad grains of sand and the gentlest of morning breezes.

"Men of Ahrioch. Warriors of Kenai. Today you embark upon a quest of retribution. Today is your first true step towards cleansing your enemy from the land. Today you tread like the heroes of old against those who would stand against us."

She paused and breathed. Timing and theatricality were important to further win their hearts and minds.

"We are but few in number but our souls are pure and given to our faith willingly. With that knowledge utmost in your heart each one of you glorious acolytes is worth a hundred of our foe. We shall be a scourge upon their earth and strike like nightmares. We shall infiltrate into the mists of dreams and annihilate them in the silence of shadows. Strike them where they are weak but think they are strong. For today we embark against their faith and their way of life. Onto Aklavik. We shall rip the heart from their beating breast and lay waste to their hope. Aklavik!"

The sun crested the low range of hills and struck the amassed grey cloaked warriors. A great chant of 'Aklavik' went up from the horde and then the first few men stepped into the sea and then onto the lowered gangplank, each wishing to be the first to embark, full of vengeance and then after crossing the Circle Sea and Porcupine Gulf to crash in battle against the monastery which sat at the base of the great mountain of Aklavik.

Vixen smiled. No need for any subtlety now or subterfuge. That time was over. Some carnage was about to come to Umiat, the likes of which it had not seen. Not a war against an army but a rampage against the people.

Chapter Eight

'The Peppercorn' burst breaking waves, still choppy from the effects of the dying storm. Sitka had been well battered by the elements and few could remember winds as wicked but the large wooden structures were well constructed and the city had survived, just as it had survived assaults before. No-one had noticed the eight adventurous types leaving the offices of 'Seton Rax and Company' the day after the storm blew itself out. The barbarian owner had turned a little sign to read 'Closed' as he locked up the establishment. He had toyed with the idea of adding 'Gone Hunting' but 'Closed' would do just fine. The lucrative private contract had finally come walking in through the door and though Seton was surprised by the customer, the quarry was an absolute delight. He just hoped the information that had been gathered was good enough to be able to find a trail.

The giant warrior hare, Is-Is, led the way, his chain mail glistening from a light sheen of protective oil that he had purloined from Pavor. Pavor himself had taken an instant liking to the fearsome Is-Is. He had heard tales of his prowess, of waging war, killing Kenai Mountain Dragons, defeating gladiators, all from Seton who had quested with Is-Is before. Plus Is-Is had had a glorious career in the Umiat Army which an old soldier like Pavor found fascinating when Is-Is regaled him with legendary stories from the time of the Ahrioch Wars as they had waited for the storm to blow over. Pavor now trotted alongside Is-Is as Eris and Percy came next, Campbell and A'Lastor followed them and finally the bulky Captain Battfin brought up the rear with the muscle bound Seton Rax.

So it was that they sneaked back to the docks and quickly set sail and found themselves closeted away, all eight, in Captain Battfin's opulent cabin.

"Right, this is what we know," said Campbell. "Vixen was spotted fifteen days ago with a large body of men by one of our watchers who was stationed at a remote island off the Tanana Strait. This island was once one of religious significance, in the ancient past, to the Ahrioch Horde."

"So we assume," continued Percy. "That our old companion Vixen is still very much involved with that foul faith and is plotting some sort of revenge after we took revenge against them for stealing the Umiat Stone and threatening Tumbletick."

"You cut off their leader's head and butchered half his henchmen didn't you?" asked Pavor, already well versed in what had happened at Beth Col in the city of Ende.

"Well technically, Egremont cut off Ahriman's head and we all did a fair amount of butchering both at Beth Col and Kantishna," replied Campbell. "But Vixen escaped that day and her capture, trial and execution is very much desired."

"So what's the plan?" asked Pavor. "Go to this island and try and find her trail? If they are still there it should be easy enough."

"Absolutely. We head east to the island and see what the Ahrioch Horde are up to," replied Campbell.

"Why do they still call themselves a horde?" asked Eris. "From what I can make out they're just a ragtag band of misfits who follow an old demonic faith who have caused a bit of trouble recently."

"Well it's their own name for themselves," replied Campbell. "They were absolutely a horde once. Large enough to wage war against Umiat and send vast armies across the sea. As to a bit of trouble, I think committing the atrocity they did at the Court of Rhyell and stealing the symbolic heart of the nation is probably better qualified as a significant issue. Anyway, there are less of them than there once was but you could hardly expect them to rename themselves the Ahrioch Collective or the Ahrioch Regional Cell Group of Limited Influence and Power, now could you my dear?"

The group laughed at Campbell's retort but five in the cabin soon fell to stern looks again as they remembered friends who had died due to the actions of their enemy. Lord Jackson of En'Tuk had fallen in their quest when an arrow struck him in the chest. Nazar Grant had been ripped to shreds and devoured by undead minions raised to defend Beth Col. Y'Bor Kaz and Beran had been hacked down by mercenary Landsknechts as they had fought to provide a little more time for their fellows to escape.

"Well," said Campbell breaking the silence. "The sooner we finish the job and bring Vixen to justice the better. Plus if she is leading a core of the devout, we can cleanse the land of them as well. We've got a good bunch at the core with us eight plus, we've got 'The Peppercorn' and her crew who are a hand picked group of blood thirsty pirates."

"That is correct," said Percy. "As soon as Mr. Battfin won his first command the very dregs and vilest scum of the fleet wanted to sail with the newly appointed Captain Battfin. I had thought he'd need to advertise but apparently his reputation is such that the very best pirates would flock to him. I'd even written a poster for him. It said 'Wanted. Skinny wiry fellows, tough. Little need for food or praise. Experienced at sea and piracy. Orphans preferred'."

Again laughter played around the ship's room of command. Light poured in through the large lattice bow windows and lit charts and maps that showed the lengths they had to sail to get to the island off the Tanana Strait.

Only A'Lastor and Is-Is were silent with their own thoughts well hidden. The others fell into easy conversations, Percy and Campbell were gregarious fellows, Eris was always a sparkling charm and Pavor and Seton were quick to call for tales of fact or fiction and keen to tell of their own business endeavours. Captain Battfin had to attend to his many duties around 'The Peppercorn' and was frequently out of the cabin, leaving the rest to while away the days as they sailed around the coast of Umiat.

On the third day they sailed by the large city of En'Tuk, the home town of Lord Jackson who had quested with many of them for the Umiat Stone. They had just finished a rather fine meal, it turned out that Campbell's comment about the ship's cook was a little unfair, and the thieving liar had just told a rather saucy tale as a post dinner entertainment called 'Gordon the Horny Weasel'. It was a well known story with a few embellishments by the Master Thief which engendered him as a fine raconteur and wit. When Seton had finished guffawing he wiped his eyes dry and asked a question.

"So if Lord Jackson of En'Tuk was the richest man in the world when he died, doesn't that mean that the second most wealthy instantly took his place? It was back on that first day that we met each other."

"Indeed it does, or did," replied Campbell putting his feet up on the large planked dinner table and leaning back in his chair. He clasped a tankard of quality ale to his chest and sucked his teeth. "Would you like to hear a yarn about that individual? It is a tale of derring-do and features a protagonist of devastating looks and ability."

"Here we go again," said Percy, fishing out his pipe and plugging some Viking Mango tobacco firmly into the bowl. "You had better say yes otherwise he might go all mauve on us. And it is, to be fair, quite a good story. I've heard it about five times already and I would hear it again to pass away the afternoon."

"Certainly then," said Seton.

"Let's hear it," called Eris placing her hands on the sides of her face and planting her elbows either side of her cleaned plate. "I'm particularly interested in anyone who has devastating looks and ability."

"Very well," stated Campbell in his most refined voice, deep, resonant but perhaps with a little too much flamboyance. "If it is a unanimous decision of our dinner guests?"

Pavor laughed his assent, Is-Is raised an eyebrow and A'Lastor nodded in agreement. So Campbell took a deep gulp of ale, placed the tankard firmly down and then sprang from his reclined position and took a theatrical stance in front of the window and began to address his audience.

"As you may well know, I, Campbell the Weasel, hold a high rank within the esteemed Guild of Thieves. As such I am often requested to perform such tasks that befit such a station. For while I am able to freelance without reproach or recrimination, occasionally, I have to still prove my bequeathed loyalties with a commissioned duty which others of lesser qualities could not. Now as Mr. Rax has already observed, upon the tragic death of Lord Jackson of En'Tuk another gentleman instantly became the wealthiest in the world. And, some of you here, right now, have already been very, very close to him. Well, within sight of him, as he was transported with ancient ceremony to his private villa, on his private island, in the middle of the vast harbour of Ende."

There were a couple of tiny gasps and comments of agreement as minds were thrown back to the day when Tumbletick and company had sailed across the horizon wide bay that formed the natural harbour of Ende in the southern continent of Kenai.

Campbell paused for a bit longer. He was pleased with the way the retelling of his tale was going. Even those who had heard it before had looks of engagement on their faces and a positive body language towards him.

"This, gentleman, had made his wealth in a similar way to Lord Jackson. Through trade and acquisition, intimidation and crime, by parley and by the sword. Much of his treasure was gained by the rugged land of Kenai giving up her jewels and precious metals to him. His men digging for the wage of a few coppers a week and he gaining tens of thousands of gold pieces a day. Because he was he and he owned the men who dug. But you will have noticed how I do not refer to him by name. Well that is because no-one really knows his true name. Maybe not even he himself knows what his mother may have whispered to him as he laid nursing at her matronly breast. Perhaps he prefers to be called Lord, Master or Sir as he relishes in his luxury, servants and guards surrounding him in the opulence of the ancients. For on his wooded isle he has built marble temples and villas that speak of an older age. A decadent and painted age of theatre, orgies and dance. An age of songs and feasts, of silks and cold hard steel at the throats of gladiators. Whereas Lord Jackson would be happy to be a public figure and emblazon his name over the doors of his many businesses, our reclusive friend closets himself away with his fantasies and drug fuelled dreams and does not even pay his dues and negotiated cut to the Thieves Guild anymore. As such, he needed to be sent a message. A message which tells him he can still be touched, at will, by us or by our brethren in the affiliated Guild of Assassins. And so it was, that I, Campbell the Weasel, was given the honour of delivering this message to the debtor."

Campbell again turned to silence. He twitched his long pointed nose and rubbed his pathetically sparse beard. He knew he didn't look like a hero and yet he so obviously was one. 'Now for the climax of the tale,' he thought to himself and then to rouse his audience a little further he took on the pose of a classical performer of the stage, one hand to his heart and the other, reaching, yearning, grasping for the gods.

"I had only recently returned from Ende, where I and some of my illustrious companions had successfully secured the Umiat Stone, before the request came to reach out and touch the target with a salutary reminder of our influence. So back I sailed, to that great harbour and took lodgings in a Guild safe house, where I could view the island's comings and goings through a spyglass of great virtue and merit. The isle is heavily masked by trees but information could be gleaned which benefited my task and for a few days I gathered and noted my observations. When I was ready and certain that the target was on the island, I donned my most shadowy gear, stole a small rowing boat and skulled my way across those busy sea lanes. It was a dark and cloudy night when the moon was but a sliver of merest slice of pale light that both guides and hides those of a secretive nature. I manoeuvred my craft with skill and grace, silent strokes of the oar beneath the surface of the sea, a constant movement of pressure against the ocean to move me towards my goal. I landed and secured the boat a mere twenty yards from the main dock to the private island. I hauled the tiny craft up into the tree line, knowing that being this close to the landing stage was the least obvious place for a thief to land. Such an incursion would be unsuspected here and unchallenged. I trod silently into the trees, over moss covered slopes and up into the heart of his private realm. Garbed much as A'Lastor is now, I flitted like a memory between the thoughts of the few woodland creatures that sensed me and completely slinked beyond the ken of others who were paid to watch."

"The island home of the gentleman had become his own fantasy plaything," Campbell continued. "I skirted round many follies and white marble temples, placed in ornamental gardens within the woods. It was a pleasant place indeed and so peaceful that I easily avoided the stomping guards who marched in phalanxes of burnished brass. All spears and wide brimmed shields. Their helmets with garish plumes might have looked the part but they also restricted their gaze from the Master Thief who crept and sauntered with impunity over their land. And so it was, that I, Campbell the Weasel, highest and most skilled of all his class, both of the quick and the dead, never to be surpassed in ability or craft, came to the vast private residence of the target. Sprawling low over the height of the island, shaped and moulded by an architect's eye, the home was a gleaming replica of some forgotten palace of antiquity. A maze of rooms and passages, of courtyards and atriums, kitchens, stores, offices and the most private of private chambers hidden within the very centre of the structure. My trusty picks soon had a servant's entrance unlocked and my nose and intuition then led the way. Gloved hands silently opened doors following well placed drops of oil on hinges. Unseen I twisted and turned from hiding place to hiding place, sometimes behind statues, sometimes wedged between the ceiling and a wall. I made my way by all the nocturnal guests and servants who meandered in assignations or purposefully strode with intent. None saw or heard the ultimate footpad, the supreme pilferer, the brilliant burglar."

"He called himself brilliant pilferer and supreme burglar the last time he told this story," interjected Percy. The rest of the group broke into broad smiles.

"They are not official titles," replied Campbell, his arms folded for a while. "So they are interchangeable."

"Ah," said Percy with a tilt of his head towards the heavens. "So long as I am clear on the matter. Pray continue, do."

"His personal quarters were not difficult to find. I could have followed the streams of maids with dainties laden on silver trays, or dainty maidens dressed as maids ready to be laid. He certainly had a penchant for buxom servant girls in flowing black and white dresses and a bucolic attitude to natural delights. And so it was, that I, Campbell the Weasel, Master Thief, made my own way into his private study as I listened to his scolding entertainment of a group of naughty staff. His office was large and well equipped, with books and trophies of his life. A solid desk with an ornate chair sat slightly away from one side of the room and an unlit fireplace and carved mantel dominated the wall behind it. My well trained eye spotted objects of great value, both of worth and sentimentality, placed in well positioned places around the room. But which to pick? Which would have the most impact? Quickly my skill identified a small figurine, quite crudely carved but in the centre of the mantel-piece. I relished it with my eye. It was ancient and from the far southern lands and from a far, far past. Older than civilisation, from the very birth of man. A fertility figure, once held by one who could only dream of what we were to become. Apart from its rarity I did not know why he should value this item so much, but, I lifted it, turned it round and placed it back down, now settled on a small calling card with a very simple message inscribed upon it. As I left and made my way silently through the corridors, out into the night, through the trees and back to my boat like a wraith through a graveyard, I smiled to myself and imagined him entering the study to work the next day. He may not notice at once but notice he would. His antique facing the wrong way. A few steps across the room to correct it, thoughts of berating his personal maid, before he spotted the small calling card with the message 'Courtesy of the Thieves Guild' embossed in a delicate golden script. Oh what knowledge and fear would then course through his veins, as I, long gone let the Guild know how the task had been completed."

"Oh bravo," said Percy, clapping loudly and with his voice slightly altered as he gripped his pipe with his teeth. "Bravo!"

Eris and Pavor joined in the applause while A'Lastor and Is-Is instantly turned back towards each other and continued maintaining their blades. Seton Rax sat with his eyes wide and mouth hanging open before he could speak.

"Is that really what you did?" the barbarian asked.

"Oh yes indeed Master Rax. 'Tis truly what I, Campbell the Weasel, did."

"Most impressive. What was the result? Has he started paying the Guild the expected percentage?" Seton queried.

"Not that I am aware of. But that doesn't matter. He'll just be very aware that we are aware and are able to 'touch' him again should we will it. Besides there are other more important things which concern us all now and the Guild is keen to see Vixen brought to justice as well. It is not good for the economy to have high profile enemies wandering around at large and threatening the peace."

Captain Battfin came striding into the cabin with a purposeful push of the door and had a quick but muted conversation with Percy. Fenton swiftly stood and went out on deck before the captain shared what concerned him with the others.

"There be a ship hailing us. Coming from the east. They have information and have been searching for us."

Chorus Eight

The slaves on board the black ship eased upon their treadmills and the wheels slowed as, in the depths of night, Vixen's vessel churned the water a little less and approached with a stealth that was unsuspected towards the island. Aklavik was an impressive sight as the dominant dark rock of the jagged mountain thrust straight from the sea and clawed towards the starry sky. To the west and north the island fell away to flatter plains of fertile farmland, villages and the homesteads of peasants and minor lords who benefited from business from the monastery and the ability to grow almost anything on the old lava flats of the dormant volcano.

The monastery was a complex structure, bulky and inorganic looking as many generations had built in differing religious and fashionable styles up the side of the mountain. Countless flights of narrow steep stairs, cut out of the rook, linked buildings and cells, storerooms and chapels. Little squares were everywhere, terraced and lined with low stone walls, individual rocks shaped to fit together without the need for mortar. In each of these tiny piazzas a solitary gnarled tree would grow, bearing a small and bitter yellow fruit much prized by the monks for its ability to cleanse the palate and sharpen the mind for contemplation and prayer.

The monastery was principally designed for the promotion of peace and dedication to the solitary god of Umiat. However, the monks were pragmatic and while many were totally peaceful there were differing factions collected together within the diverse buildings. One faction who shared its many walls were of a warrior ilk. It was one of these monks who, in his plate armour and with his mace at his side, was keeping watch from a turret in his group's wing of the jumbled hermitage. It was he who saw the black ship move without sail or oar across the little harbour that supplied the many monks and it was he who rang the alarm bell above his head as he watched dozens of armed men pour out of the boat and begin tramping along the wooden planks of the dock. The hollow booming of hobnailed boots merged with the peeling of the bell in a melody of impending death. Soon the sound of metal against leather as swords were drawn from scabbards and the screeching yell of two hundred zealots merged to form a cacophony that reached the ears of rapidly waking monks and servants around the complex.

Vixen and Hoarfrost stood on board the deck of the black ship and watched as their shrieking soldiers streamed off, a frenzy of Hell fed maniacs, towards the maze of monastic design. Outer walls were easily scaled by grappling hooks and ropes. Gates, not designed for defence, were soon smashed from hinges and the horde seeped into the buildings and began their butchering work with relish and fluidity.

"And so it begins," said Vixen to Hoarfrost. "Would you care to join them?"

"Naturally mistress. I have a strong need to let some blood free from those monkish frames. Will you partake as well?"

"Of course. I wish to bathe in gore and claim some souls for Ahrioch before the rising of the sun."

Hoarfrost leapt off the boat, followed by Vixen. They strode through the shallow sea, the thighs of Vixen smashing the surface into froth, Hoarfrost found the going easier with his knees well above the water. Together they made land and dashed up a broad set of stone stairs where the tide would sometimes reach. Their men had peeled off into groups, confident that little resistance would be found among the soft and pliant monks. Tonight the monastery would be an abattoir, it would be swift and easy work. The two followed behind a group of their men who had just broken into a chapel, kneeling on the floor in front of them were huddled a bunch of monks bobbing in frantic prayer to their god. Hoarfrost was first to push away his own men to get at the enemy, with a double handed sword that he wielded in one vast fist he ran and began hacking away at the backs of the monks. They did not run or turn and fight, they just died. Vixen was then beside him and as he impaled others, she grabbed their praying heads, pulled them back and began to cut throats with a favoured knife. She laughed in glee at the cascades of blood on the tunics of the monks. She built up a rhythm. Cut out a throat, drop the carcass and move on to the next victim.

"Go," she screamed to her men who watched behind her. "Find yourself some others! This knot of scum are for us to enjoy."

Her troops obeyed and soon just her and Hoarfrost were left with the sound of prayer dwindling. The vast warrior beside her soon grew bored with elaborate sword strokes against such a foe and stepped back to watch as Vixen executed each man in a methodical manner. He leaned against a column of stone and marvelled at her ritualistic technique which soon had the floor awash with thick crimson, hiding the intricate mosaic beneath. With all the monks dead, Hoarfrost bowed to his mistress. She smiled radiantly, dagger in hand, panting slightly with a curl of red hair clinging to a cheek, she stood above the corpses, a vengeful demon.

"More, let's find more," she breathed in deeply, the smell of death exciting her on to additional murder. "Lead on Hoarfrost. There's work to be done."

As death swarmed around the multitude of buildings, the one wing with the warrior monks, closed and barricaded their doors. Stronger doors built for just such an event. Yet not strong enough to keep out the calls of the dying and the orgiastic cries of the assailants. Through thin slots in their thicker stone walls, glimpses were caught of flittering figures, dripping blood from their swords and with horrifically drenched hems on their hooded cloaks. The sect of monks in the outpost was small and now unfashionable. Where once they had been strong and an influence, now only their building spoke of their older power. Few feet crept the vast halls to the early morning prayers now. Due to the nature of their order, many of the Rose Cross had left to seek adventure and take their peculiar mix of militarism and healing around the continent of Umiat and beyond. The few who remained grew old and wearisome and locked themselves away in their fort on the extremities of the monastic complex. Twenty remained in a structure that could have house twenty times that number. With them a handful of servants from the local villages cared for their dietary and cleaning needs. The monks doled out maces and warhammers to these servants and all congregated as a token force in the magnificent foyer, behind the single thick gate to the outpost, clinging to the mountain, hanging over the sea. They awaited the assault that they knew would eventually come.

Silently, mailed gloves gripped hard on the shafts of blunt heavy weapons. While their faith encouraged the destruction of enemies by force, no blood was to be deliberately shed. So bulky smashing maces and hammers were used. The warrior monks continued to stand mutely, listening to the wailing, outside, in the dark. Then closer unknown voices, approaching their own gate. Loud barks, commands, then bulky crashes against the nail studded doors. The wood began to briefly bow and vast hinges strained in their frame as rocks from broken walls were used to batter against the bolted portal. The rabid and raging foe was keen to clear the entire monastery of faith and the pounding on the gate increased in fervour and frequency.

A young servant boy, named Tobias, stood in the midst of the remaining monks and held onto a war hammer, far too heavy for him to swing. He looked with frightened eyes at the grim faced warrior monks and thought how it was okay for them in their crafted armour with years of training behind them in martial skills. He was just a serf from the country given an opportunity of a bed each night and meals in exchange for servitude. Now he was wrapped up in a fate too awful to contemplate. The pounding at the gate increased further, prayers began to be spoken, clearly and brave, no raucous rants to fire up the blood and stir the soul. They would stand and fight in the entrance to their annex, where a little space availed itself for combat, not curled up, hiding in a corner, alone, hoping to be spared as the enemy searched them out with vengeance burning their minds to then thrust a yard of steel through the quaking flesh of discovered monks.

The gates finally burst in splintered rage. One huge panel remained intact and crashed to the stone slab floor as its hinges failed, the second part of the door, now mostly destroyed swung open from the force and behind it a torrent of men rushed in, yelling, wide eyed and already swathed in blood. The monks and servants heaved up their heavy weapons in their hands to repel the onslaught. Within the airy atrium they had hoped for some room in which to attack and duck and fight but the last thoughts of many was how swift and pressing the demons of Hell are. The cascading killers of Ahrioch fell upon the defenders, cutting, hacking and biting. Pushing their bodies into a scrum of dying monks and peasant aides.

The young Tobias never got to find out if he could wield the war hammer, crushed between two mailed monks he felt the thrust of a sword gash into his guts and twist and hack its way back out from his body. He died with an expulsion of vomit, blood and excretion, the smell of sweat and fear burning his mind as the pain and darkness finally took him.

The monks fought back hard but ineffectually and with unpractised and old hands. The force of the Ahrioch Horde that assaulted them were all veterans, skilled and eager to kill. None were left alive. The monastery was ransacked and set to the torch and the evil that caused it howled with delight and cavorted with body parts as they danced victoriously in blood flooded halls, lit by the flames of destruction.

Chapter Nine

The ship approaching 'The Peppercorn' was a wickedly sleek and fast pirate sloop and it masterfully pulled up alongside after a short, tight, leaning curve. Ropes were thrown and pulled taut and the two vessels came together and wallowed to allow the captain from the other ship, a tottering jaunt along an extended gangplank. Captain Battfin and Percy Fenton received the other man and after quickly whispered words he departed, the plank was lifted, the ropes released and the two ships ended their brief embrace.

The group of adventurers gathered again in the cabin with intrigued looks towards their pirate companions.

"Well," said Fenton, addressing them in sombre tones. "I think we have found part of the trail of Vixen. A few days ago there was a violent and devastating attack on the monastery at Aklavik. There were apparently no survivors. Local peasants saw the smoking ruins and when they summoned up the courage to approach, found the hallowed stones and stairs of that fair edifice dripping still with deep congealing blood."

"So she seeks to lead raids against Umiat," said Campbell. "As suspected. Now we know she has transport. We also can confirm the sighting of her in the east of Kenai as highly probable and know that she has chosen to raid a location which was vulnerable but has religious significance."

"How do you know it was Vixen?" asked Eris. "I mean it's an assumption isn't it? No witnesses, just a gory scene."

"I think it is safe to assume on this occasion," said Fenton.

"Does it change your plan to head to the island?" asked A'Lastor in a rare comment. "If we sailed to the monastery I may well be able to pick up certain, scents. A hint of their intentions and next steps. I would suspect that they are still in the area of the Porcupine Gulf."

"I agree with A'Lastor," said Campbell immediately. "Those of us with tracking abilities might well be able to glean a lot of information from the gory scene, as Eris puts it."

"It seems to me that we are hunting for her over a very large area," observed Pavor. "And she is obviously using a boat to move around and the sea doesn't leave many marks to follow."

"But now we have two reports. It gives us a closer proximity," said Campbell, lifting a dagger with a skilled move and then cleaning his nails, deftly scraping up dirt with the pointed blade. He then moved to a large map on the wall and began to point with the knife around the chart. "We also know that she has travelled from point one at Beth Col, where she ran away from a knife fight with me, to point two on the island off the Tanana Strait, to point three, the monastery at Aklavik."

"And another thing that has been confirmed," said Fenton. "We now know that she does have a large force of men with her. And new information, exactly as Pavor points out, she has a vessel."

"I'd still recommend going to the island with the stone circles and the Ahrioch heritage where she was spotted by your man on the mountain," said Seton. "I think we can assume that she won't return to Aklavik, as she has destroyed it and that she must have some form of base. So why wouldn't she head back to eastern Kenai?"

"Are there any other areas of extreme religious importance in the far east of Umiat?" asked Pavor. "Apart from the monastery I thought it was all pretty sparse and just thousands of islands around the Porcupine Gulf and they are of no use to anyone except pirates and thieves to hide on."

Campbell, Percy and Captain Battfin all looked at Pavor.

"No offence meant gentlemen," the wiry warrior proffered by way of an apology.

"None taken," said Campbell. "But a point well made. Thousands of islands there are. Should one want to, or have the need to, you could hide out for decades. Could you get the fleet to up some numbers in the gulf Percy? Might be an idea to increase our resources in the vicinity."

"No problem," Percy replied. "What about Pavor's other point of other locations of any religious significance?"

"There's nothing really until you get to Ve'Tath," mused Campbell in response. The thief had travelled extensively around Umiat in his past and was racking his remembrances of the multitude of small settlements to the east beyond the last major river of the continent. "Sagwon is a large town to the north-east but it doesn't have any major religious structures because the monastery is, sorry was, so close. There are loads and loads of villages though along the coast. They all have shrines, a couple of small churches perhaps. Do you think she might only be going for what she sees as legitimate faith targets then Pavor?"

"It's possible. But one attack does not a pattern make," he replied.

"Hmm," thought Campbell out loud. "I think perhaps, knowing Vixen as we do, that an increase in the number of ships to patrol the coastal towns as well as investigating the islands of the Porcupine Gulf will be needed. Then 'The Peppercorn' heads for the remains of the monastery and we attempt to utilise our talents there to find out any other useful information. Agreed?"

While there were many confirmations to the authority of Campbell's question and decision, thoughts did turn to the problems that faced them of hunting Vixen down over such an expanse of sea and little lumps of land. Eventually, though, all were fully behind the plan and there were consolatory thoughts that at least they were getting closer to the traitorous spy.

So 'The Peppercorn' picked up the trade winds and with sails cracking and rapidly rippling, they pushed on through the waters of the Sea of Kaltag and towards the east. Preparations for what they would find at the monastery mostly concerned sharpening blades, for comfort and to partake in an activity rather than any concern of engaging with the enemy there. Is-Is and A'Lastor spent much of their time together, examining each others blades and talking long into the inky nights of swelling seas about how to keep and edge sharp on curved or crooked weapons. Is-Is had never fought with a xyele before, his massive strength was usually enough to hack through a foe when he fought with his straight two handed sword but he was intrigued with the speed and agility that A'Lastor could muster when they had sparred together out on deck. A'Lastor in turn was obsessed with the kukris that were the giant hare's favoured devices for close quarter and quieter work. The hunter's instinct and fighter's need for devastation combined with interest in the way a kukri would work against flesh. A'Lastor's darker side was also drawn to the myths associated with the taking of blood upon drawing the specialist knives and he watched intently when Is-Is always cut his own thumb a little to allow the kukris to feed after sharpening them.

Eris spent much of her time sparring too, though with words rather than weapons against the caddish wits of Percy and Campbell who both playfully traded witticisms of erotic intent with her. Both men had heard the stories of her dangerous nature and ability to bring men sternly under control and then take them out with a well placed kick or secreted dagger, yet, both continued to flirt and toy as each grew more enamoured by her voluptuous charm. Pavor, however, would often chide the two younger men and remind them of their quest and professional nature if things became a little too crude by his own protective reckoning. As an added bonus for Pavor, Eris would then give him a little kiss on the cheek as a thank you, with a comment towards him like 'noble protector' or 'honoured bodyguard'.

Seton went out on deck many times, enjoying the blasting wind of the sea dashing his hair horizontally behind him as he scanned the horizon for ships. He also enjoyed getting to know the rest of the crew. Captain Battfin helped him in this enterprise by finding him simple and laborious jobs to do which the barbarian enjoyed both in terms of exercising and maintaining his massive bulk but also as an occupation to help the days pass. Days passing though meant that Vixen and her

Ahrioch Horde had more time to hide and the faint trail would grow fainter.

The days turned into a week of mainly boredom for those not entertained by the duties of 'The Peppercorn'. Gazing over the bulwarks at a grey and rolling sea was monotonous, the brown green coast of Umiat lacked any real majesty and there were no sea monsters breaking the surface of the sea and bringing fear from imagination to reality.

However, league upon league was swallowed up and the day did come when they sailed between two large islands that filled the horizon and marked the entrance to the Porcupine Gulf. For those that had sailed into Rampart, this passage was mundane and corridor like, but for Eris and Pavor the sights of rocks rising to each side of the boat in long walls of granite was a spectacle worth dropping their jaws for.

"Three days till Aklavik," shouted Captain Battfin as after eight hours they left the channel and arrived into the calmer gulf.

"So long a time," moaned Seton Rax, gazing at the large sea surrounded by islands.

"Would you rather we had walked?" asked Pavor who had stood on deck with Eris for the entire day, sightseeing.

"No. Not at all. It's just so tedious being at sea. This is supposed to be an adventure. A hunt," the barbarian replied. "But I'm sure we won't have to wait much longer. Three days to Aklavik and then we trust to those skills of A'Lastor and Campbell to find some clue as to where she is."

"And if they can't, messages have been spread around the fleet and by now the official Umiat authorities must have been informed of the loss of the monastery," Pavor replied.

"We'll find her," said Eris, putting her arms around the shoulders of both men. "It's obvious isn't it? And if it isn't us that actually gets to put the collar around her traitorous neck then it will be someone else. And I have a feeling that she'll be brought our way. Campbell and Percy are important men in Umiat and seem wrapped up in her destiny."

"I'm sure you're right Eris," said Seton with a hint of melancholy. "It's just I want to capture her so much. The reward is just fantastic I know but I lost good friends on my last quest which she was involved in. Admittedly two died within five minutes of meeting her and then one died who I'd only just met that day and then another new acquaintance a couple of weeks after that. But I also lost Nazar Grant, Beran and Garraday on that journey. Death swathes himself around her and whispers with love into her ears."

Eris and Pavor pulled faces of impressed shock at the barbarian's maudlin last words.

"Come on guys," said Eris hugging them closer to her. "Let's get some rest below decks before Seton here slips into some more melancholic musing. We need our blood up when we finally meet her."

"I'm sorry Eris. Sorry Pavor," replied Seton. "But one can not help thinking that even with the illustrious warriors and men of skill and a bunch of bloodthirsty pirates with us, we are heading up against a tougher foe than we three have ever faced before."

"Have you been drinking Seton?" observed Pavor. "Maybe not but I think we need to get you out of the sun for a while."

Seton Rax & Company

With that comment they headed off for the shade of the cabin and an afternoon repose. 'The Peppercorn' continued her journey unabated. Spray lashed out from her bouncing bow, the rhythm of the wood on the waves with a full sail was a lullaby to some, to others a constant pleasure. The leaden, dark waters of the Sea of Kaltag and the Circle Sea gave way to brighter blues in the gulf but the waves still rose and fell around them marking out a timeless cadence to those who could hear it. Captain Battfin stood at the wheel and solidly held 'The Peppercorn' on a true north line and the ruins of Aklavik drew closer.

Chorus Nine

The village on the cape north of Sagwon had had some notice of ill tidings from the south. A fast messenger on horseback had galloped in the previous day to impart the news that Aklavik had been raided by demons and that a peculiar black ship had been seen moving north without the aid of oar nor sail. Word of mouth was faster than the technology Vixen had at her disposal but it mattered not as she ordered it to change direction and the set of wheels on the starboard side where whipped into a faster rotation.

The ship gently turned to port and then both sides began rotating at their most frenzied and constant thrashing. Waves undulated out to the stern in an increasing arrowhead shape, overriding the gentle swell of the Sea of Umiat. Startled children looking for shellfish at the low tide saw the approaching ship first and started running back to the little hamlet. The lord of the ramshackle settlement was roused from his breakfast of ham and eggs and climbed to the top of the narrow tower attached to the side of his wooden manor house. It was the only stone structure in the village was often used to look for the spouting of whales who past by twice a year in great herds. Behind the village the great Schwatka Mountains ended their traverse of the continent, to the south only the road to Sagwon, elsewhere was the sea. From the sea came their way of life. The lord raised an old gnarled hand to his brow and he spotted the strange rectangular black boat powering towards the flat sandy beach revealed by the retreating sea. With no alarm bell at this outpost of Umiat he simply let roar a command that mixed with the commotion in the huts where the children who had first seen the ship cried to their parents. Most of the able bodied men had set to sea at dawn to fish far to the north. All that were left were the lord, his household and the women, children and old men of the village. Those old men were tough though, leathered and hardened by years at sea. The lord was a cunning veteran of the Ahrioch wars, a strong and noble knight once, who cared for his people and taxed them lightly. The small force that the Lord swiftly gathered with their ancient swords, harpoons and the odd shield, watched as the craft slipped up onto the sand, rasping onto the beach. Little waves lapped around its bow and then hatches opened on the deck and grey cloaked men clambered out to leap onto the land. Well more than a hundred, storming up towards the wooden collection of huts, yelling, screaming, a horde of sword wielding deviants who slathered at the mouth in anticipation of out pacing their fellows and being the first to hack into peasant flesh.

The lord barked a couple of quick commands and harpoons were launched by ancient but well practised arms. The fastest of the foe were struck in the chest and guts by the great jagged metal heads meant to penetrate and snag a whale. On men the weapons rent great holes, rupturing cascades of stomach contents as innards were thrust out from the wounds, mouth and bowels. Yet there were not enough harpoons. Not enough arms to cast them. There were too many bounding berserkers and the enemy soon crashed into the little knot of defenders and ransacked their torsos of limbs, heads and life. The raping and butchering of the huddled women and children took a little longer and was a harder game of hide and seek than a stand up fight. Then the torches were lit, what was wanted was taken and the bodies left where they lay. The little unmarked hamlet was wiped from a map that hadn't shown it was there in the first place.

The fishermen who were at sea saw the columns of smoke rising into a placid sky. They feared the worst immediately and cursed each other for not listening to the rider who had brought the rumours of terror from the south. They finished with the hauling in of fish, letting nets drop to be swallowed by the sea. When they made it back to the place that had been home they found the dead already covered in crabs, sickeningly feasting in crusty crowds and they fell to their knees and howled in despair.

Chapter Ten

The crew and passengers of 'The Peppercorn' looked upon the ruins of the monastery of Aklavik. The destruction was rife and devastating. The fires that had been lit had raged strong and deeply into the roots of the vast structure where many amphorae of olive oil were stored and fuelled the burning flames. The foundations had cracked in the searing heat, buildings collapsed, great towers of faith and wisdom had toppled into the sea leaving the large basement stones jutting out from the surface while below the crafted stones drowned. The books and leaves of learning of the monks had burned well too. Beauty had been scratched into a ruinous scar. Blood had stained the polished stairs where generations of gentle men had trod barefoot. As they looked upon the destruction they saw movement within the wreckage. A handful of holy monks who had been away attending to the funeral needs of a dignitary in Sagwon had returned and now piteously scraped up remains and fallen stones. These were weeping men of devotion, attending to murdered souls and attempting to reconstruct the impossible.

"Well what are we going to learn from this?" asked Percy to his fellows who were lined up either side of him.

"We'll deduce a lot I'm sure," replied Campbell. "For a start we know that she now has a significant force. Fire can only do so much. Men were used here and they appear to be very committed to their task."

"You and I must walk among the ruins Campbell," said A'Lastor bluntly. "No one else need come ashore and enter into this charnel house. I fear there will still be sights there that would be unpleasant for even those of our experience."

Campbell nodded and bit his bottom lip in thought.

"Agreed," said the thief after a short time. "A'Lastor and I will disembark and search for the signs that we may be able to find. Percy, if you could raise the appropriate flags and release some homing pigeons to the rest of the fleet, I think we should encourage others to stay away from Aklavik for a while. You know the kind of thing to say. I don't want too many vivid eye witness reports getting back to the wider world. Although I fear that it is too late now anyway."

"Right you are Campbell," Percy responded and scampered off to the signals officer.

"There is a jetty there which is still intact," A'Lastor said pointing to a small dock near to a large pile of tumbled ruins at the base of the mountain. "Let's take the ship's launch and get this done now."

Many faces turned away from the destruction as clouds of bloated flies, disturbed by the few monks, flew up from the ruins. Captain Battfin barked the necessary commands and Campbell and A'Lastor were lowered to the sea in the longboat. Campbell took the oars and his athletic frame soon had the little boat powering towards the nearby rickety wooden wharf. A'Lastor sprang out from the bow with a rope when they were near enough and tied the boat securely to a long post at the end of the dock. Some monks cast distraught faces towards the black garbed figure of A'Lastor and the shady looking Campbell but soon ignored them and turned back to their grisly tasks of collection, cleaning and inept rebuilding.

"Quick, this way," said Campbell striding off and up into the maze of rubble strewn stairs. He clambered through broken rent walls and skipped up steps avoiding unpleasant uncollected lumps of dead monk thick with maggots and putrefaction.

A'Lastor casually followed, his movements more assured, graceful and fluid. Very soon any eye watching from 'The Peppercorn' had lost its ability to see the two as they disappeared down into vaults now opened to the sky. As soon as both were sure they were completely hidden, far in the depths of an old cellar, piled high with mounds of rubble that had crashed through its erstwhile ceiling, they stopped.

"As you already suspect A'Lastor, I know what you truly are. The benefit of my position within the Guild gives me access to certain information. You can take your mask off here and feed," said Campbell. "You must be famished. Is there any, nourishment, still hanging around here?"

"A few scant morsels still cling to what was once their home," A'Lastor replied unbinding his headgear to reveal his flawless face. He then reaching into a pocket to remove the spiked metal tube.

Campbell could not see what the demon was snaring as he walked around the cellar deftly swiping the air here and there and then sucking deeply on the pipe. After a while A'Lastor sighed in near contentment, put the tube away and sat cross legged on a prominent piece of ruined masonry.

"How were they?" asked Campbell, intrigued by the feeding habits of the demon.

"They were not nearly as, nourishing, to quote you, as a dark soul. But they will suffice for now. The equivalent of a thin soup, with little flavour, if compared to your appetites, Master Thief," said the demon looking up into a shaft of light cascading through the broken vault. "They were not sanctioned to die. But they were here and I can take advantage of the opportunity to eat if I discover any carrion."

Campbell gazed with a delightful smile as he took in the near perfect features of the underworld bounty hunter.

"We at the Guild were extremely pleased that you had joined up with 'Seton Rax and Company' you know?"

"Well if I hadn't you might have asked me to discontinued my little jaunt around Umiat mightn't you?" A'Lastor replied simply.

"I doubt that we would have done that A'Lastor," said Campbell in conciliatory tones. "We are happy that a few freelancers of your ilk wandering around our mortal world. We just wouldn't want too many about. Bit suspicious if all the bad types were captured too quickly and then returned looking extremely lifeless. And despite all of that killing and feeding we think you have some beneficial other uses for us."

"Thank you Master Thief. Though there are not as many of my kind left now as you might well think. Hell has been a tough place in recent millennia and my race have not been seen as necessary among some of the Lords on certain levels of the pit. Still, I'm here to claim some of the fouler souls, to devour them and to cleanse them from existence."

"Yes. Yes," Campbell salivated in delight at the power that was with him in the dingy remains of an old cellar in a destroyed edifice to faith. "And now you can claim Vixen. Claim Raven Hill. A soul much corrupted and darker than all."

"And not her own. It belongs to Ahrioch and will taste all the more divine when I swallow her," A'Lastor stroked the pipe, now back in his trousers, running his gloved hands over the material of the pocket.

"Yes," said Campbell. "Only that is going to be a bit difficult you see because we are going to have to execute her, most foully, on stage in front of the vast audience that will gather in the capital city of Rhyell. And, well, a demon sucking the remains of her escaping, wonderfully seasoned and blackened soul, may be a bit conspicuous. So we will have to think of a way round that now, won't we?"

"Yes, you will," replied A'Lastor matter of factly. "I know where she is right now. Roughly. She is easy to sense and track. The whore reeks of evil and I will delight in her capture and death."

"Does she really seem evil to you? A demon?" Campbell leaned forward intrigued.

"Yes. We have our factions in Hell. Our enmities. Perhaps to your eyes I appear as good because I track down and claim those who have committed wrongs. But I still fall on the wrong side of the light. Much like yourself Master Campbell."

"How do you sense her A'Lastor?" Campbell asked.

The ninja clad demon paused and thought through his response. Campbell continued to be held by the being's great beauty, enhanced by the playing of light and shadow around his perfect form.

"It is like a heat. Deep in my head. When I face her the warmth swells and grows. Then the sensation colours to a deep pastel rouge. When very close it will be all I know and it is an intense ravishment for my senses. I sometimes have to fight hard to keep my conscious self aware of the physical realities surrounding me. With some of the lesser creatures I have tracked, it is easy enough. With a great evil, like the capture of Areithous, which is when I last truly fed, it was nearly too much to remain focused. Ahh, the lust. It was over powering, delightful, everything I desire. He was a dark and evil being. Vixen might well be blacker still and I will likely be in a state of orgiastic ecstasy when I am near to her."

"Don't worry my friend," Campbell comforted. "She has no such hold over me. My needs are of a differing nature. With Is-Is with us, Captain Battfin, Seton and Pavor and the crew we have enough muscle to combat her men. Eris and I will be pretty immune to her charms. You can track her and Percy has some uses too. Mostly in providing the shipping, but some uses. So were is she now my demonic ally?"

A'Lastor waved vacantly to the south.

"She is moving, quite slowly, out in the gulf. Your assumptions were correct. She still needs to land though to feed and water her men I would guess. So I suggest we head off into the gulf and I will act as your guide, sitting at the prow of 'The Peppercorn'."

"So we are agreed. You help us track down the cracking traitor and we capture her. Then we will find a solution that enables you to feed on her soul yet not reveal your identity to a vast and baying mob when she is executed."

"Agreed. It shouldn't be too difficult," A'Lastor said and began re-swathing his face with the black cloth headgear.

"No indeed," replied Campbell. "It all seems so ridiculously easy when you have a demonically fiendish friend who can just point us in the right direction by sensing her."

"It's not as easy as all that you know," said A'Lastor slightly hurt. "I have to focus in and concentrate a little as well. It is not like some arrow guiding the way with its head always accurately pointing where she is. As I say, it can seem quite vague and like a mist. But it does give the general direction. So, yes, good news really."

The thief and the demon then clambered out of the cellar and picked their way through the ruins back to the wooden jetty and their secured launch.

Once back aboard 'The Peppercorn', after the brief row back, they were quickly surrounded by the others who were eager for news.

"Not gone for very long there Campbell," said Percy enquiringly. "Any luck?"

"Yes," replied Campbell immediately. "Of course. You have within your midst two of the finest trackers the world has ever seen. It is not difficult for two such as us to pick up clues. For instance within one congealed footprint of blood we found some grains of black sand which would indicate that at least one of her men has recently been on a volcanic beach. Another clue was found in a chipped piece of stone where perhaps a monk ducked and an Ahrioch sword struck an engraved column. The piece of metal that was left within the rent had a slight scent of coconut to it, indicating that recently its owner must have hacked open one of the wonderful fruits upon an island to the south of the Porcupine Gulf."

"Coconut? Fruit? Really?" said Captain Battfin, an arched eyebrow framing a piercing stare at the thief. "I think it's a nut."

"What ever it is, the flesh and milky middle left a distinct aroma for one as gifted as I to track down as a second clue," said Campbell confidently turning to all in the group. "There were a couple of other clues too but if I am to be doubted I will not share the insights gathered with you."

His voice was raised to a level that indicated, in a truly pained manner, that he was hurt at the sense of slight towards him.

"No please do go on. It's, you're, fascinating," said Eris leaning on the bulwark of the boat and thrusting out her chest a little more than was necessary towards the thief. She was confident that such a blatant flirtation would bring him back to his raconteur ways.

"Fine, I shall," Campbell replied. "There was one final vital piece of information that yielded up the couple of extra clues. We found it deep in a recently ruined cellar."

A'Lastor turned to look at Campbell, a sharp precise turn that was not his normal, usually controlled manner.

"Well?" said Seton. "What was it? A note from Vixen?"

"Nothing so easy as that my magnificently muscled friend. No the final clues that will lead us to them were down in a cellar. A cellar that was smashed open from a toppled tower. Vixen herself had been in that room and had delighted in torturing a few bound and gagged monks. We found their still undiscovered bodies. To be true they were a little rotten now but they had been out of the worst of the sunlight and only a few flies had found their way there to spawn a mess of maggots within them. I believe from the scene that she tortured them before the burning of the monastery. One because that makes more sense and two because some legs were seen sticking out from beneath the crashed ruins meaning the destruction came after the group of monks had been placed down into that pit."

"Come come," interjected Percy. "Pray tell us how you knew it was her handy work?"

"Well as you know we travelled with her for sometime, around Rampart and Kenai and I have known her before that, in dalliances betwixt the Guild and her previous employers, the Secret Service of Umiat. Well, I knew at once she had been there from a footprint in the soft cellar floor. Exact size and shape of a boot that she favours and the depression caused was consistent for a surface of that quality and resistance and a person of her weight. And I also knew she had at least been involved in the torturing by cut marks on the monks that had been made by a dagger that she carries."

"Really?" said Captain Battfin. "Are you sure?"

"Of course I'm sure. If you remember I have also fought against Vixen in a knife fight in the private chambers of Ahriman when we were at Beth Col. I have seen that dagger, unsheathed and thrust at my face, as well as being maintained aboard 'The Ardent Panda' and numerous other occasions in our travels together. It had twenty seven teeth of steel on one side of it for any particularly nasty pieces of work she may need to do. And upon the eyeless skull of one of the monks I found wounds that would be consistent with such a blade. So I put it to you that Vixen and the Ahrioch Horde had been here and that recently they have been on a volcanic island to the southeast of the Porcupine Gulf where coconuts are known to grown and that we should start looking there as soon as possible!"

"Hadn't we already sort of guessed that she must have a base among the islands?" said Pavor as Campbell still held his hand high in the air in some dramatic pose of intellectual deduction.

"Yes," said Percy. "That is why we have the fleet out looking for her."

"But," replied Campbell with aplomb. "Now I have proved it and by the very nature of the volcanic sand and the peculiar aroma of the coconut I will be able to take us straight to the island where they had once been and we can look for clues there."

"They might be hopping about more than one island," said Eris.

"Ah, but they might not," said Campbell. "I suggest we set sail immediately and continue on our quest."

General agreement came and Captain Battfin soon had the crew tacking 'The Peppercorn' towards the south and east. As the adventurers and pirates set to their interests and tasks, Campbell went to stand with A'Lastor at the prow.

"What do you think the chances are of her landing on an island with a black volcanic beach and a bunch of coconut trees?" Campbell asked in a whispered conspiracy.

"Around there parts?" A'Lastor replied. "Highly likely."

"You don't think I went over the top?" the thief asked.

"They probably expect a little flamboyancy from you and I would imagine that those that know you best think you are actually hiding something or just trying to build your mystique," A'Lastor gazed towards the horizon. "For a moment I thought you might have revealed my little secret. Hunter of evil though I am, I would prefer my true heritage to remain a secret."

"How is that old demonic sense right now?"

"It grows ever stronger and glows broadly ahead of us. We are travelling in the right direction. She is among these islands."

"Excellent. I'll turn my mind to how we can conclude our agreement and let Captain Battfin know that his course is true."

Campbell turned and wrapped himself a little tighter in his cloak against the breezes of the sea. He walked away from A'Lastor to find Captain Battfin. The demon bounty hunter leaned hard into the joint at the prow of the ship. The need to feed was growing strong. The scant fare of the monk souls had only gone to remind him of his hunger. At this point in the trip he did not want to cut some crew member's throat as he slept. Pirates would be good fodder, sinful beings, who would be fat with nourishment. He might have to arrange for some accident late at night, after all, sailors often fell asleep at their post in the crows nest and could fall into the deep if the ship pitched steeply on a rogue wave. A'Lastor tried to turn his thoughts from his stomach and towards the pinkish pastel glow in the front of his mind.

Chorus Ten

Vixen met with Hoarfrost in the private cabin of the black ship. It was small and dark, most of the vessel being given up to space for the treadmills and wheels or the hold which currently contained the strike force of their men. They had now annihilated the monastery plus a total of three coastal villages. Terror was taking a grip as rumour and evidence spread of a black ship bringing demons at will to devour, rend and kill the citizens of Umiat. For all the hundreds they had destroyed Vixen and Hoarfrost had lost a handful of men to lucky strikes from the pitiful resistance they had encountered.

"What now my mistress?" asked Hoarfrost. "More fishermen and peasants? The men's morale is still high, due to your leadership and the slaughter you have delivered."

"But?" replied Vixen looking enquiringly at the giant warrior, hunched in the deeply shadowed cabin. "I sense there is a lack of satisfaction on your part."

"Your perception is always accurate," Hoarfrost replied shifting his bulk a little in the cramped conditions. "I am a warrior and I thirst for something, more, challenging. A larger town or a military target. One where I can test my mettle more than against these soft women and whining babes."

"Hoarfrost, I understand your concerns but you must remember that we are instigating terror against our enemy. A warrior as honourable and mighty as you can understand that as a legitimate tactic. Plus we would even with you at the front of our dedicated and dangerous men, inevitably eventually lose against an amassed and determined foe," Vixen paused. "While I too long to test myself against someone who can truly wield a weapon, we must stay true to our cause and plan. Their society will be far more troubled by devastating raids in rural communities than if we launched a full scale war against their mighty capital. Let them turn inwards against each other with the fear gnawing their nightmares. Let them blame their own leaders for failing to stop us rather than joining in a rally of nationalistic pride against a common and known foe. We must be the unseen bite in the night. Let them awake and find themselves diseased."

"Mistress I of course bow to your decision and recognise its wisdom," Hoarfrost paused again and knew that Vixen was taking in the sight of his pensive eyes despite the shadows of the cabin.

"You are still contemplating something my captain," Vixen nudged verbally.

"Yes mistress. Permission to speak freely."

"Granted Hoarfrost. Of course granted. What am I without the advice of a trusted follower?"

Hoarfrost remained still and quiet. Vixen was a great leader but one steeped in blood and vengeance. To put his ideas forward risked her wrath and he was convinced she could create a particularly cruel punishment for anyone she considered disloyal or traitorous. Eventually, convinced that his views were valid, he spoke.

"Well, your predecessor could and did use his skills, his art, to raise the dead. Additional warriors for his ranks. He could summon demons to strike absolute terror into the heart of the enemy. Well, we have lost a few men and if we continue our current campaign then we will be whittled away," he fell silent again. "The enemy gets in the odd lucky strike. They have rare fellows who will stand and fight before being reaped like corn. Yet even a scythe needs sharpening as stalks can and do dull a blade. Why can we not utilise the arts that Ahrioch can provide?"

"Your point is made with a true heart Hoarfrost. I too have thought to test my skill with imps, lesser demons and perhaps to reanimate a corpse. Ahriman may not have been a great leader of men but he was more schooled in the mystic ways of demonology and necromancy than I. And, while I hold his spirit within me and I am absorbing some of his knowledge, I would still need his books to be truly proficient. And the books are back in Beth Col. I hope still safe after the debacle which occurred there."

"Then should we not travel to Ende and reclaim them rather than fighting as we are? Raise the Horde still further and fight on a larger scale with greater allies. Allies from Hell who will tear and rend and eat with even more passion than our current troops?"

"I fled Beth Col to meet with you and the other faithful to execute my current plan. While we still have enough men to carry out that mission then I would intend to do so. One monastery and a handful of villages does not a campaign of terror make. Yet I appreciate your advice," Vixen calmed a little from what was an increasingly voluminous voice. "Perhaps your idea does have merit. Perhaps I have been remiss in my studies. Perhaps a few more atrocities will have the peasants of Umiat rioting in Rhyell."

"Yes mistress, yes. A few more raids then return to Beth Col. Learn and rebuild a larger army. Read and digest from the ancient books of power. Beth Col was burned only a little in their attack, the outside walls and gates only. The last I heard it was rebuilt and secure. We still have men of faith guarding it. Egremont and his assassins fled too fast with the crack Tumbletick to destroy our religious heart. You will be safe there, I guarantee it."

"Hmm, I wonder Hoarfrost. The city of Ende holds no true allegiance to us. It is too diverse, too neutral and chaotic for my liking. There are too many eyes there that do not look to our temple for their inspiration. Eyes that would see us return even if we did so under cover of darkness and disguise. But there is also merit in your guidance and it is wise," Vixen now fell silent and mulled over the idea in her mind. "We could return and rebuild further. I should develop my arcane arts and demons and undead are useful weapons. We have written a message to the people of Umiat but has it truly been sent? I will reflect on this Hoarfrost but my instinct would be to raid a few more settlements. Perhaps we can find one that could even challenge your martial skill?"

"I will of course support your decision fully and whole heartedly mistress," Hoarfrost bowed his head further than it was already stooped and he smiled slightly, unseen due to the angle of his head and the darkness of the room.

"I sense your joy Hoarfrost," Vixen commented. "I said perhaps we could find somewhere to challenge you. But come now and bring your mistress joy for we live today and relish in a victory. However small."

The giant captain raised his head again, still smiling but with a differing intent, he stood stooping and scooped up the voluptuous red head and carried her to the small bed at the back of the cabin. He lowered her gently to the cot and kissed her with a firmness that reciprocated a bite of his lower lip from her. Hoarfrost reached to unbutton her bodice and became further aroused when she knocked his hand away and started to release the clothing herself.

No one on board the black chip heard their throes of passion, fuelled by the remains of bloodlust from the day's battle. The wheels of the ship continued to thrash at the sea, thrusting up white foam from the depths of the waves as the warriors wrestled in lust.

Chapter Eleven

'The Peppercorn' dropped anchor in the bay of a mid sized island, one of many uncharted such places around the Porcupine Gulf. A typical volcanic cone jutted from the sea, long dormant it was now covered in lush vegetation and trees. The blackened shallow sands of the bay played nicely with the gently lapping sea and a myriad of patterns were briefly seen, only to soak away, as the little waves left brief white kisses on the dark beach. Coconut trees jutted out at all angles, some striving enough to hang almost horizontally over the sea, others with proud vast leaves, showing off clusters of the ubiquitous nut beneath.

Campbell stood beaming on board the deck. Seton Rax, Pavor, Eris, A'Lastor, Percy Fenton, Captain Battfin, Is-Is and most of the crew stood looking back at the proud thief. Then they turned and looked back at the idyllic isle and wondered at the skill of the tracker in their ranks. A'Lastor alone had any thoughts that differed and his demonic mind was questioning whether luck was a true property that could be gathered and spent by humans.

"Huh? Huh?" Campbell the Weasel gestured to the island. "What did I tell you? Shall we disembark and go and investigate then?"

"Fine. Well done Campbell," said Percy. "For all we know you've just brought us to an island you know. Like the one that Captain Battfin was marooned on all those years ago when he was but a fledgling pirate."

Captain Battfin kept a stern face.

"You recall an unhappy time for me Captain Fenton," the massive black pirate said. "Though the island I was left on was similar 'twas not this one. Not enough goats."

With that Captain Battfin gave his broadest smile reserved for very rare occasions and set about deciding which of the crew would remain as guards on 'The Peppercorn' and who would come ashore in search of Vixen and her men.

"Right," said Percy, momentarily taking command. "The ship's launch can carry about twenty men at a squeeze. I suggest the eight of us are on the first trip then we can ferry back and forth the rest of the landing party. There's no sign of their vessel but that doesn't mean that they are not on the island. Secret coves, camouflage, magical hiding spells, you know all that sneaky stuff."

The pirate cast a look at Campbell who gasped in mock shock and raised his hands to his chest in derisory innocence.

"If Campbell is correct," Percy continued. "And they are on this island then we need to ensure we don't go stumbling into any traps. There is a lot of vegetation for the Ahrioch Horde to launch an attack from. So we'll probably send Campbell and A'Lastor to scout off ahead while we form a beachhead here."

"No problem," said Campbell calmly.

"It will be a pleasure," A'Lastor added.

So the launch was lowered containing the eight adventurers and twelve of the toughest hand picked pirates. Weapons were readied in case of any ambush when they were most vulnerable but as the little boat gave a final lifting heave in the surf and came to rest on the shore, no attack came. Bodies leapt over the side and scampered up the beach, remaining alert, quick twitching heads scanning the trees and lush thick undergrowth. A couple of pirates began rowing the launch back to 'The Peppercorn' to pick up the next twenty pirates at a frantic ferrying pace. Soon the shuttling boat had a hundred souls on the beach and Campbell and A'Lastor slipped off along the sands with a scout's speed and alertness. The remaining adventures set to work on cutting wooden stakes from the wide choice of slim jungle trees and then setting them into the firmer earth betwixt the beach and the lush interior of the island. They soon began to weave a thick thicket of randomly jutting spikes of vicious bamboos and other hard woods to form a bristling defence.

As the rudimentary fort was beginning to shape up, Campbell kept close on the heels of A'Lastor who ran on with a purposeful stride. About a mile along the beach the demon turned sharply left and headed into the lush undergrowth.

"She is moving again," said A'Lastor over his shoulder, pushing his way through vines and bushes. A vibrancy of greens surrounded him and purple flowers shaped like jagged cones were in abundance in this particular part of the jungle. "She was on this island and now she is moving. Over there, the other side, we landed on the wrong coast."

"But she is close," replied Campbell, his hand shifting a strand of creeper from his face that had vicious spikes lined along it. "Don't be too hard on yourself. Your senses brought us in the right direction. You can't expect to be pinpoint accurate if all you get is a glowing warmth in your mind."

"Yes that is all that it is," A'Lastor replied and the thief sensed sadness in his voice.

"Well? What is your recommendation?" Campbell asked trying to build some confidence in his ally but realising that his own tone could be perceived as slightly cutting. "Do we carry on for more information or report back?"

"We carry on. Information gathering is always of benefit plus I can not tell if she is on foot or at sea."

With that A'Lastor took out his xyele and began to chop away at some stubborn vines in their path. Campbell drew out a long bladed knife and also began hacking away where necessary.

Within a couple of sweaty minutes of clearing foliage they sensed a clearing ahead as the intensity of the light grew around them and the vegetation began to thin. Campbell sniffed the air and through the humidity and jungle stench picked up the familiar aroma of death.

Carefully they emerged into a clearing and saw the slaughtered remains of an indigenous tribe. Clustered around a large wooden hut, raised about six foot from the land, with a thickly thatched roof but basically open at all sides, were the corpses of about thirty men, women and children. Campbell shook his head in disgust.

"Definitely the work of Vixen and her men," he said. "But why kill these people as well? No one is going to hear about it, although technically they are people of Umiat. This was just for sport I feel."

"Perhaps," replied A'Lastor who was already waving his pipe in the air and wrapping the triangular blades around the invisible wisps of remaining souls. "I need to feed again and besides it provides us with the information. These were killed very recently, within the hour, they are still very fresh."

"Then we are very close to her," Campbell paused, watching A'Lastor as he feasted in his unusual manner. "You can tell if they were dark or good souls, can't you?"

"Yes. These are mostly innocents. But even here away from other influences there are a couple who are tinged with darkness," the demon replied.

"I've been meaning to confirm something with you," said Campbell. "Is it a fact that you can only take a life if someone has been sanctioned for a kill but you can devour any souls you find?"

"Pretty much correct," Said A'Lastor. "I can fight back if someone threatens me, eat whatever I find but only hunt down one who has done wrong in the eyes of a legitimate authority."

"Thought so," replied Campbell looking around at the massacre. "What say you then? Do we press on or return to fetch the others?"

"We still continue to press on. Find out if they have left the island or not."

A'Lastor finished eating and they moved to cross the clearing. As they passed the large communal hut Campbell raised his hand and pointed down to some markings in the earth.

"Well A'Lastor? What make you of that? I think we have found a genuine clue this time," Campbell went and lowered himself on his haunches, squatting closer to the scratches in the ground. "These were cut into the earth after the villagers had been killed. Someone held a discussion here, after they had murdered these people and they couldn't help but be illustrative during their debate."

A'Lastor looked down and also could see that it was definitely a man made etching in the dirt. A thin trickle of blood had been bisected with the stick that had made the lines, hence Campbell had been able to conclude it was done after the killings and was therefore likely made by Vixen and her crew rather than by the villagers themselves.

"It looks like a bird's head with its beak open about to eat a nut. Or a claw grasping at a jewel. What is it Campbell?"

"It is a map my friend," Campbell laughed. "They've only gone and drawn a map of where they're cracking going! Some idiot sat here and drew the tip of Kenai. They are going to head back to Ende. I'm certain of it. It makes sense. Quick. We are only about a mile from the others. Let's get Percy and a couple of the others to see this. Won't do any harm in backing up our assumptions with some other people's confirmation of our interpretation of the clue. Is the crimson cloud still moving in your mind?"

"Yes it is. Heading south," A'Lastor replied throwing his arm in the direction of the red glow. "She must be at sea."

"A'Lastor let's run quick. Show them this and then back to 'The Peppercorn'. The chase will then be on."

"Why not straight back to the ship?" A'Lastor enquired. "Surely they'll believe us."

"No, it is as I've said. When we have some genuine evidence it will help convince them. Percy and Captain Battfin were a bit scathing when I was being poetic at Aklavik. There's a bit of me that does want to see those pirate faces concede that I, we, are indeed the ultimate trackers."

With that Campbell was off and pushing his way down the path they had cut earlier, already it seemed to be closing up again with tendrils of plants seeking to reclaim the space or loose vegetation falling into the gap. A'Lastor was right behind the thief when both burst out from the bushes and onto the beach. Turning to their right and running over the sand, avoiding little crabs that scuttled everywhere and the waves of an approaching tide they soon had the needling defences of the base in their sights.

"You are back quickly again aren't you?" said Percy looking up as he rammed another stake in between the thickening wall. "Anything to report?"

"Yes. Come with us. Bring Captain Battfin, Is-Is and Seton Rax and company. We've got some of Vixen's handiwork to show you and someone has left us a clue that even you could decipher."

So the eight were swiftly gathered and departed leaving the pirates with orders to continue burgeoning the defences. More as a way of keeping them occupied rather than the need for any protection. A'Lastor and Campbell keenly ran in the lead with the rest of the group, heavier footed, enduring the arduous effort that running on sand provides.

Campbell took his bearings and slowed down, their earlier tracks had already been washed away by larger waves that had made it all the way up the beach. Campbell had to look for other signs. He picked his way through a large scuttle of fist sized crabs, recognised some particular bushes and then plummeted into the undergrowth and towards the dead villagers. Captain Battfin, Seton and Is-Is had to hack away at more vines and encroaching leaves to get their bulky frames comfortably down the improvised track. Their slashing and cutting set nearby perching birds fluttering in a busting fluster into the sky. Their flapping and squawks of resentment mixing with the rustling of the jungle as life swarmed all around them before they entered into the clearing and into a scene of carnage and death.

"What did you want to show us then Campbell?" asked Percy. "Some deserted old hut and some pile of crabs?"

"The crabs weren't here before. Look closely at what they are covering."

The group gazed in disgust as hundreds and hundreds of crabs crawled over the lumps of butchered meat. They could see pincers scooping out eyes from decapitated heads and hear the constant clicking as claws sliced away flesh playing a ghoulish staccato beat over the surrounding sounds of the jungle.

"This way," said Campbell and led the group through the piles of competing crustaceans to the scratched markings at the back of the clearing. "So we have a slaughter of innocents and then this particular piece of information."

"Well it is a depiction of the tip of Kenai," said Percy bluntly. "Plus the fact that the crabs weren't here before indicated that the killings took place very recently. So that would mean that whoever did this is either still on the island, readying to depart, or already has and is heading back to Ende."

"We'll make a tracker out of you yet," said Campbell. "And where do you think the new nominated leader of the Ahrioch Horde would be going to in the vast and rambling city of Ende?"

"Beth Col," said Percy.

"Beth Col," said Campbell. "Back to base after committing her crimes."

"Pity we didn't destroy it when we were last there," added Seton.

"Pity?" replied Campbell. "Good that we didn't you mean. We now can be pretty certain that they are heading back to Ende and because we left them with a headquarters we can make a strong assumption as to where they will go. Yes good news indeed that we were in a bit of a rush the last time we stood on that unholy ground."

"Back to 'The Peppercorn' then," said Captain Battfin. "You could have just told us this. We have wasted time."

"I wanted you to see it and decide for yourselves that this was the right course of action this time," said Campbell.

"Fine. Let's go then," ordered Percy heading back towards the beach. "I do agree with Captain Battfin though. This has been a cracking waste of our time."

The handsome pirate scowled and strode off, kicking away some crabs that were crossing his path and sending them into shallow flighted arcs that ended with a tumbling roll when they crashed back to earth.

"Watch out!" shouted Pavor suddenly. "There's a big one after you Percy!"

The group turned towards Pavor's pointed arm and saw a lumbering shell at least three foot wide traversing at pace towards the pirate. Percy faltered in his stride and sneered in disgust at the vast shell, claws held aloft snipping the air and with its mouth parts moving in a manic rage or anticipation of a live meal. Percy drew his sword and calmly thrust the steel into the soft face of the crab and watched it shudder and die. He withdrew the blade, one foot on the shell for purchase and then wiped of most of the thick black blood with a foppishly conjured handkerchief.

"Anyone want to carry this beast back and boil it up," he said. "Might be a fair amount of meat on it for Cook to whip up some delights with."

The group laughed but no-one volunteered to carry the chunky carcass back to 'The Peppercorn.' The jollity was short lived though when more large crabs began to emerge from the jungle's edge. Three footers were common, some at least as broad as a fathom were now coming towards the group.

"Looks like the little ones were a swift vanguard," Eris said with a tinge of concern and a rapidly drawn dagger.

"Yeah," said Percy, very conscious that he stood alone and away from his comrades. "And by the looks of it these big ones are happy to go after live meat. Not just carrion."

"Quick! Back through the forest!" shouted Campbell.

"They're coming from the forest!" retorted Captain Battfin.

"They're coming from the sea. They're attracted by the smell," said Pavor.

"There's no need to be personal Pavor," shouted Percy, still attempting some humour and lunging his sword towards another crab that skitted intelligently away. "I think we better get away from here."

"Well 'The Peppercorn' is that way," shouted Campbell, twitching in all directions looking at the encroaching wall of shell and pincer. "Is-Is, you lead the way and everyone else follow him and keep in a swift and straight line."

Is-Is had no look of concern on his scarred and furry face. He just reached to the scabbard on his back, drew his two handed sword and sprung off in the direction of the shore. The others fell into a line behind the mighty hare and sprinted after him. Is-Is did not break stride or change direction as he cleaved through a five foot wide shell that lurched at him from the tree line. The sword cracked through the hard outer casing and into the soft crabmeat within. Then the hare's blade was used to carve a passage through the gentler plants of the jungle. Leaves, flowers and chunks of vine flew around him as he continued to run and chop away with his sword.

It was short work for the hare to make it to the beach through the narrow strip of flora that divided the clearing from the sea but as Is-Is ran onto the black sands of the shore he realised there was more work to do. As the others followed his path they had all sensed the crabs cracking their way through the undergrowth towards the clearing or turning towards them but as they arrived at the beach they were struck by the sight of a giant hare in full chain mail hacking and thrusting away at an army of shells with yearning eager claws, the sea lapping at his ankles.

The eight adventurers found themselves in the middles of a wide swathe of vast crabs that were emerging from the sea and heading towards the unexpected meal. Most were dark reds and browns, with spindly legs that moved mechanically and lifted their bodies far from the ground. They moved quickly and with intelligence, yet their black stalked eyes seemed devoid of any emotion save hunger.

Is-Is was lopping off crab extremities at a frantic pace before Captain Battfin joined him with his two cutlasses thinning the ranks of the scores of crustaceans. They were soon in little knots of combat, Eris and Pavor were fortunate to be with Seton, his battleaxe was making a good impression against the hard shells. Campbell and

A'Lastor were fighting together, dodging attacks and then when the opportunity availed itself slipping in a blade to finish off a crab. Is-Is and Captain Battfin were in the area with the thickest density of foes and were labouring hard to clear a way to escape down the beach. Percy Fenton had side stepped a couple of snaps before he leapt across the backs of three of the larger crabs and then made his way to part of the shore devoid of any threat.

"You want to get away from those crabs," Percy shouted. "They're trying to get to that clearing and feast on those villagers."

"A coward you are Percy," shouted back Campbell, with a nail like strike of his dagger through a shell. "An expert on crabs you are not!"

With the advice given Percy then fled off towards the wooden corral where he still expected to find a large body of protective pirates.

Is-Is and Captain Battfin were still having the hardest time. Seton, Pavor and Eris had created a large heap of dead crabs around them, Campbell and A'Lastor had fought and dodged their way to safety. Then a full fathom and a half wide beast locked a toothed claw around the thigh of Captain Battfin and gripped hard. The heavily scarred black pirate screamed in agony, with no armour on his legs, only the toughness of his muscles tensing stopped the beast from severing the limb. Is-Is was swift to react and brought his sword down in a wide vertical arc, the steel sliced though the crabs appendage, separating it cleanly but leaving the claw still holding the pirate's leg. Captain Battfin stumbled in shock, dropped his cutlasses into the ever deepening sea which was now up to his shins and attempted to rip the pincer from his thigh but it only resulted in more pain. Is-Is batted away more crabs sensing the blood of man and beast merging in the waters. Seton Rax seeing an opportunity left Pavor and Eris and ran, splashing by a couple of creatures to the side of Captain Battfin. The barbarian helped Is-Is in keeping the crabs at bay while the pirate gave up on trying to remove the claw and retrieved his cutlasses from the water before the depth grew too much or a riptide pulled his blades away.

Further up on the beach the black sands were now sticky with the dark blood of dying craps and the groups of warriors were relieved to see that the beasts started to turn from them and to begin feasting on their own dead. Easier meat than the adventurers who fought back with shiny blades of death. Is-Is went to support Captain Battfin with a strong arm and limping badly they made their way to safety with Seton knocking a few uninterested crustaceans out of the way. Eris and Pavor had joined with Campbell and A'Lastor and as soon as all were certain that the crabs were now totally occupied and happy relishing in the throes of cannibalism it was the Master Thief who knelt beside the wounded Captain Battfin and examined the damage while the pirate struggled to still stand.

"Hmm," said Campbell after taking a very close look at the gripping claw and wounded area. "The jagged bits of the pincer have dug deep and you seem to losing a lot of blood."

"Really?" said Captain Battfin through strongly clenched teeth. "You think I can't tell?"

"Yes, we need to get that wound cleaned and bandaged very soon," the thief continued, prodding a little with his finger at the edges of the thigh wide injury. "Why didn't you take off the claw?"

"You don't think I've tried," Captain Battfin roared back and then swooned with the exertion of the retort. "It's locked solid since the cracking thing died."

"You tried to unclamp it by pulling the claws apart, now didn't you?" said Campbell with a sarcastic lilt to his voice. "Why didn't you just do this?"

With that question the weasel like little man with a scraggly beard reached towards the severed part of the claw and inserted his hand into the rent. Grabbing the necessary piece of cartilage he pushed the controlling part of inner crab workings and the claw instantly opened and fell to the sand while the thief still held onto the other end.

"I think that even I will be able to carry this part back for the cook," said Campbell. "Some fresh crab claw flesh of this size is sure to be delicious and more of a mouthful than saying 'fresh crab claw flesh' again."

They made their way back to the landing site, the odd turn of a head to check that no more shells were scuttling after them. Is-Is continued to aid Captain Battfin along the ever narrowing strip of sand, the wound was serious but not enough to slow up the pride of the pirate for now.

As they neared the completed defences of the beachhead, above the high tide mark in firmer earth, they saw Percy waving to them. His pipe was already lit and a broad grin was on his face.

"Why didn't you just run away like I did?" he called to them. "Surely people of your talent can outpace a few crabs!"

Many thoughts returned to the comment that Campbell had shouted at the fleeing pirate but most could only manage to smile at the charismatic and debonair Percy Fenton.

However the smiles soon disappeared and turned to frowns as a look of aghast astonishment suddenly flowed across Percy's features and many of the pirates behind him too. The pipe fell from Percy's mouth and embedded itself in the soft sand, spilling a glowing ember of firmly compressed tobacco. A short blue grey trail of smoke gently lifted on the breeze. The adventurers, with stomachs churning at what could have caused such a change in demeanour in their friend, turned to look behind them.

A wide area of beach was lurching upwards and towards them. At first confusion reigned amongst the company. Then it was obvious. The beach was falling off the back of a shell, in some areas in large sodden clumps and streams of water, in other drier places it cascaded like the sand of an hour glass. This was a giant crab come to feast on the living. It emerged from over the entire width of the beach, large parts of its shell still wet from where it had been beneath the sea. The crashing sand revealed barnacles the size of human heads locked onto the dark brown, almost black carapace. The eyes were on stalks longer than a fully grown man and the legs that started to rise and thrust out from the sand, striving towards the band of pirates and warriors must have been ten yards long and were thick and bulbously jointed. Its mouth was made of blades of bone and opened and closed in an alien and methodical manner. The shell itself was at least twenty yards across but it was the pincers pushing their way out of rising slumping mounds of wet black sand which inspired the most fear and caused all who saw them to now race to behind the barrier of wooden spikes.

Is-Is still supported the wounded Captain Battfin and the two were last to the protective wall of sharpened stakes. As they slipped by the entrance and into the scrum of pirates and bounty hunters, Is-Is dropped his injured companion, turned and started to tug on one of the stakes, pulling it from the sand.

The giant crab was now fully out of the beach, leaving a vast and collapsing hole behind it as the sea and sand flowed to fill the enormous pit which it has created. Its huge claws were snapping the air and leading its assault towards the men who had been killing its brethren.

Is-Is was the first to act. Massively strong he lifted the stake in one hand and with a couple of strides launched it, javelin fashion, towards the monster. The wood flew true but merely bounced off the thick carapace with a hollow clattering. Is-Is frowned, turned and began tugging at a larger more solid sharpened pole. The crab was now very close, some pirates had the foresight to run, to flee out of the only entrance to their circular wooden perimeter which easily could trap them if the monster made it by the solitary warrior, Is-Is, who stood in its way.

Is-Is gauged the distance between him and the lumbering mass of crab. He looked at the keenness of the spike and then at the softer underside of the vast shelled beast. The paler underbelly of the crab was probably about fifteen foot from the ground, Is-Is was tall and strong and knew he could thrust the wood into the monster from below.

"Is-Is, no!" shouted Campbell from behind, figuring out what the hare intended to do. "It must weight a couple of tons. You'll be crushed."

Is-Is casually scratched his jaw, then holding the shaft like a pike he advance slowly towards the monster. Seton

Rax, shaking his head, took action and ran after the hare with his battleaxe. Pirates were running into the sea, fleeing the beast and swimming for 'The Peppercorn'. Eris and Pavor lifted Captain Battfin under his shoulders and tried to get him to the launch with a group of braver pirates who backed away from the crab with swords drawn in futile desperation.

Is-Is now picked up the pace and ran towards the giant crab, he ducked under a rapidly swung claw and thrust the nine foot stake up beneath the mouth of the beast. The skin was yellow here and the hare trusted that it would be soft. With all of his might and all the pace of his attack the point struck home, splintered and skidded off the surface of the skin. Is-Is lost his grip and the shaft fell to the sand beneath the crab. The paler underside was not soft at all. A pincer approached the hare again, Is-Is leapt backwards, drawing his sword in mid flight and landed beside the brave Seton Rax who now joined him in the fight.

"A valiant attempt Master Is-Is. But, I suspect this is a tougher foe than even a Kenai Mountain Dragon."

Pavor, Eris and Captain Battfin had made it to the launch and were clambering in to be pushed into the surf by their bodyguard of pirates, who also then keenly leapt aboard themselves and started to row with all the enthusiasm of the fearful. Campbell and A'Lastor stood next to a forlorn looking Percy who gazed at the departing vessel, swimming pirates and then at the gigantic crab. Other, loyal members of the crew remained with Percy, Campbell and A'Lastor, all with weapons drawn but standing still, waiting for a command.

"Come on then!" Percy finally shouted. "We can't just leave Is-Is and Seton to fight alone against something like that! Charge!"

As Is-Is and Seton heard the cry to back them up in battle they spread out and dealt with a couple of sweeping claws each. Neither however had sharp enough weapons or the strength to damage the chunky curved pincers and their blades were batted away. They were however both agile enough to dodge the attacks and their separation caused some confusion to the crab and it pivoted and scuttled in sudden indecision about which of the two potential meals it should make a play for next.

Percy arrived with his mass of men and they started to attack the eight legs which supported the crab high in the air. Ending in tough spiked points the legs were weapons in themselves as they rose and fell, impaling the sandy beach and striking out at the men around them.

The pirate cutlasses were also ineffective against the creature which was tougher than any plate mail armour and the men began to think of retreat quickly. They might have to swim for it or maybe the launch would return. Percy sensed the futility beginning to rise.

"Hold true men! Attack the joints. Distract and fend it off!" he shouted, battering a leg that came perilously close to catching him in the shoulder with a downwards thrust.

"Go for the eyes!" countermanded Campbell. "Attack the eyes!"

"Attack the eyes?" returned Percy. "They're at least twenty foot from the floor and on the end of cracking stalks!"

"Well you're not getting anywhere hitting its legs are you?" Campbell retorted with a raging vehemence slipping under one thrusting leg and battering the tip of a pincer with his long knife.

The crab's peculiar gait, lumbering body, twitching legs and rapid mouth movements disconcerted the attacking pirates and heroes. Campbell's suggestion of targeting the eyes was ignored as all were attempting to escape the claws and legs and the exoskeleton covering was not even be chipped by their puny weapons. Soon the crab's first kill came. The tip of a leg caught an unwary pirate on the back of the neck, the man instantly buckled under the weight of the thrust, collapsed to the sand, and was compressed briefly into the beach forming his own shallow grave in the soft surface beneath him as he was impaled by the pointed leg. The crab with unnerving speed retrieved the killing limb, pivoted around in a rickety scuttle and picked up the body with a pincer and drew the corpse to its mouth. Machine like in its mastications the man was mauled in one continuous thrust into the cutting, chomping orifice.

Several pirates turned and fled to the sea and attempted to swim towards 'The Peppercorn'. Others in desperation redoubled their efforts to injure the crab as momentarily it was still, apart from its grisly feeding.

Is-Is stepped calmly back and sheathed his sword. It had been keenly sharp and well cared for but now was dulled and chipped due to the formidable armour of the crab. The hare had been swayed by Campbell's comments and drew out a couple of throwing daggers. The stalks that supported the eyes were swaying slightly and had the width of a man's wrist to them. Is-Is felt he could hit the targets and swiftly aimed, then threw his first knife. It missed an eye and toppled in the air and over the carapace of the crab to embed itself neatly in the beach. Is-Is tossed the second knife a foot in the air as skilled as a juggler, caught it by the blade, aimed and let loose his second throw. This time the dagger arced perfectly and the lethal tip made contact with a stalk, the steel pierced the soft flesh and the blade sank deep, up to its hilt, ejecting black ichor from the far side along with a good six inches of blood stained metal.

The result on the crab was terrifying, whether through loss of sight, pain or shock the beast dropped the remains of the mostly chewed pirate and immediately started to attack the men around it in a frenzy. Two of its foes were instantly clamped together in one huge claw, the men's screams almost stopped the blood of the other pirates and warriors as they were crushed together, killed so claustrophobically by the pressure of the pincers and their own bodies pressed together. The crab did not attempt to eat the remains, it went for more kills, opening its claw to attack again. The crew and passengers of 'The Peppercorn' who remained on the beach retched as they saw the two unfortunate corpses fall to the sand as one unrecognisable clump of flesh and mangled clothes.

"I don't think that cutting its eyes off is going to kill it!" shouted Percy, rolling away from an attacking limb. "Everyone for himself!"

With the order to retreat given by the senior pirate in the crew, every one of the buccaneers bolted away. Some went into the trees, to emerge further down the beach, others went straight for the sea. The launch was bravely returning in an effort to rescue some of the fleeing.

Is-Is however thought of Captain Battfin, still lying within the compound of stakes and walked backwards, keeping an eye on the thrashing crab, to within the area of defensive fencing. The large black pirate was struggling to keep his eyes open and was fully laid out on the ground. His wounded leg, cut all the way round by the spiked clamping pincer should not be causing him this much trouble thought the hare. Is-Is wondered if this crab species had any poisonous qualities to it to help in the dispatching of live food. The hare looked around, the giant crab had scuttled after a large group of fleeing pirates, chasing them into the surf. The launch was still being rowed into shore, turning to port slightly to avoid the colossal crustacean. Then Is-Is saw Seton Rax, Pavor and Eris rushing to aid Captain Battfin as well. Together, the two men lifted their wounded friend, Is-Is and Eris acted as guides to where they expected the launch to make land, all the time keeping an eye on the crab.

The monster itself, with revenge for its pain deep in its ancient mind was picking out pirates from the waves with ease. For eons it had been the greatest hunter of the depths around this isle. A few thrashing men, struggling in the choppy waters were simple prey. It took its time and devoured three in a continuous thrusting into its evil dark maw. Bits that dropped into the surf could be scavenged by smaller members of its kind.

With its one remaining working eye it watched, while it fed, as the launch landed a little way up the coast. Other tasty morsels clambered in, the boat was packed, over loaded as a vast hare in sparkling chain mail and a long haired barbarian pushed it back into the sea. The crab thought to itself about taking a few strides towards the boat and crushing it to spill the contents into the depths but why walk all that way when it could simply scoop up some more swimming seamen from the sea in front of it now. Plus there was some extra treats still on the beach if the other crabs hadn't already found the two men that had been mashed into one. All in all the crab felt that it had been a very successful day. Usually these human creatures stayed very far away from it and its kind, knowing that they could do very little harm to a creature of its formidable prowess. It took another couple of men from the slightly deeper water, grabbing them gently and submerged them. Then it walked further into the sea and sought out one of its favoured hiding places, a deep and dark sodden cave. It would enjoy the drowned pirates later. It knew it would be some time until the hunt would be as good as this again, with food so stupid and slow. It would sever the wounded stalk when it had rested and fed and grow a new eye. The crab scuttled over the edge of a ravine and sank slowly, swaying a little as it free fell into the abyss and to much deeper, darker water.

Eventually all the survivors made it back to 'The Peppercorn'. The crab disappearing beneath the waves had been a welcome sight but the ship set sail as soon as all the swimmers had clambered up hastily thrown ropes and the launch had been retrieved. Pirate eyes still looked to under the surface for any sign of a following black shell and claws for a decent length of time even after 'The Peppercorn' was more than a league from the coast.

The ship's carpenter who doubled up as a surgeon was called to inspect Captain Battfin's leg. He took one look at the wound and shook his head, tutting a great deal with his tongue on his teeth.

"Unfortunately," said the carpenter eventually. "Our dear captain will have to keep it. He won't be needing my services with neither saw nor lathe for a wooden replacement. Captain Battfin will just have to go on two legs for a while longer, he'll not be gaining iconic status just yet."

Eris and Pavor cleaned the wounds to the surgeon's direction. Captain Battfin had lost a lot of blood and the sun had been hot and it was this which had officially accounted for the swooning that Is-Is described to the surgeon when he had lifted him aboard. Campbell, Seton, A'Lastor, Is-Is and Percy relaxed around the rest of the cabin while Captain Battfin received more medical attention laid out on the table. Eventually it was Campbell that spoke first.

"First Eblis in Rampart and now this cracking crab! What is it about us lot and monsters with massive pincers?"

The room shook with relieved laughter. They were all okay. They were pretty certain where Vixen was heading and 'The Peppercorn' was making good time westwards with most of the crew intact. Briggs the First Mate was at the helm as Captain Battfin was being seen to and he was more than a competent sailor who would see them safely out of the Porcupine Gulf.

Chorus Eleven

Vixen and Hoarfrost stood at the prow of the black ship. Its strange rectangular hulk ploughing through the water with no masts or sails behind them, just the flat fighting platform. They were already passing from the Circle Sea into the Sea of Kaltag, the last island of the Tanana chain was to port and on the distant horizon Vixen could just make out the high plateau of the independent island of Rampart that managed to survive between the two great powers of Umiat and Kenai with a strange mix of free trade and adventure tourism.

All the men and slavish crew were below decks, the wind was strong but not loud enough to cover their conversation completely, so they spoke in hushed tones.

"Our power will build," said Hoarfrost. "We have shown our intent and dedications. Follows of the faith who were at the fringes will now see that our cause is just. They will see that Ahrioch has the power to act. His teeth and claws are sharp and that we have touched the lives of our enemies. They will flock to us now. To you now. You can build upon the base of the dead we have sent to Hell. Souls for Ahrioch to feast upon."

"Yes, yes, Hoarfrost," Vixen replied. "All good hyperbole and rhetoric. Good for your flocked faithful. Good to be shouted from the temple roof. But I am still concerned Hoarfrost. We must still be discreet at the right times."

"Discreet mistress? We have struck hard and fast. We have done well."

"We have bloodied the steps of a monastery and wiped out some peasants. Some in Umiat might be thankful to us. The church will be less powerful or gain support through sympathy. Some well versed in politics will gain in station through advocating strength while others will be dismissed for failing to protect the land."

"Mistress?" Hoarfrost's smile and victorious verse had gone.

"Do not worry my fine captain. It is just the musings of one who once resided there, disgusted by their machinations. I can see the faces now who will use our efforts for their own advantage. But really Hoarfrost I am convincing myself that your guidance to return to Beth Col is the right course. It is time to apply the power within me to the dedication of the arts of demonology and necromancy. For when we return again it will not be against peasants or yielding monks. We were not a suicide mission. We were messengers. Now we must, as you say, grow and build, convert and enslave. Become truly powerful."

"With you as our leader we will," Hoarfrost reached out and tenderly touched her shoulder, a sign of respect and loyalty.

"But as I say Hoarfrost. Carefully. With discretion. Ende is a sprawling mass of chaos and compounds of individual intent. No one true direction. Many there will still trade with Umiat while there is wood and furs and gems to sell. They will continue to trade back their own gluts of meat and corn and cheese to us. The principalities of mercantile brigands are shaping our city rather than the leaders of faith. We must avoid their eyes for a time. They have much to lose should we succeed. There will be another battle for us to fight if they do not join with us."

"We will succeed and quickly. With you grace and skill and the soul of Ahriman within you, we will succeed," Hoarfrost, the giant warrior, killer of thousands, bent forward and kissed Vixen's forehead with a childlike tenderness. "Do you still sense Ahriman within you?"

Vixen looked back up into his eyes after the question as her protector now stood, so tall and mighty before her.

"Yes I still feel him. I know that he will help me no end in my studies once they come. As I have already said, combined we will be stronger. I did think him a weak leader and a poor warrior. Then when I saw him pronounce every complicated word of the transference spell correctly, even though he had been hit with an arrow through his arm and one in the thigh, I knew he was great. Flawless pronunciation through the pain. That beast Is-Is had deliberately wounded him so that they could execute him later. The agony he must have been in. Yet he completed the spell and his soul left his shell of a body to come and reside with me."

"Truly he was of great skill," Hoarfrost eulogised.

"So we return to the scene of a recent defeat. Return to see if, as you say, the loyal have rebuilt. Return to see what effect our campaign of destruction has had on the ways of the people of Ende. Yes, you are right Hoarfrost. We return and we build. Go below now. I wish to be alone. Encourage the captain to enthuse the slaves to run faster in their wheels. I want to be in Beth Col in three days."

"Three days it shall be my mistress. I will run in a treadmill myself in order to get you safely there."

Hoarfrost disappeared through a hatch and Vixen strained her sight towards the island of Rampart. One day the neutrality of even that fortified isle would be erased. All would worship Ahrioch with her as the High Priestess. The sea winds pulled her long red hair away from her face as she closed her eyes in silent prayer for strength and victory.

Chapter Twelve

The legendary strength of Captain Battfin was further enhanced by the speed with which he recovered from the wound to his leg. With the cycle of two suns he was back at the helm, guiding 'The Peppercorn' with all his skill. Catching every gust and the slightest zephyr, racing with the rip tides and skirting the edges of deep unseen maelstroms, the seasoned pirate powered towards the western arm of Kenai.

A'Lastor took his customary position, tucked into the prow. He was in constant communication with Campbell and the two became more and more convinced with the belief that Vixen was heading towards Ende. Each passing league at sea had A'Lastor nodding slowly with confirmation. Percy had sent several messages by both flag and pigeon to maintain a lookout for Vixen and the black ship but in trusting the counsel from Campbell, orders had been given to focus on the trade routes to and from Ende as well as the city itself. While the harbour was gargantuan and a ship could slink in at any number of docks in an anonymous manner, the description and reputation of Vixen's vessel would make it hard for her to arrive unnoticed in the city.

Then the sightings did come in. Pirate vessels disguised as merchants signalled that the black ship had been spotted travelling west off the Kenai coast near Kantishna. The talk in the cabin was all of success. Vixen was easy to read. She was heading back to Kenai, to Ende and then most likely to Beth Col. There were five on 'The Peppercorn' who knew exactly where the religious compound was within the maze of streets, within the mass of population in the largest city of scum and villainy there was. Vixen could not possibly know that she was being tracked by old and new adversaries yet they suspected that she probably thought of her old companions a lot. They must play on her thoughts and nightmares. Her last moments with them had been ones of ultimate betrayal. She had thought herself victorious and then found herself in defeat. Campbell in particular also reran those final scenes in his head. The knife fight, the mutterings of the wounded Ahriman, his decapitation at the hands of Egremont. How Tumbletick had been held under a sacrificial blade awaiting the piercing blow. How Ahriman had not fought back and then how Vixen had suddenly fled.

'The Peppercorn' sailed on, the sense of Vixen in A'Lastor's mind grew paler but was still always to the west. The seas grew rougher around the coast of Kenai as the waves crashed into the forbidding coastline of granite cliffs and mountains. The adventurers and crew bided their time with daily chores and thoughts of what was to come.

In Captain Battfin's cabin, Campbell and Percy were discussing what was to be the plan. Is-Is sat in a corner sharpening his sword, still dull in places after the encounter with the giant crab. Blade maintenance was not something to be rushed at the best of times and long jaunts at sea enabled the hare to care for his broadsword with particular attention. Pavor and Eris were interested in the tales of Beth Col and what had transpired there before yet Seton Rax was quiet, chewing at the skin of his mouth behind his bottom lip, feeling little lumps of substance slip between his teeth. Memories of the undead guards, the

Landsknecht mercenaries and of the riotous mob flooded back to him in scarlet flashes of blood spraying on walls and roars of pain as zombies fed on his friend. Campbell and Percy Fenton though casually chatted about what had occurred there as well as slightly more seriously about the plans for their return.

"This time it will be different", continued Campbell. "No sneaking in this time with just a small and elite team forced into a quick and decisive action. No improvised battering ram of a flaming cart loaded with wood and soaked with lantern oil. No rioting inhabitants of Ende to provide a diversion. This time it will be a designated assault."

"Right, we've got just shy of two hundred pirates with us on 'The Peppercorn.' All good men," stated Percy. "However, seeing as Beth Col was pretty much intact when we left it last, I think we can assume that they will have bolstered their defences. Built more towers. Mended the gates. Got in more guards who can keep a lookout. The sort of thing that you or I would have added had we been left with a compound after a bunch of assassins had crept in and killed our leader."

"Yes," replied Campbell. "Let's just hope they have only designed defences against that kind of incursion. They probably think that they are safe versus a significant force marching against them due to location and the loose alliance of those who live in Ende. I mean what kind of a lunatic would land in the harbour and march an army through the streets? However, I strongly feel that if we got our force up to five hundred we could very simply do just that. Land and march our men straight to their temple and assault it. The princes of Ende will be worried for themselves when they see a small army arrive at the docks. I suspect that when they realise the attack is not aimed against them they will turn their backs and lock themselves away. They may even join in the attack in an effort to settle old scores, attempt to gain some territory or some other advantage that would increase their standing with the powers of Umiat as well as reducing another power of Ende. They by the very nature of our actions will benefit. No, I don't think we will be under any threat from any of the major powers except the Ahrioch Horde themselves."

"The way the locals responded to bags of money and some mind altering leaf being thrown into the compound would be a good indication of what they value over one of their many religions," added Seton sullenly.

"Exactly," said Campbell with a snap of his fingers. "The locals won't cracking care either what goes on just as long as it doesn't effect them."

"Simple then," said Percy. "We get some more of the fleet together, wait off the coast and amass and, as you say, then a significant force will just march through the streets and attack Beth Col. Even if Vixen isn't there it will be worthwhile."

"Oh I have a very strong feeling that she will be there," said Campbell. "But we better make it a thousand men. We are going this time to destroy Beth Col. To wipe it from the face of the map. Do you know what I mean? I want no stone left on another. Annihilated. Left as a scar within the city. Extirpated. Destroyed completely. Crack! This time it will be dust. Not just a handful of us and some drug fuelled rioters. This time a dedicated and knowing force of men. An army on a bloodlust mission."

"Well that's quite clear and impassioned," said Eris. "Is there any room for a woman on this crusade? So far the only action I've had since leaving Sitka is verbal fencing with you and Percy and running away from giant crabs. A girl can get bored you know."

"Of course Eris," Campbell quickly replied. "Of course. We all know of your skills and I am sure, absolutely certain that you will play a vital role in the destruction of Beth Col and the capture of the slut Vixen who does your fair sex harm with her every action."

"Well," said Percy, pushing back his chair from the table and standing. "I think we all feel just as enthused about this as Campbell. This time it's no sneak attack by an elite few. A proper battle awaits. I agree that even five hundred pirates might not be enough for the kind of demolition work we've got to do this time. I've got a few pigeons left. We'll get your thousand together Campbell. It's a big chunk of the fleet but Vixen and her cohorts represent the biggest threat to all of Umiat at the moment. It will probably take a fortnight to get everyone together that we need. Maybe even three weeks until we can all hook up off the coast. I'll instruct that the rendezvous be Point Kuskok to the north of the last great mountain of the eight great peaks of Kenai."

"Good," replied Campbell looking at the map on the wall. "Yes, Point Kuskok will be good. I wish it could be faster but I understand the logistics of communication by pigeon. Make sure you choose good men Percy. A thousand of the best. Ready and willing to fight."

"Oh, they will be," said Percy going to the door. "They will be."

Percy sauntered off to release his remaining messenger birds. He was always amazed at how useful they were, able to fly around and somehow find their designated ship anywhere at sea. Pavor went with him as he too had developed a keen interest in this method of communication. Campbell tried to calm down but was seething after his rant against Vixen and Beth Col. He was hunched over the table, restlessly turning his head from side to side and breathing heavily. Eris stood and went to sooth him, massaging the back of his neck and shoulders and ensuring her bust was pressed firmly against his head.

"We all believe in you Campbell," she said and kissed him on his crown. "We will follow you. We will be victorious and we will capture Vixen. Then it's back to Rhyell and rewards and treasure for all. I'm particularly keen to get one of those titles that Princess Annabella Blaise has promised to hand out. Who would have thought that a lowly dancer could make her way to a position of high rank?"

"Thanks Eris," the weasel looking man replied. He grabbed one of her hands and kissed it as gallantly as he could with her still standing behind him. "I know she'll be there. No escape this time. Plus I know the exact title that I want bestowed upon me."

Seton Rax, who along with Is-Is had not said much during the discussions, cradled his double handed double headed battleaxe across his lap. He drew a finger along the edge of its blade. It too, like Is-Is' broadsword had been sharpened after the crab encounter.

"This time we ain't going in blind though," the barbarian said. "We know the layout of the main temple and that is where she is bound to be."

Is-Is nodded sagely in the corner and drew a whetstone down the entire length of his sword. The slicing, grating sound of stone on metal felt cold in the cabin, yet comforting when a warrior like Is-Is was producing it.

"You are right Seton. No hit and run. No snatch and grab," replied Campbell.

"What did we call the entire mission last time? Y'Bor came up with it," asked the barbarian still drawing his finger along the long arch of steel.

"Operation Bellomancer," Campbell stated immediately. "A person who has the ability to be able to divine the future through examining the flights of arrows. If I recall."

"I don't think we need a name for this mission," stated Seton sucking the blood from thin fresh wound, gently sliced by his axe. The long haired bounty hunter looked over to Is-Is again and with a grim set jaw admired the edge that the hare had fashioned again on his sword.

"No. Neither do I," said Campbell, now very calm and determined. "Neither do I."

Chorus Twelve

It was night and the sea was dark. No stars or moon, just black clouds to hide the ship as it churned the waters and pulled alongside the dock. Vixen and Hoarfrost were first to jump down to the wooden jetty, their men followed and with no torches lit they all took the stumbling strides of the nearly blind, searching for the warrior in front to guide their own way through the trees. With a skeleton crew left on board, the black ship's wheels started to reverse and the boat slipped away, turned and then the paddles strained against the resistance of the sea and the momentum of their weight, as a forward motion was called for. The boat eventually powered off to the emptier waters of the south. With the trees acting as a screen, flints were struck and a few bulls' eye lanterns lit. Their enclosing cases and one aperture allowed controlled beams of orange light to scope out the paths to the palace at the top of the island. When the expected guards, clad in bronze breast plates, stepped out from their hiding places and presented a wall of pointed lances, Hoarfrost turned his lantern and shone it on to the face of Vixen as she pulled back the hood of her cloak to reveal her startling red hair and stunning features.

"You will escort us to your master," she stated clearly.

The guards smartly snapped their lances to their sides and saluted. Vixen's visage was recognised and responded to. The going to the palace was now simple. Darkness had been an ally in landing on the isle, not in hiding them from the sentries but from spying eyes that might have noticed them disembark from the black ship.

Vixen did not have to wait long to see the master of the house. He was already waiting, dressed in a white gown, hood down, he stood in front of twelve other similarly dressed figures who all each held a large flaming torch. The man was completely bald, had no eyebrows and was extremely pale. He had thick pink lips, hanging from his fat face, which shone under the firelight. He was corpulent beneath his robe and his rotund stomach caused it to bulge, straining at the cloth. He extended two fat hands, covered in gold rings and gems, his nails were long and had been painted red. Vixen strode up to him and smiled as he fell to his knees, his hands still extended to grasp the proffered arm of Vixen. He kissed her many times around the knuckles and Vixen noted with disdain that he left great gobs of saliva behind which trickled down her fingers. Apollyon was a useful servant to the Ahrioch Horde. His wealth provided donations when he was called upon. Although Vixen was disgusted by some of his more theatrical performances and parties, which he held in the name of Ahrioch, his gold was useful to the cause.

"We will speak in private," she said commandingly. "See that my men are well fed and pleasured as they see fit."

Apollyon nodded and vociferously started calling out to servants who bowed and scraped and ushered Vixen's warriors away to the communal dining rooms. Vixen then followed the obsequious dribbler, with only Hoarfrost still in attendance, through the passages and corridors of the palace until they came to the man's private study. He showed them in and locked the door, leaving the key in its hole as an additional block against prying eyes.

"My mistress," the bald man said. "It is such a pleasure to see you here again in my humble home. Have you come to worship with us? I thought you were away conducting good works to the north. Now that you are High Priestess you honour me with your presence. I was delighted when the guards reported that you were here. I rushed out with my friends so that we could welcome you in person. I haven't seen you since before the unpleasantness at Beth Col. Naturally I knew of your elevation to leader with the loss of Ahriman. I was so glad that you survived and are now already taking our faith in the right direction."

Vixen remained quiet and let Apollyon continue to blather. She knew it was an act, or maybe the influence of some stimulant. He opened an elaborate cabinet filled with crystal decanters and smaller vials containing liquids of many colours. He selected a square, medium sized vessel that glittered a thousand shards of light as he poured some honey coloured drink into three silver goblets.

"Something to ward off the cold of night. It is particular favourite of mine. A whiskey from a monastery in the northwest of Umiat called Rinkabar," Apollyon said handing the goblets to Hoarfrost and Vixen. "It is a superb vintage. A very fine year."

"Yes I know the skill of the monks there Apollyon," Vixen replied sternly.

"Mistress please? I protest. Although we can not be seen in here there may be people listening and we do have company," he spluttered in response to her having used his real name.

"Hoarfrost is my most trusted man, Apollyon, and I will use your given name if I see fit to do so. But thank you for the drink. It is very fine."

"I trust that their premises will be safe for a while in the mountains," Apollyon said with no hint of sarcasm as he returned the decanter and shut up the cabinet. Its gold woven inlay around dark wood caught Vixens' eye as an object of particular beauty.

"Yes," she said. "It will be safe, for now. So now I know news of our escapades have reached you in detail Apollyon. Not just 'good works to the north'. I trust that you have profited from it somehow."

The fat man winced as Vixen pronounced his name again, his shuddering setting his gut to a slight wobble under his robes.

"Yes and yes," Apollyon said turning to the High Priestess of his faith and her indomitable protector, Hoarfrost. "News is cheap, gossip travels fast and is given away freely. The ability to be first to have the chance to sell materials to the orders who wish to rebuild is more expensive and you have to move even faster than wagging tongues. But business is business and your actions means work for some of us. Now what can I do for you? I take it that you have not come socially, so I will dispense with that charade, for the moment. Although if you could stay and conduct a ceremony with us I would be grateful."

"Fine. I will do so," Vixen said. She was amazed by how quickly Apollyon could flit between characters. It was an act. She downed her whiskey in one go and placed the goblet on the mantel-piece next to a small figurine. "What I need is simple. I need to get me and my men transported to Beth Col in secrecy. I need some heavy weaponry to reinforce and bolster Beth Col. Ballistae, catapults and onagers. Weapons of war to defend your temple Apollyon. I also need a donation. I have yet to see how well Beth Col has been rebuilt but gold is always useful. I may need builders but I will need mercenaries."

"You shall have whatever you wish Raven Hill, my mistress," Apollyon replied and sipped his whiskey delicately. He marvelled at the honey notes and the wisp of heather wrapped around lightly smoked kelp. "In return you will preside over one of my entertainments. As High Priestess, you need not participate, unless you wish to. I will also require you to elevate me to the rank of bishop. For this you will get your secret escort to our spiritual home, ten great weapons of war with bolts and stones to fire and a donation of twenty thousand gold pieces."

"Excellent Apollyon. I accept your conditions as well. Upon safe delivery of me and my men to Beth Col, with the artillery delivered and the gold in my possession, you will be nominated as Bishop of Ende. We will also attend one of your ceremonies. I trust from your twelve white clad friends that you were planning on celebrating your devotions to Ahrioch tonight?"

"But of course. I engage every night in some form of celebration."

"Then tonight I will bless you and your adepts with my presence. For we must be swift. I take it you can have everything arranged for delivery with exceptional speed?"

"Yes mistress," Apollyon bowed deeply, his sweaty head shimmered with her reflection.

That night Vixen managed to maintain the decorum expected as she sat on a throne and watched as Apollyon and his twelve acolytes writhed and thrashed in an indiscriminate heap beneath her. It was a valid form of praise to her dark Lord, but it was mostly enjoyed by fringe sects. As she looked upon the sweating mound of moving bodies her thoughts turned to a reunification and a common form of worship. One strain with the same end view. Sacrifice and consumption of the victim was one thing, orgiastic devotion, another.

The morning came and Hoarfrost oversaw the embarkation to a galley provided for transport. The trireme would row them swiftly to the most northerly point of Ende's harbour. Vixen followed the men, bleary eyed, beneath a heavy cloak of disguise. The worshipping of Ahrioch had gone on till just before dawn and she had had very little sleep. She hoped to catch some more as the ship crossed the harbour but the noise of three banks of slaves rowing would not allow that. The trireme was sleek, black with golden trims, its oars moved in graceful unison as it powered through the water to its goal. This was however a piece of theatricality, a whim of Apollyon to be transported in style befitting an ancient emperor, not a warrior at the head of an armada. The trireme had no battering ram attached at its bow, just an effete gilded carving of a naked elf. Its perfect golden form led the way back to Beth Col.

Upon docking, messengers under the employ of Apollyon ran off to various warehouses to arrange for delivery of the heavy weapons and the delivery of gold. Vixen bit her lips in thought. Here she was, landing in a three tiered trireme, with close to two hundred men about to march through the streets. Deliveries of a large sum of gold and ten siege weapons had been arranged and she wanted it all to be unnoticed. It was bound to be the worst kept secret of the day. At the very least something big was bound to be spotted at the Ahrioch Horde's compound, Beth Col. At best she might be able to keep the fact that the High Priestess was in residence. Her major hope though was in association with the master of the island and his well known fake warship. If she could remain invisible all might be well. Vixen summoned Hoarfrost before the men started to clamber down to the lowered gangplanks to the wharf below.

"Gather six of your best men captain," Vixen ordered. "I wish to cross the city by other routes than the rest of our men. Let them form a diversion of clattering yahoos. I doubt they would be unnoticed anyway so instruct them to sing and chant as they march. Draw the eyes of the mob away from us."

"It will be done," Hoarfrost replied and stepping away from Vixen soon collared a couple of corporals and four troopers that had all served him well in the past. They gathered in a tight bunch around their leader and waited for the rest of the men to leave the galley and then march off noisily, north into the sprawling slums and decadent old mighty edifices of Ende.

A few minutes later Vixen gave the command and her bodyguard escorted her as they might any other noblewoman in the city, who, through business of her own, had to walk the dangerous streets.

Vixen cast her mind back to the last time she had walked north from the docks to Beth Col. Then she had snatched Tumbletick away from his protectors and with her men spirited him away in darkness to be prepared for sacrifice. A lot had transpired since then and she still planned to take her revenge on the surviving members of that adventure plus the misshapen dwarf himself. The streets were crowded. Ende was bustling and she prayed to Ahrioch that this deception during the day would work and no enemies would confirm her journey to the temple. She looked tentatively under the cowl of her hooded cloak. Through the chinks of her bodyguard's burly frames she saw locals, peasants and scum scatter away from her group. Bedraggled urchins, braver than the older beggars, or more desperate, called out for alms from the 'pretty noblewoman'. A correct assumption seeing as how the filth ridden mites could not see her face. Her guards kicked out at some of the more adventurous and they made their way back to the sewers of the back alleys. Again Vixen found herself thinking of how Ende needed to be purified and cleansed. A cull would be called for when the Ahrioch Horde had truly gained power. Not just in Umiat but here in Kenai as well. Then Ende could easily become the glorious capital of the two continents, combined through faith and her leadership. The slums would be cleared and great public works constructed. It was a dream shared by many of high rank within the religion, past and present. A unified style of grand architecture, solid and resilient, a pure line, designed to inspire, work and last for a millennia. Vixen slipped back to reality and urged on her protectors. She was keen to make it back to Beth Col. Whatever the state of affairs currently the compound would need much work to be completely safe. It must become fortified. It must be able to protect her and her studies.

When eventually they did make it to the walls of Beth Col, Vixen took some comfort that much of Hoarfrost's beliefs were instantly confirmed. There were more wooden watchtowers prickling above the curtain wall that surrounded the complex. She was pleased to see that clusters of iron spikes had been sent into clumps of concrete all along the top of the perimeter of the wall as well, to discourage and wound any who climbed over. The gates had been replaced, currently they were open though as her band of men had arrived and had gained entrance through the correct use of known passwords. She crept in on the heels of her small army and quickly ordered Hoarfrost to shut and bar the gates. She felt nervous, needed the doors shut behind her and the defences bolstered still further. The household steward came running over and threw himself at the feet of the High Priestess of Ahrioch, grovelling and snivelling instantly about not knowing she was arriving.

"Get up, get up," Vixen ordered. "Listen carefully. I want my apartment made up quickly. If there is not a bath there, in Ahriman's old chambers, waiting for me when I do get to the rooms, then I will have your head. Also we will be expecting delivery of a donation plus some heavy weapons shortly. The weapons are to be set on the roof of the temple and guarding its entrance. Only those deliveries are to be accepted until I change any orders. Do I make myself clear?"

"Yes mistress. Yes!" the man scrambled to his feet and ran off barking orders at underlings, kicking and hitting them to inspire a swift response.

"The men, Hoarfrost, can barrack around the complex," Vixen said to her captain. "You know the guardhouses and common rooms better than most anyway. We will find you a house closer to the temple for your own personal billet. I'm sure there will still be some vacant after the defeat which occurred here. But first you and I will inspect the library which is where I will be spending most of my time. Then to the temple's heart to say some small prayers of gratitude for a safe arrival back to Beth Col. And then my bath."

The library was intact and had been well cared for despite the attack on the complex. No heathen had made it into this sanctuary of learning and the religion's head librarian, Em'Lee and her staff had it extremely well maintained. They were praised highly by Vixen and instructed to gather the books and scrolls she would need to begin her studies first in demonology and then necromancy. The diminutive and highly attractive brunette, Em'Lee, soon had the other lower librarians scurrying away efficiently to collect the works she instantly brought to mind.

The main heart of the temple, with its sunken floor and mosaic hexagram had been purified and cleansed after the slaughter that had occurred there and Vixen performed a quick rite of thankfulness before retiring to the chambers that had once belonged to Ahriman and were now hers. The bath was full and hot and aromatic with oils. The steward had done a good job. Vixen stripped, leaving her clothes in discarded expectation of bliss and she sunk into the water for an hour of relaxation before her labours would truly begin.

The next day saw the placing of the artillery around the main temple of Beth Col. The ballistae were modern and could fire broad bladed bolts big enough to sever a horses head or penetrate deeply into massed ranks of men. The onagers were designed to unleash shrapnel, like rocks or spiked iron balls, in a low arc to devastate any group of attackers over a wider area than the accurate ballista or catapult. The catapults were of an older design but virtually identical to the ballistae. There were however subtle differences, the catapults were powered by twisted cords rather than an elastic bow of iron, but catapults too fired evil bolts rather than stones which many a non warrior thought. All were specifically equipped with an anti-personnel inventory, rather than a true siege arsenal, as that was where the expected threat lay.

As the days turned to weeks Vixen was spending her time solely devoted to study, while Hoarfrost saw to the training in the use of the siege weapons and hiring of additional mercenaries to bolster their numbers. While he had been unable to find recruits as good as the Landsknechts the donation from Apollyon was immensely useful in the retaining the loyalties of those who did not feel the passion of faith, just the lust for wealth.

Em'Lee, the head librarian, provided Vixen with the works she need and aid with some pronunciation. The High Priestess applied herself well to the study and conjuring of demons. Raising the dead would come when her own confidence had grown. The capture, holding and then commanding of denizens of the pit had to be her first aim. With the permanent perfect hexagram in the temple she practised the art with imps at first. Many came through to the material plane in an imperfect form, with limbs missing or parts of the body just a sloppy sticky ooze. They would gibber and moan at being torn from the abyss and pace about within the hexagram. Vixen ensured that any that were damaged were disposed of while fully formed imps were sent back to the abyss. In time as she practiced she started to bring forth larger and more fearsome creatures like nupperibae and abishai, devils than existed in their thousands among the ranks of Hell. These devils were more intelligent and useful than the imps, the nupperibae had an almost human appearance apart from being grossly deformed and the abishai, known as the scaly devil, were winged and lizard like. Vixen considered releasing these to patrol the passageways of Beth Col but felt that perhaps still she was not that skilled in controlling them. What she really needed was one large devil or demon that she could control. With the soul of Ahriman, now very much animated within her due to the nature of her studies, she found that the words and knowledge started to come to her more easily than she would have suspected. But then she was an exceptional woman. The guidance of Em'Lee was still vital in combination with encouragement that the soul of Ahriman provided but Vixen still felt she shone and was a natural. What would have taken someone adept to the calling of the dark arts weeks, took her merely hours. By the end of thirteen days she was ready to call up a major demon to the physical plain, ripping it from the abyss to serve her. She was ready to summon a nabassu, commonly known in the realm of nightmares as a death stealer.

Chapter Thirteen

The fleet that Percy Fenton had mustered off Point Kuskok had started sailing for its final destination two days ago. It now rounded the most westerly point of Kenai and then turned north into the harbour of Ende. From the city no alarm was raised, no fear felt, it was just another seven ships slipping in the busiest sea lanes of the world.

Just short of one thousand pirates were aboard the seven ships. 'The Peppercorn' led the way followed by 'The Brazen Manticore', 'The Ardent Panda', 'The Boreas', 'The Dantalion', 'The Medusa' and 'The Revenge'. All were fully rigged with stiff cloth sails to take advantage of the strong winds, the smallest ship of the group was a two mast brig and held fifty fully armed buccaneers ready to assault Beth Col. The largest, 'The Ardent Panda' was a full scale ship of the line, a classic warship, with four masts and carried three hundred men.

The attack would be a rampage inspired by years of fighting at sea. This was no organised army. The only considered bit of battle tactics would be the use of a battering ram, against the gates of the compound, that had been in the hold of 'The Dantalion' for years. Campbell the Weasel, Percy Fenton, Captain Battfin and Is-Is had all been to Beth Col before. They knew the gates could be smashed and also knew that the walls could be scaled with grappling hooks and a determined foe could easily drop down onto out buildings built against the inside walls of the temple complex. This time however the plan was a full frontal assault and then to spread out in individual combat. The battering ram would then be taken to the central building and main temple to shatter its only door which faced the gates, enabling one swift and simple move. The eight adventurers would then, with forty hand picked men, devastate any living thing within the temple. But Vixen must be taken alive. With Vixen captured the eight would retreat to 'The Peppercorn' and depart for Rhyell with their bounty while the remaining cutthroats dismembered any remaining followers of the Ahrioch Horde and then dismantled the entire structure by fire, hammer and hand.

Campbell had stated how the plan was simple and would not fail because it was so accessible to all. Death and destruction. He stood at the prow of 'The Peppercorn' with A'Lastor and smiled as the demon indicated that their quarry was directly ahead with another confirming lift of his head. Campbell placed a hand on the shoulder of A'Lastor.

"Are you ready for this my friend?" the thief asked. "Because this is what we have all been working towards. You will get your reward with a successful battle at Beth Col."

"Yes Campbell. I am more than ready. Today we capture the hunted."

The seven ships led by Captain Battfin on 'The Peppercorn' closed to a tight formation, sails were furled and with a grace unsuspected in pirates, they all pulled up alongside two adjacent wharfs simultaneously. As they heaved to, willing dock workers caught lines and tied the ships fast.

"This must be the most welcomed that any invasion can ever have been," said Percy dryly as he watched from the deck of the lead ship. Is-Is nodded and gave a final patting check around his body that all his weapons were in place. Pavor and Eris were both pacing with anticipation of the fight and capture of Vixen. Seton Rax hefted his battleaxe to a comfortable position for marching and awaited the gangplank to be lowered.

Captain Battfin gave the order and men began streaming off the ships and mustered on the dockside. A thousand men clustering together, bristling with blades, a few heavy hammers, six manhandling a battering ram and it all seemed like a common occurrence in the port city of Ende. Ende was a huge city, the vast majority of the population of Kenai lived there, more than a thousand thousand souls rubbed shoulders in their slums and compounds. Living rough in dilapidated old cathedrals or warehouses. Existing very well behind high walls in villas with neatly trimmed gardens and nights out to the theatres that still put on plays in areas policed by mercenaries hired by rich citizens to keep away undesirables. With the army of pirates taking up a tiny portion of the dockside, the inhabitants were not too concerned, but they did at least take notice now and many did slink away. There was the sound of shutting doors and closing bolts but most just ignored the invasion force as just another matter that did not involve them, especially when the army marched away to the north being led by a ninja, a weasel like man, a barbarian with a bare torso, a flamboyantly dressed foppish cad, one scary scarred black fellow, a buxom brunette, a thin wiry warrior and one enormous hare covered in daggers, knives, chain mail and carrying a huge sword. However, others who noticed the indiscrete entry of faces that had been very well described had specific instruction to report such an event. More than one of the faithful was picketed out at vantage points around the docks, perched up in high towers and they ran with the news to their mistress. They were fleet of foot and sped to gain the time needed to respond to the expected event.

The amazing memory of Campbell the Weasel led them straight and true through the slums and by the decaying decadence of ancient structures that made up most of Ende. As predicted the local powers and princely brigands simply looked away with the realisation that this was not a private army hired to harass them. So it was that with a short forced march, pumping with anticipation of the bloodlust to come, the pirate army saw before it the compound of Beth Col.

It was set in a slight dell within the mounds and slopes of the city. The twenty foot high, whitewashed wall that surrounded it looked different now. When a few of them had last been here there had only been four wooded watch towers built on the inside. Now Campbell could count twelve. Also large iron spikes were set at jaunty angles all around the top of the wall. The thief also spotted wooden machines of war set on top of the central temple, with its flat roof it was an ideal location for weapons of mass destruction. The block like structure and total compound was more heavily defended now then when they had attacked months before.

"Looks almost as if they were expecting us," said Campbell to the other seven adventures as they stood with their army behind them. The sun was high above their heads and all the locals were locked away or had scattered into the surrounding alleyways when the force had halted. "Still we had reports from our ships and spies about her movements. Why wouldn't they have heard about us as well?"

"Should we at least make a call and enquire whether they want to surrender and give up Vixen?" asked Percy looking at the siege engines with the nervous eye of a man who had faced them at sea and knew all too well of their power.

"No," Campbell retorted immediately. "We stick to the plan. Beth Col is to be destroyed and everyone in it killed. Everyone killed except Vixen."

"Bring forth the battering ram!" shouted Captain Battfin.

There was an eerie calm as the six men, three to a side, carried the wooden trunk. Thick handles had been thrust through it to support the weight of the bole plus the large metal head that encased the end, shaped like a fist. There was no movement in the watch towers or on the roof of the temple. Whether there were warriors waiting on the other side or not, none could tell.

"Is she in there?" Campbell whispered to A'Lastor. The demon nodded.

"Attack!" cried the Master Thief.

The six pirates with the battering ram ran towards the double gates of Beth Col. In their previous attack a cart, loaded with wood and on fire had been forced to crash here. It had taken out the gate and part of the wall as well. This had been repaired but there were signs of where large cracks had been patched up. Although it was a large compound, this was no fort. It was essentially a temple surrounded by private residences and courtyards that had in time all been acquired by the Ahrioch Horde and a wall had been erected around their possessions. The iron fist, secured to the hefty log of solid wood, smashed into the centre join of the gates. At the first moment of contact it was obvious that the reinforced, thick oak gates, barred from behind were still no match for the half ton weight, at a ramming speed, punching a great ball of iron into the weakest spot. The bar behind the gates simply snapped with a resounding crack and the wooden portal swung open to reveal the entrance to the religious heart of the Ahrioch Horde. The battering pirates dropped the ram and were first into the compound, swiftly followed by a swarm of eager warriors, they flowed in and began to form a bunched mass in the main courtyard. Ahead of them lay the blocky temple of Beth Col, white and three storeys tall, there were only windows on the top floor of the building with lead running in a criss-cross design throughout their circular shape. Directly opposite the main gates of the outer wall was the door to the temple itself and in front of this door stood ranks of warriors, guards and mercenaries. Maybe three hundred men, armed with swords and at regular intervals in their lines small teams of men clustered around six wooden siege engines all facing the rush of pirates who pushed their way through the bottle neck of the gates and now started to spread out further in the open space in front of the temple. Despite their overwhelming odds at this stage it would still take some time to get the entire force through the gates which were only wide enough for maybe six abreast. The pirates had imagined finding Beth Col as a heaving throng of people not be confronted by all the inhabitants in one massed rank with two ballistae, two catapults and two onagers in their midst. The pirates began bunching up and not running off into the individual combat situations they thought they might. No one was foolish enough at this stage to engage an enemy in such a formation. They needed to have a large numerical superiority before a charge could be attempted. By being faced by an unexpected rank upon rank of warriors the pirates continued to be confused. Each thought that standing by the side of his fellows was the best response to this situation and so they continued to bunch up in a bulge of men in front of the broken gates. Then there was a response from the Ahrioch Horde. An extremely tall warrior stepped forth from within the mass of the Ahrioch Horde and strode a few yards in front of his army to stand isolated from the rest.

Seton Rax and company stood at the front of the pirate army still attempting to form up within the space provided with its ever increasing numbers. Campbell joined A'Lastor from within the scrum to find Is-Is already staring deliberately at the large warrior who had identified himself as a particular target by emerging from the Ahrioch Horde soldiers. Captain Battfin soon also found his way to the front rank of the buccaneers to take his place as a leader as well. So it was, that an expected violent raid of individuals swarming about Beth Col found themselves instead as a bunched up group, being pushed from behind as other pirates attempted to push their way in, as those inside backed away from the face off with a determined and professional looking foe.

In the front rank of the pirates now stood, Seton Rax, Eris, Pavor, A'Lastor, Campbell, Is-Is and Captain Battfin. Percy must have been somewhere behind, urging on the cutthroats at the rear of the attacking force.

Hoarfrost stood at the front of his men, guards and mercenaries hired for the defence. He looked with a soldier's eye at his enemy swelling before him. His spies had reported quickly and they had been ready with their predetermined response against a large assault. All non essential inhabitants to the expected battle had fled Beth Col. To defend the temple door was imperative and only those who could fight well would be needed. The pirates had gained entry exactly as planned, he as captain now just had to time his next order to perfection. He gauged the numbers of his foes, he wanted to wait until about half their number were within the compound walls and half without, this would also mean that the threat opposite him was still not at two to one with his and at a force size where it would be likely to brave an assault. It also provided the largest target before they might charge. He raised his arm, a cruel toothed sword in his hand, he paused, then sliced the air in front of him. At his command several things happened at once. Archers appeared from prone positions in the watch towers and instantly kicked down the ladders which provided access. Teams of men also appeared on the temple roof and grouped around the siege engines there. On the ground the command to attack meant one thing only and its sound was more fearful and devastating than any war cry. In a strange pre-battle silence the noise of twisted cord releasing with explosive force, the rasp of huge bladed bolts being ejaculated down grooved shafts by released triggers, metal bows springing back into their desired non taut state, the crash of wooden arms hitting a crossbar and releasing a large amount of flints shaped like axe heads, all combined.

The siege engines from the ground and roof of Beth Col unleashed a controlled fury and hurled their projectiles against the five hundred men and one woman in front of them. The bolts they fired landed first in the flesh of their victims, punching vast gashes in bodies, skewering men together and knocking corridors of death into the army. The stones landed next, sharpened flints that withered the force with vicious wounds and confusion. At least a tenth of the amassed army inside Beth Col died in that volley. Bodies fell in the violence, screams rang out and fell silent. Groans of the wounded came next. The pirates still outside the compound continued to push and now found that some space availed itself but it was caused by the dead falling to the ground. The survivors looked around after checking themselves to still be alive and listened as the cranking of the weapons indicated that the enemy had already began to reload. The archers now started their attack from the watchtowers. They lobbed a rain of piercing death down on the pirates who were still outside Beth Col. The resulting pandemonium was pleasing to the marksmen of the Ahrioch Horde. As men died, others tried with more effort to enter the gates, pushing their own, some ran and sought shelter down alleys between nearby buildings, leaving the field of combat. The pirates pushed harder trying to escape the arrows, not realising that they were attempting to gain entrance to a killing field as they tried to flee another. Corpses were trampled on, more than one injured man was killed as he was trodden on by uncaring boots of his colleagues. The cries of dying men now mixed with the twang of bow strings and the mechanical sounds of the siege engines. Seconds that had felt leaden and slow had only just ticked by and about eighty pirates were now lost to death, while others were fearfully wounded.

"It's a cracking ambush!" shouted Campbell who was one of the first to recover his wits from the debacle. He quickly checked to his left and right, the confused and startled army was looking for direction and leadership despite years of experience at sea, or because of it. The army which would have been swinging on ropes, fighting in rigging and charging over decks if they had been on an ocean was now standing still on land, the dead slumped amongst their ranks. Campbell looked left again and, to his horror, saw Pavor kneeling, holding Eris in his arms as she lay on the floor. Pavor was cradling the beautiful bounty hunter as she slowly drifted away from life and his unspoken love. Her leg had been ripped off by a ballista bolt, that after tearing through her lower hip and upper thigh had slammed into the guts of a cutthroat behind her. Pavor was kissing her pale face and hugging her, urging her to live. Blood had already ceased to pump from the massive trauma, her heart had stopped with her last feelings being the unimaginable pains of the great rent and the tender touches of Pavor's lips.

Pavor gently laid Eris' body to the blood soaked flagstones of the compound courtyard. He stood slowly, he felt emotion greater than he ever had. His stomach churned with regret, anger and shock at the randomness with which Eris had been taken from him. She was everything that he had desired and loved. Now she had been ripped from him by a method that was not befitting for one so beautiful. If she had been marked for death then she should have been taken in a glorious battle against warriors, not by a machine aimed at her by engineers. He was surrounded by pirates feeling indecision and fear, there was no response. He knew what to do though, his decision was made. Grim faced he drew his rarely used sword and simply charged. His plaited ponytail streamed behind him as his legs ran with a rage he had never before felt. The battle cry that roared from within him was one of utter grief and hatred. Hoarfrost backed away from the lone assailant who had broken ranks and secluded himself quickly behind his own men. Pavor soon crossed the small void that separated the two groups and he crashed into a wall of warriors still screaming in despair.

"No!" cried Seton Rax in an agony of his own, desperate to try and halt the foolish solo assault of his friend.

The pirates and adventures gasped in loss as another of their comrades instantly collapsed under the attack from the defending Ahrioch Horde. Pavor didn't even get in a single thrust of a sword or punch from his iron shod fist. He simply buckled and fell to the ground within a bunch of enclosing, hunching, scrum of killers who stabbed and cut and hacked to death the lone brave man. Then they stood again, returned to their previous lined ranks and revealed the chopped and bloodied corpse before them.

It was however the catalyst that was needed, the shock to the combined system after all the confusion. Before the siege engines could fire again they must attack and it was the voice of hundreds, not one leader, that cried into the air with their own various calls to attack.

The pirates stampeded forward, rage and desperation to slam against their foe. The need to engage the enemy before the massive siege engines could be primed again was the uppermost thought in their minds. Is-Is found himself at the spearhead, he was so fast that he left the enraged mass of men behind him. The hare led with his broadsword levelled like a lance and he headed straight towards the men who had felled Pavor. The pirates behind the gates now had room to flow in and they too rushed forward, still targeted by the archers above who looked to pick off individuals with their bows.

Is-Is eyed the men who had killed his friend. They still stood in a defensive rank behind Pavor's corpse. Is-Is charged at a bewildering speed, yards ahead of any of the other pirates. He crashed into the Ahrioch Horde as he leapt over the bloody remains of his dead friend. His sword bit into the throat of an enemy. As the point severed the man's spine the hare punched out with the hilt of the sword straight into the face of another foe. This brought the six foot blade into a horizontal position in front of the crashing mass of hare. The first victim was now nearly decapitated and the rest of the sword collided against a wall of warriors with all the weight of the mail clad Is-Is behind it. The pirates were not far behind now and they smashed into the Ahrioch Horde with an avenging force. Weapons were hacked and thrust into enemies which seemed like meaningless meat. Through ribs and limbs of foes who could not tell who they have just killed or who was attacking them. Under the noon sun of Kenai, men struggled in a rage unnoticed by the rest of the city of Ende. The pirates pushed hard with their greater numbers and the warriors loyal to Vixen found themselves pressed against the wall of their temple. Panic began to take hold as the sweating crush of buccaneers thrust against them. Elements of the Ahrioch Horde began to peel off from the edges of their ranks to fight in more space. Those still in the ranks further back waited for the men in front to die and fall for then themselves to be pushed forward in the eagerness to engage from warriors behind.

The archers of the watchtowers now fired into the backs of the pirates where they had a clear shot. The majority of the battle was occurring on only one side of the temple with skirmishing taking place at the peripheries as groups broke off from the edges to take the fighting into other areas of the compound. Percy Fenton was indeed at the rear of the attack and noticing the sniping from the wooden towers led a reasonable band of marauders to deal with the shooting platforms. Under fire from deadly shafts, the pirates, used to climbing rigging during storms, found no difficulty in heaving their way up the towers, daggers twixt their teeth. It did not even occur to them to raise the ladders back up, climbing the wooden scaffolding was a simple task and ladders can be kicked back down when an assailant is near to the top. The archers soon found themselves frantically fending off cutthroats clambering over the ledges of their high hides, a loosed arrow might send one pirate to fall to his death but another would then strike a knife into the kidneys of the marksman as he never found the fletching for a follow up arrow. The towers were soon cleared of the threat and Percy and his commandoes returned to the fray.

The pirates fell particularly heavily on the men who had fired the siege engines. Death was dealt out brutally for most but tortuously for those. They were dragged out from amongst the ranks to be toyed with a while in more space before their own death. The weapons themselves were also attacked, smashed with the few heavy hammers that had been brought along for other demolition tasks.

It was a numbers exercise now. The forces from Umiat had more men, the Ahrioch Horde recognised this. They were dwindling in the crush. Any who had been cut off or had run to other areas of the compound were easily surrounded and dispatched. Hoarfrost recognising this had to resort to his next strategy. The siege engines were now smashed on the ground but had performed well. His archers were gone, his men were still capable and vicious but outnumbered maybe three to one at this stage. The engines on the roof which had also fired in the first volley were now reloaded but the battle was too close to the temple wall to get in a decent angle of attack and he would not risk hitting his own men no matter how desperate the situation. The captain of the Ahrioch Horde was by the door to the temple. His men would fight even harder in the next stage, the lust of the zealot in their hearts. He pounded on the door and it opened, from the inside. He was first through but followed quickly by others, who turned with discipline and plunged through the portal like a bursting pustule draining away after an initial tense spurt. Members of the Ahrioch Horde who were engaging the enemy at this moment knew their role and fought with a revived intensity. Their comrades needed a little time to get as many into the temple as possible. A semicircle of the faithful held back the assault in a wide arc from the wall of the temple a good thirty foot either side of the central open door. Behind this front the warriors within all turned and slipped away into the darkness of the corridors behind them. The thin ranks of warriors left did well to hold off the pirates for a while but as the door to the temple slammed shut and the boom of a lowed bar reached them they knew their fate. At least a third of their original number, maybe a hundred and twenty had gained access to the thickly walled squat building. The forty or so brave warriors who remained outside fought with the mania of the blessed, sacrifices defending the core of Beth Col, their High Priestess, and comrades. To a man they fought steadfastly but with none behind to step into the gap as they fell the line shrank fast into small pockets of surrounded men and then ended its defence of the courtyard.

Is-Is and Seton Rax were engaged in defeating the last of the Ahrioch Horde outside of the main temple of Beth Col, butchering away at the remnants of the front rank. Fenton and Captain Battfin were leading squads of cutthroats checking out buildings for servants or fled warriors. None contained any of the enemy and the pirates began to return to the area to the front of the temple, knowing that the job of cleansing the compound and the destruction of the structure would only come once the central temple had been eradicated as well. They were surprised to find the rest of the out buildings so deserted. They might have expected servants, priests or pockets of resistance from hidden warriors keen to cause other ambushes, but none was found.

Campbell stood slightly further back with A'Lastor. Bodies were everywhere, wounded too, but the wounded of the Ahrioch Horde were being hacked to Hell by special parties as they screamed final prayers to their dark lord. The mashed remains of Pavor were at Campbell's feet. His corpse had been trampled on by many during the course of the battle. Eris' body lay with those who had died in the first volley. With the work now completed against the remaining Ahrioch warriors, Seton Rax and Is-Is walked over and joined with Campbell and A'Lastor.

"Time to grieve later," said Seton sternly avoiding the clump of death near Campbell's shoes. "We have to clear the temple now, and from memory, those corridors are going to be tough to deal with."

"Correct," said Campbell. "We don't know what resides within but at a minimum we've got to think there's at least a hundred and fifty men skulking around inside. There were zombies last time too, plus some pretty tough mercenary types. We have got to do it though and we must take Vixen alive. No fires, just yet. Can't risk that."

"Watch to the roof," said A'Lastor with a nod. "The men have departed from there too but they may return to drop death down upon us from that vantage now it is only us out here."

Campbell quickly agreed and called for men who were skilled with bows. They pilfered the remains of the archers and clambered up to the watchtowers, defences now used in the assault to keep an eye out for any enemy that may seek to sneak back to the roof and use the remaining engines of war.

"Maybe we shouldn't have destroyed the siege engines on the ground," said Seton. "We could have turned them against the temple. Sure one of those bolts could have cracked open the wall in places."

"Indeed," agreed A'Lastor. "Imagine if they are all lined up in behind the door. We could have sent down a couple of ballistae strikes and cleaned half of them away."

"Fair point," said Campbell. "But we are where we are and let's not be too hard on ourselves as we have to ensure we take Vixen alive. So it is going to have to be hand to hand. It will be costly through the corridors though. I suppose we could always try and smoke them out."

"It is too large a building," replied Seton suddenly looking down at the body of his dead friend and remembering his bravery he showed in a smoking out operation. "I don't think we'd be able to get it right and there is always the chance Vixen could choke to death and the mission is failed again."

"There must be access from the roof," pointed out A'Lastor who was still thinking about it. "They got the weapons up there, there were men there and now they have gone."

"Correct," Campbell nodded. "They are all probably lined up in the main corridor and then hiding around the building. Probably thick with mercenaries too. I know I keep labouring the point about the mercenaries but they were the toughest opponents we met here last time."

"They would be likely to expect a full frontal attack at this point," added Seton. "Though last time if I recall the zombies were also pretty nasty."

"There may be an option for some subterfuge," said A'Lastor, Campbell turned to the demon and realised his observation.

"Sorry A'Lastor. Of course. We need to diversify approach. If I recall the private chambers are up on the top floor," said Campbell. " A small and dedicated team could grapple their way up there and sneak in through the roof. Try and snatch Vixen away as she skulks in her rooms. A little bit like last time."

The thief looked at A'Lastor, then at Seton and Is-Is. The demon hiding behind his ninja gear turned back from looking at the roof and nodded, Seton and Is-Is were both nodding too.

"The four of us then, plus Captain Battfin. Percy remains outside to command the men if anything goes wrong," suggested Seton, putting the axe back into its strapping on his back and taking a grappling hook off the belt of a nearby pirate who walked by.

"Good group," said Campbell. "Strong and dangerous. Let's do it then. And let's do it now. If it is to be done then best it were done quickly, is some damn good advice I've always followed."

More grappling hooks were sought and soon found. The five adventurers stormed round to the far side of the temple and started to swing the clawed iron grips. All managed to heave them high enough first time and with a fine enough trajectory to land solidly on the flat temple roof and they all caught on a lip of brick work when pulled tight. The three men, one hare and one demon started to climb the white walls of Beth Col and were soon standing on the roof.

"So far so good," said Campbell. "That was a bit too easy."

The hatch that led to the floor below was prominent and already swung open. Is-Is, shaking his head at the carelessness of the defenders moved confidently and with no hesitation quickly dropped down the shaft of light that lit the corridor below. Two kukris were already in his paws as he landed, ready for any close quarter combat in the restrictive passageways of the upper floors. No enemies were about. Captain Battfin dropped down, then Seton and A'Lastor, finally Campbell was the last to enter the upper levels, landing with the quietest of thuds that marked him out as a thief of immense ability. Campbell pointed the direction he wanted them to move, guessing at the direction of the private quarters from their visit nearly a year before. The passages were dark and quiet, a couple of turns and they found themselves at the top of a flight of stairs with the corridor continuing to their right.

Is-Is took the lead now, confident and purposeful in the dim light. He remembered the way, the way they had ran before in the desperate search for Tumbletick and the Umiat Stone. He remembered the door he had kicked down and then set a swift arrow off into a flight that stuck it into the forearm of Ahriman as he was about to strike down the sacrificial blade he held into the chest of his friend.

Campbell quickly whispered the directions they would take when on the other side of the door. Seton, A'Lastor and Captain Battfin all nodded their understanding. The door to the private chambers would be opposite this one, maybe still behind a purple drape.

Is-Is tried the door first, attempting a silent entry rather that a smashing lash of his broad feet. The door opened. The octagonal antechamber was bare, no braziers or pedestals but the drapes did remain, alternating red and purple, fully covering each of the eight walls. The squad crept in, the room was devoid, silent. Pulses racing they approached the purple drape with the door behind it to the private suite of rooms. Is-Is grabbed the material, nodded and then pulled it down with a violent rip. Captain Battfin kicked the door open that was behind it and then he and Seton Rax were the first two to rush into the collection of rooms to snatch Vixen. A'Lastor and Campbell followed, darting in to each room and finding all devoid of life. The furniture showed signs of recent use and Campbell sneered when he found an ornate bath and vials of oils that were half empty. A'Lastor joined Campbell in the room with the bath and as they were briefly alone Campbell risked a quick question.

"Well A'Lastor? Do you sense her?"

"It is all a red mist before me, you are but a shadow within it. She is in this building," the demon replied.

Campbell returned to the octagonal room, Seton was cursing under his breath Is-Is and Captain Battfin stood still awaiting orders.

"Well it is going to be a bloodbath then," the thief coolly stated. "No opportunity for a quick hit and run."

"She'll be in the very heart then," said Captain Battfin. "Where Percy and I got to last time. The marble floor, lowered amidst tiers, demonic devices held in a mosaic. There were undead and Landsknechts there last time."

"Maybe with all her men guarding the ceremonial approach this time," mused Seton. "They have got to be in here somewhere. We all watched a load of them enter."

"Right," commanded Campbell. "We still must act quick. We'll get fifty good men to climb up here and meet with us. We'll then assault from within the building when the other guys attack the front door head on. We'll surprise them."

Captain Battfin took the initiative and went back to the roof to pass on the observations and orders. Is-Is moved to guard the top of the stairs while the others waited for the return of Captain Battfin and the selected men. Soon a steady stream of pirates began to arrive and the passageway on the top floor was crowded with blood lusting buccaneers. The remaining fearsome bunch of pirates outside were ready to assault against the lower floor.

"We sweep down when we hear the violence start," said Campbell. "This flight of stairs leads directly down to the main corridor where our enemies will no doubt be staunchly defending against our encroaching men. Be brave. It is likely to be ugly and cumbersome down there. Anyone fought in a mine before, attacking a castle? Well I reckon it is going to be like that. Brutal."

The pirates left outside the temple readied themselves. Percy had easily understood the plan and sent six of his men to reclaim the battering ram. Volunteers were called for to be the shock troops who would enter first as soon as the door was breached. Bolstered by the knowledge that a decent force of men were already in the building to offer a surprise attack the volunteers who most sought glory and bragging rights, stood forward. Twenty scarred and burly warriors drew short cruel stabbing weapons, still stained with the blood of those who had fallen before.

"Oh my glorious boys!" roared Fenton in delight looking at the bunch of bravos who would go in first. "Long will we sing of you! Drop them all dead. Carve forth a channel of victory! Damn them all to Hell!"

The ram was brought forward, the six selected to operate it tottered to the door and then began swinging the weighty trunk. No run up this time just a mighty well placed heave. The dark iron fist knocked with the force of a giant, the door, strong though it was, could not withstand the sudden crack of metal, the hinges burst and the door crashed inwards.

The scene on the other side was as expected. The wide ceremonial approach down through the temple was packed with warriors. Four wide the Ahrioch Horde stood, their bravest at the front as well. Rank after rank was set, cascading back down the corridor and into the darkness and gloom. The ram was dropped and over it leapt the pirate shock troops, rushing in to engage in a bloody mutilation of crushed and hemmed in combat, this time worse, more terrifying than the battle that had raged outside the temple. More enclosed, more claustrophobic, more intense. The churning violence of blades backed by maddened muscles met at that front of combat. Four on four, men met and hacked away as if at a rock face. To hear the echoes and roars of rage and pain, to see the carnage build and climb in piles of slumped meat as the cutthroats fought and hacked way at the Ahrioch Horde was to see one of the weirdest battles ever fought. Some might have seen combat as Campbell had said in tunnels under castles as miners met defenders, but they were usually rare and individual struggles. A few men who might have dug under ramparts and then lit fires or placed crude bombs to bring down the fortification's walls. This was an assembly line of death and murder, the eagerness of men to rip away the next soul that stepped up to a gap and instantly be faced by weapons and teeth and fists. Pirate and zealot died to be replaced by another body, the next to the slaughter. Each man did hope to win honour and praise, his name in a song. Each man hoped to kill more than perhaps three others before he himself would be killed. The Ahrioch Horde fought with desperation and the zeal of fanatics combined. This was a last stand for them. There was nowhere to go, nothing to lose. Their mistress and their temple were to be defended. They fought hard and at times gained ground against the pirates. Pushing back in the lines of men who confronted them. Stepping over the dead to engage with the next combatant. It was as swift and as brutal as Campbell had suspected.

Then Is-Is and the others arrived, hitting hard from a side corridor. He had led the counter attack as soon as they had heard the door smashed in, yet even in the short time it took them to rush down the stairs many had already died in the corridor. The hare was devastating as usual but his killing prowess was enhanced with the benefit of surprise as he appeared from the dark against his foes. The Ahrioch Horde at that point died quickly, shocked at the sudden unexpected attack from within. Is-Is turned left to carry on the assault towards the last of the closed doors of the building, he had sixteen men in front of him who suddenly responded. Other pirates behind Is-Is turned right and attacked the column of zealots from the rear, murdering confused acolytes of Ahrioch as they struggled to turn to face the new threat. The butchery now ensued on three fronts. Pirates fought at two ends of a trapped bunch of Ahrioch Horde, murdering away and cutting down men in order to reach their own comrades and at the other front a giant hare fought with intense accuracy with a couple of kukris and stunned the remnants of the horde there. It was bad enough facing one giant hare but when he was joined by a ninja wielding two xyele and reducing the men to piles of chopped limbs the fear grew. Zealots at the rear tried to turn and started banging on the door to the Chapel of Ahrioch. But the doors were locked, stubborn, unforgiving and did not open. The men were meant to die if they could not hold off the assault. Is-Is tore out another throat with his crooked knife and watched the man fall to his knees trying to block the rent with his fingers. The hare kneed the man hard in the face with an armoured leg and sent him to his death. Is-Is' left paw swung round with the additional twist of his body sent into motion by the strike of his left knee. The kukri he held in that paw slipped neatly through the ribs of a man about to strike out at A'Lastor. With his lower lung and liver gashed by a near foot of wide sharp metal the man died of pain and an immense haemorrhage. A'Lastor fought with grace and violence combined. His slightly curved blades flashed and slashed at the bodies before him, parrying swords and cutting out guts, tearing throats and piercing torsos. The two of them fought savagely side by side. Backed up by a few pirates the two cleared their way through the remaining Ahrioch Horde and found their way to the locked, bolted and barred doors to the temple's heart.

Behind them the last remaining few enemies were cut off and had cutthroats vengefully attacking on two fronts. Captain Battfin bloodily swathed devastation through the desperate men. His cutlasses were the perfect size to deal with this corridor environment, they flashed and twinkled in the gloom and great gushes of blood sprayed, following their swipes, to splat against the passageway walls. Seton Rax had not even entered into the combat. His double handed double headed battleaxe needed more room to operate in effectively but he had been prepared to jab with it had the occasion called. Soon however, Captain Battfin and his men had only one thin rank of four Ahrioch Horde raiders left to dispatch. A yard away other pirates assaulted them from the other side. These final four men, who had gleefully killed monks at Aklavik, raped village women and children before cutting their throats, died just as the others did. Unable to put up any valid resistance to attackers from two sides the four were severed from their souls by countless vicious hacks. Their blood seeped to the sides of the passage, their bodies slumped to the carpet of dead that clogged the floor and their dying yells fell silent and all that was left was the ominous looking double door that a few knew led to the least holy scene in all of Kenai.

The survivors took a little time to recover their strength while looking at the charnel house around them. They also looked to the doors and listened in case they suddenly opened and another fresh wave of killers emerged in an attempt to drive them from Beth Col. One solitary room remained to be cleared. The rest was cleansed. Vixen would be behind these last doors. She would be in the tiered room with a sunken floor and a permanent hexagram marked out in mosaic. Is-Is and Seton Rax took up position by the ornately carved black wooden doors. The dead members of the Ahrioch Horde who had tried to open them had already given the clue that they were likely both locked and barred. There was little room to bring up the battering ram again, it would be difficult to move it over the mounds of dead. It was hard enough for the survivors to pick their way through to be ready to enter the final part of the temple. So Seton lifted his axe ready to break the door down or chop his way through. Is-Is was ready to support the barbarian if any foe attempted to attack through as he hacked the door. With space left for the swinging of the axe, Captain Battfin was standing by Percy Fenton who now made his way close to the front of the action. Campbell and A'Lastor were next in line and behind them was the rest of the cutthroat band, nervously anticipating the final stage of the battle of Beth Col. All was silence. Seton lifted his axe, looked to Is-Is who nodded in reply and twirled his kukris. The broad curved blade of the heavy two handed axe came down hard against the door powered by its own weight and the might of Seton. The resonant crack of wood suddenly splitting shot down the corridor and brought attentive glances to the fore. Seton ripped the axe from the wood with a great tug and heaved again and again and again. Great splinters began to fall on the floor as the door protested in vain against the strength of the steel. Seton hacked away at where he could feel more tensile resistance in the wood. It must be where the bar lay behind. Three more heavy thwacks and light appeared through a jagged wound in the door. The bar could clearly be seen behind the widening gap. Seton concentrated and brought the axe down viciously on this final barrier. The bar cleaved in two, snapping violently, its ends flying up as its middle crashed down to the marble floor of the temple's main chamber. The single massive strike had, in breaking the beam, also violently lifted it out of its bronze holders. All heard the tone of the two pieces falling down the tiers on the other side. It seemed musically pleasant after the discordant cacophonies of battle.

Is-Is pushed open the doors and stepped through with Seton Rax to gaze upon the brightly torch lit chamber which was vacant apart from three very different individuals and the hexagram mosaic. The room was square at the level where Is-Is and Seton stood, large enough to accommodate many worshippers who would sit on the six tiers which led down to a sunken circle. A pit of white marble with the black hexagram design. The tiers were shaped to make the transition from square to circle a gradual change. There though, standing on this lowest level of the pit was Vixen. With her was her bodyguard and captain, Hoarfrost and contained within the boundaries of the hexagram was a tall, winged, fanged and clawed demon, gazing hungrily at the potential feast of Is-Is and Seton Rax.

Captain Battfin, Percy, Campbell and A'Lastor now entered the heart of Beth Col and took in the scene. Vixen was looking directly at them, imperiously, her stunning features set into a mask of hatred. Hoarfrost, so tall and powerful stood beside her, his sword drawn ready to defend his mistress' life. The demon began turning and pacing within the confines of the hexagram. Two equilateral triangles were at the centre of the design, set into a six pointed star. Their points touched the circumference of a circle. A slightly larger circle was around this one so that it made a ring. Within the ring where each of the points of the star touched the circle there was an elaborate black cross marked in to the design. Between each of these six crosses there was a word. They could easily read these larger clearer words in the outer circle which the demon never trod upon, however within the zone where the demon paced there were the thirteen sections made by the star and the circumference of the inner circle. In these areas were designs and lettering forming words which none could make out, but the demon could not pass the words of power. Tetragamaton, Elohim, Messias, Sother, Emanuel, Adonai Jah. The demon was tall and thin with a scaly and sinewy form. The head was very long and had two small bony white horns. It had large ears that were bat like and yellow tusks protruding from its wide salivating maw. Its long arms, thin and lithe, spoke of power and demonic strength. Its fingers flexed and showed razor sharp talons, instead of nails, which retracted when its hands became fists of rage at its confinement. On its back a pair of vast wings, leathery and black moved like a churning dark sea, it wanted to fly.

"It's a nabassu," said A'Lastor calmly, breaking the silence. "A major demon from the lower levels of the Abyss. Extremely dangerous and rare."

"Can we kill it?" asked Seton Rax from the side of his mouth not taking his eyes from the beast for a moment.

"Yes, we can," replied A'Lastor. "If it doesn't kill us first."

Campbell turned and shut the doors, although heavily hacked they still closed quite well, testament to the craftsman who had created them. He turned back and looked to the bottom of the room.

"You're trapped Vixen," he shouted down. "We have caught you hiding out in the scene of your ultimate treachery. Fitting that your demise will start in the very building your master died and you fled from me."

"You crack Campbell," Vixen spat back. "You think you have caught me? I only have to say the word of unbinding and this demon will be released. It will strike down upon you all with the frenzy of Hell. I'm not trapped! You are!"

"Say the cracking word then Vixen you whore!" Campbell shouted back with an aggressiveness that called for a conclusion. With a roar befitting a mighty warrior, the little thief was the first to run and leap down the first tier towards Vixen and her two final defenders. Is-Is and Captain Battfin responded more quickly than anyone else and were soon bounding after Campbell. A'Lastor and Percy waited with Seton Rax at the top of the room, confident in the others skills to deal with the final situation.

"Astaris," called Vixen and the nabassu, instantly released from the invisible bindings of the hexagram leapt six foot straight up and spread its wings. It let loose a cry of delight, hunger and rage. All in the room felt the huge blast of air as the demon's wings propelled its bulk still higher into the vault of the temple. Then looking as if it meant to rend the room asunder, the nabassu made frantic crawling movements with its taloned hands, kicked with its legs, batted the air with its wings and flew straight towards the six adventurers. Its mouth was wide and open, its tusks glistening with demonic spit, it screeched again the terrifying call of its kind. Campbell, Is-Is and Captain Battfin faltered a little in their strides as they were confronted by the beast plummeting towards them. They readied their weapons to defend against the demon's onslaught but then had no need. The nabassu, in its powered flailing flight, aimed higher in the temple, its yellow eyes were focused on the group standing on the top tier and one individual in particular caught its attention. In a row the three stood, facing the oncoming demon, they felt in turn aware, aghast and afraid. A'Lastor, Percy Fenton and Seton Rax, waited the brief second for the demon to strike. Its black broad wings beat twice more, its claws reached out ahead of it, it moved with a devastating speed and the individual it had targeted realised he was going to take the full force of the strike. It crashed into Percy Fenton, grasping with its taloned hands and feet all at the same instant, it thrust him backwards as it still flew and smashed him hard against the wall of the temple. The demon immediately began scrabbling away, digging with swift twitching strikes into the body of the debonair pirate. Percy did not have the reflexes to respond to the nabassu's attentions. Within another second the razor sharp talons of the beast from the Abyss had cut through the pirate's jerkin and outer skin. The next couple of tearing scratches of its claws had sliced through his stomach, splashing and spraying blood and guts in an explosive torrent. Then the demon was down to the intestines and bowels and started to throw them out of the cavity it had created and around itself and the room in a reckless manner.

Shocked and stunned at the speed of the attack and the ferocity of its movements, Seton Rax roared and swung his axe hard at the head of the demon. Despite its frenzied clawing and beating wings to steady itself as it held onto Percy, its thin horned head remained completely still, focussed on the killing of the man beneath it. Its feet were grasping at the hips and its talons continued to dig but the head and neck stayed still.

A'Lastor too responded and drove a xyele towards the scaly torso of the beast, heading for where he knew it still had its own vital organs. Seton in the half second it took to make his sweeping blow towards the nabassu was stunned to suddenly see the head twitch to the right at a terrifying speed, instantly stop again and focus its slit like eyes on the face of the barbarian. The nabassu hissed a screech of alien anger just before the axe head made contact with the neck. It was like hitting granite. The sharp heavy blade dug in only a quarter of an inch and the shock of the sudden stop shot up the shaft and caused the barbarian's wrists to crack due to the unexpected halting.

The hissing of the beast turned to a roar but whether in rage or pain Seton never knew. A'Lastor called out a word in his own unknown tongue as the tip of his xyele met the scaled flesh of the demon. With the blade held horizontally the slightly curved sword bit deeply. A'Lastor called the word again and again and shoved with all the ferocity of his own demonic kind. The sharp steel side of the sword gradually cut its way into the body of the beast, leading the blunt side to widen and split the innards of the nabassu. A'Lastor was leaning onto the pommel of the sword, he dropped his other weapon and then had two hands on the hilt, shoving the xyele in further. The demon remained looking at Seton as the steel emerged the other side of its relatively thin frame. Seton looked in horror as the face of the demon contorted into its own version of shock. It understood the words that the others did not. It knew dark magic when it heard it. Its mouth widened to unbelievable size as it cried in pain, still holding the corpse of Percy Fenton against the wall it gave a final beat of its bat like wings. As it died it vomited a gut load of blood, bile and demonic fluids in a broad spray over the barbarian it continued to stare at. Seton was still holding the shaft of his axe, the blade being stuck in the neck, as he received the spewing death throes over his body. 'Not again' thought the barbarian throwing his mind back to when another creature had vomited blood all over him. Then, with its death, Seton watched as the demon fell to the ground. The axe came loose and the nabassu rolled down a couple of tiers, slumping the corpse of Percy Fenton with it, leaving a trail of pirate innards to slip and quiver on the marble floor. A'Lastor had had to leave the xyele in the body of the demon, it was too far in to easily remove, but he reached down for his dropped weapon and then stood to see the barbarian, covered in blood, from the splatter of Fenton and the final gory hurlings of the beast, staring at the ninja garbed A'Lastor in awe.

At the moment the nabassu died, Is-Is, Campbell and Captain Battfin turned with grim faces and advanced on Vixen and Hoarfrost. The giant Ahrioch Horde captain stood nearly as tall as the tip of Is-Is' ears, a formidable veteran of many a battle, he raised his sword. Vixen stood stunned at the devastation she had just witnessed. The demon she had raised should not have been dispatched so simply by mortal foes. She thought she had heard a smattering of immensely dark magic from the figure she did not recognise, but now she had to worry about three well known adversaries.

"Deal with them Hoarfrost," she ordered, a hint of fear creeping though in her voice. She then drew her own dagger in anticipation of another knife fight with Campbell.

"Is-Is, Captain Battfin, you two deal with the giant," said the Master Thief. "Me and Vixen 'ere have got something to conclude."

With that the hare and the vicious captain of 'The Peppercorn' advanced on Hoarfrost. He went to engage them but then violently lashed out with his sword at the dagger of Vixen, knocking it from her hand to clatter to the stone floor. He then. Dropped his sword, grabbed at her mouth with his broad left hand, snatched her arm that had held the dagger and stepped behind her in a pinning move that both painfully half nelsoned her whilst it also muzzled her quiet.

"Take her," he cried. "Take the bitch! Just let me live!"

The three advancing warriors stopped. Sensing a subterfuge but when Hoarfrost continued to hold her and begged again to be let off in return for his mistress it was Campbell who responded with a long and raucous laugh, slapping his thighs and bending double with the exertion. Is-Is and Captain Battfin remained alert though, checking that Hoarfrost did indeed have Vixen held tightly. Campbell continued to laugh. He was finding it hard to breath with the effort. He started to calm himself, stood and wiped a tear of pure enjoyment away from the corner of his eye.

"Excellent," the thief said eventually. "Excellent. Of course. How very fitting that you Vixen should be betrayed at the very last by those you thought would serve you. You crack Vixen. You are going to pay dearly for what you have done. Is-Is gag and bind her. I think she may well have some power in her voice now. That's why he's holding the whore's mouth so tightly shut. Make sure she can't use it or struggle free."

Is-Is nodded and produced some binding leather ties he had in one of the pouches strapped to his body. The big paw of the hare replaced Hoarfrost's hand and as a duo the peculiar pair bound up the struggling High Priestess of the Ahrioch Horde. Vixen had been captured. Seton Rax and A'Lastor, as official bounty hunters, came down, by the ripped remains of Percy Fenton and to the body of the nabassu where A'Lastor heaved out his xyele. Then they took the remaining tiers down and officially received the quarry of Vixen. She tried to struggle a little but Is-Is and Hoarfrost had bound her with exceptional tightness. Seton Rax and A'Lastor had no trouble in moving the body of Vixen in whatever direction they desired. They paused slightly by the body of Fenton and gave his remains a courteous nod. Vixen, despite her own incarceration and gagging, said a curse in her mind against the High Captain of the Pirate League, still vengeful to the last. Together, Seton Rax and A'Lastor, bundled her off up the tiers to begin her trip to 'The Peppercorn' and then onto a deep dark dungeon under Rhyell castle where she would await the outcome of her trial and execution.

Is-Is, Captain Battfin and Campbell waited for them to depart and stood silently in the now gory temple with the last surviving member of the Ahrioch Horde that they knew of, other than the doomed Vixen.

"Thank you for that. Hoarfrost isn't it?" said Campbell, rubbing his chin and looking at the giant warrior. "You made the final bit of the plan a lot easier than it could have been. I was looking forward to the knife fight with her though. I'd been waiting a long time for that. There's no way she would have got a lucky kick in this time. I would have disarmed her and then with a movement faster than anyone has ever seen, leapt behind her, pinned her to the ground and bound her. But you did that all for us now didn't you? Gave her up so you could live. Maybe you thought you were saving her by not fighting? Well that is not the case. You would have done her a better favour if you had of killed her you know. Boy oh boy is she going to suffer for what she has done. But I suspect you know that though."

Hoarfrost stood, stern faced, listening to Campbell and his tirade. Taking in the threat that Is-Is and Captain Battfin still presented.

"So you want us to let you go in return for something I would have been able to claim anyway?" continued Campbell, pacing back and forth. "A reward for your fantastic betrayal of a great betrayer. Unfortunately for you though, old chap, I'm not that keen on those who betray others. No matter whom they have betrayed. I've also lost a fair few friends today and I'm not in a very forgiving mood. I also made a promise that no-one and nothing would survive this day that had any connection to the Ahrioch Horde and Beth Col."

Hoarfrost sensed the way the conversation was going. He made a quick grab for his sword that lay on the floor. Is-Is responded to the expected move and kicked the blade away. Weapons were drawn, Campbell stopped pacing and moved against Hoarfrost with Is-Is and Captain Battfin. The gigantic remaining warrior of the Ahrioch Horde attempted to defend himself with a punch of his massive fist towards the hare who engaged slightly before the others. Is-Is deftly avoided the blow and struck back. Hoarfrost raised his arms in defence but the knives and cutlasses were swift and sharp as all three adventurers fell violently upon him. The three were a blur of vengeful violence. The torches flicked and the calls of the dying man ceased but still the adventurers fought. Memories of Eris, Pavor and Fenton flooded their minds as the blood splattered around them and pooled towards the demonic hexagram mosaic. By the time they had finished their final piece of work, Hoarfrost's corpse looked as indistinct a set of remains as those of Percy's. Is-Is, Campbell and Captain Battfin sheathed their weapons and walked away from the violent vignette. There was no point in recovering any of the bodies of their fallen friends. All were far too mangled either through attentions of the nabassu or the stampede of battle. The ruins of Beth Col would serve fittingly as their tomb.

As they reached the courtyard and caught up with Seton, A'Lastor and their prisoner the remaining pirates had already anticipated their orders and were beginning the destruction of the entire complex. Maybe just short of half their original numbers remained but it was enough of a force to act as a demolition crew. Fire would help bring down the buildings too, already smoke was billowing out of the roofs of several out buildings and pirates were now gleefully entering the central temple of Beth Col to find things to burn there as well. Others were hacking up the wooden watchtowers to place in pyres by the walls where they could burn their fallen comrades while at the same time heating the walls to make the breaking of the stone much easier. Some pirates were laboriously heaving away, with the heavy hammers that had been brought along, at the corner stones of buildings to start the process of complete destruction.

About twenty other buccaneers returned with them to help man 'The Peppercorn' back to Rhyell. Vixen was to be held in the captain's cabin, under a strict watch with always at least two of either Is-Is, Campbell, Captain Battfin, Seton Rax or A'Lastor watching her. The streets of Ende offered up no protection for Vixen. The crowds showed no resistance to the small band of adventurers and pirates who bundled along a gagged and tied, red haired female for purposes of their own. It was just another sight, another violent occurrence, in a city as diverse in its pleasures and crimes as Ende. Whatever was happening it didn't concern the other inhabitants directly, so again they ignored it.

'The Peppercorn' upon leaving the harbour of Ende had many on deck watching a thick column of smoke rising to the heavens from a location few had known before. Beth Col was finally burning and the fires aided the pirates who remained as they fulfilled Campbell's desire that no stone should be left atop another. Beth Col was destroyed.

Chorus Thirteen

Campbell and A'Lastor stood at the prow of 'The Peppercorn' where they could often be found together if either one of them wasn't doing his part in keeping watch on Vixen in the cabin. They had been talking for a while about their adventure and were now discussing the final scene in the last room of the temple.

"Why did that nabassu thing attack Percy so violently?" asked Campbell. "I mean it could have easily have gone for me. I was in the lead when it was released but it just flew straight over our heads and went for Fenton."

"Demons of its type are similar in their outlook to my kind," A'Lastor replied. "It can sense those who have done wrong. It would have seen threats differently to the way you perceive them. Rather than the warrior out in front in an attack against the one who had summoned it, it would see the creature in the room who had done the most wrong, committed the most sin as its main adversary. Who, or what, was most dark in its sight."

"Wow," said Campbell with an expulsion of breath and swiftly pondering the observation. "In the company that was kept in that room? It went straight for Fenton. I sensed no doubt, no dilemma in its deliberations."

"Exactly. He must have done some very bad deeds in his time," replied A'Lastor, looking out to sea stoically. "It didn't even go for me. Another demon."

"Speaking of that my friend. How come Seton could only cleave his way about the width of my finger into the beast and you managed to shove half a yard of cold steel into it?"

"Ah. Nabassu are an extremely tough form of demon. All scaly and leathery and with thick bones underneath. You have to know exactly where to place your blade. Plus I have some other secrets that can help in the dispatching of certain foes. But like I said in the chamber, the thing can be killed if it didn't kill, me, first."

"Very good A'Lastor, I understand. And what about the mist? Has that gone now that Vixen has been captured?"

"It has dulled a little but I still sense her. I will sense her until the very moment I suck down her soul and end her life fully on this material plain. Have you given any more thought as to how I am going to achieve that in full view of the large crowd expected at her execution?"

"Yes, indeed I have. I have an excellent plan that may involve a little disguise and theatricality. I still have to work out very important element of the occasion though. But yes. There is no doubting now that you will get to feed upon the soul of Vixen."

"Then I am satisfied indeed Master Thief," replied A'Lastor.

"I too am satisfied," said Campbell. "Vixen is captured and Beth Col destroyed. We hunted her down swiftly considering the leagues and leagues of ocean travel and that is mainly thanks to you. We would have got her eventually though with the network at our disposal but you certainly sped up the process. But we have lost good companions too. Swiftly taken. Such is the cost of our trade I fear. But, as to the payment of our trade, we will all get our rewards. I suspect that Captain Battfin may do well out of the death of Fenton. Could be an astronomically swift rise through the ranks for him now."

"Yes indeed," said A'Lastor. "There was of course mention of land and titles for the capture of Vixen, as well as the traditional bounty. With three of our party dead and I having no interest in either land, title or gold, I hope your princess will be more generous still in what she bestows."

"I am sure that she will be," replied Campbell. "Especially as the Ahrioch Horde is now destroyed as well."

"Destroyed?" said A'Lastor. "You can not destroy an idea. A faith can not be butchered and buried. Ahrioch himself still reigns in his castle of skulls in the Abyss. He will still desire followers here. And did we kill all of the followers?"

"There was no one left alive in Beth Col when we left," Campbell said slightly hurt.

"And what about the black ship they sailed in?" asked A'Lastor. "We did not find that moored up and empty. What about the servants of Beth Col? I saw only warriors in the dead. What about the priests? I saw only those in the garb of guards. No I would think it an assumption indeed that the Ahrioch Horde is destroyed."

"Well I think that perhaps for the interest of my meeting with Annabella Blaise we should say that the Ahrioch Horde is wiped from the face of Kenai. Or at least the city of Ende. That would probably represent the truth as we understand it. An equivocation that will enable me to stand proud and true," replied Campbell. "Changing the subject a bit, did you get to eat at all while we were at Beth Col? A sneaky soul or too when no-one was looking?"

"Yes as a matter of fact I did," the demon replied. "I wasn't sure how long your legal process might take with Vixen."

"Oh less than a week. Less than a week," Campbell repeated himself.

'The Peppercorn' thrust on northwards. It had a good working sail plan set and caught decent ocean breezes. The sea was not rough and those that could tried to relax as much as time would allow out on the deck as the cabin felt uncomfortable as an improvised brig with Vixen as the solitary prisoner. She was not roughly treated except for when they had to feed and water her. The fear that Vixen may have the ability to use magic meant quite a lot of force was used to ensure she took on nourishment and liquid without being able to talk.

Seton found himself thinking often of Pavor and the love he must have felt for Eris for sometime. Probably from even before they had joined together as bounty hunters. When he was a doorman and she a dancer. The barbarian thought to himself that now it might be time to retire from adventuring as well as from tracking down villains for money. He had lost too many friends now. Too many. He thought back to all his time down dungeons and deserted mines, fighting in ruins and the Old City of Rampart. He listed those who had been killed when on a quest with him. He soon reached twenty and then it was difficult to count any more. On his last two adventures he could number eight. Yes perhaps it was time to take the money and change the usage of his property in Sitka to something more mundane.

Captain Battfin spent all the time he was not on guard duty in guiding 'The Peppercorn' towards Rhyell. His thoughts were mainly with Percy when he did let his mind drift. It was a glorious death for a pirate. Imagine being ripped to death by an avenging demon as your permanent end. So much better than drowning or being taken out by a random arrow or knife in the back. He had atoned for his sins well with such a demise. The legend of Fenton was secured within the pirate community and the huge black pirate, Captain Battfin, would do much to bolster it still further with gregarious tales of his friend.

Is-Is sat mostly in silence. He took more time watching Vixen than any of the others. He knew that she feared him most of all and it was perhaps Is-Is who loathed her the greatest for what she had done to Tumbletick. The hare took great pleasure in doing weapon maintenance close to the red headed traitor, ensuring she constantly had the sound of metal being sharpened slicing through to her mind and imagination.

Vixen herself remained quite calm. She resented the force feedings but understood her captor's intentions. She was bound and gagged and constantly watched so she spent her time in conversation with the soul of Ahriman. With her studies she had found that she could access his consciousness much more effectively. She needed to learn the transference spell from him but it was difficult and garbled. The term, conversation, did not really apply as thoughts could cross between the two but most actual words were indistinct. A strong thought like 'yes' or 'no' was clear but getting the sounds of arcane magic clear was tough. Still she tried. Ahriman understood the gravity of their situation so the two great entities of the Ahrioch Horde worked on getting the understanding across, otherwise it was likely to be their last few days if they could not escape the confines of Vixen's body. So she began to learn the spell that would enable them both to depart her frame, slowly and with difficulty by individual thoughts shaping up the phonemes and syllables of the magic.

'The Peppercorn' ploughed on until the moment came, as it had to do, that they arrived in the capital of Umiat and quickly unloaded their solitary piece of cargo.

Chapter Fourteen

Vixen was slumped against the roughly hewn rock wall of her cell, deep beneath the castle of Rhyell. The kind of dungeon she had sent many to in her time as Head of the Umiat Secret Service. Now she was chained with heavy manacles and her mouth was still gagged. She constantly had two guards in the cell with her as well. She felt the odd tinge of pride that she was so dangerous to the authorities of Umiat that she needed this constant surveillance. It did mean also that there was always a torch burning in the cell and she was thankful that she hadn't been left in the pitch black. She estimated that she must have been here for nearly two days. They had dragged her straight to this location from the docks and she waited patiently for the next stage of the process with contempt. She wondered who it would be that they would send to soften her up. She wondered if she would get a trial or if it was being conducted now and she was not required to attend.

The guards did not talk in her presence and just watched her, watching them. She was growing very stiff and cold with the rock behind her and her arms elongated and hanging in their chains. At least she was in a sitting position with her legs stretched out in front. If she had been forced to stand for this length of time she felt certain that even a strong individual like her would now have collapsed in exhaustion, to hang in even more agony in the restraining chains.

She heard the footsteps and the jangling of keys. Perhaps another changing of the guard, they did so regularly, or perhaps her visitor, come with the tools of his trade. Perhaps the executioner had come to collect her.

The thick door to the cell, made of black wood with a small grilled window had the key inserted. Her guards were always locked in with her as well for added security. The key was turned and the solid sound of the mechanism moving and the bolt retracting from the rock walls seemed deafening in what was fundamentally such a silent cell, deep in the granite beneath the castle. It was so quiet that she could hear the licking of the torch flames and the breathing of the sentries clearly.

The door was opened, it dragged slightly on the floor and had to be jarred hard to enable entrance. The head gaoler came in, a classic of his sort, Vixen had known him once very well indeed. He was a willing participant in interrogations, drank too much and had a sweaty pallid look to him from working too much underground. She often wondered what diseases he carried after inhabiting this realm for such a long career. He didn't look at her but gestured with his head that the two guards should leave. They swiftly did so. No-one it seemed wanted to be in her company for long any more.

The gaoler then brought in some more flaming torches and put them in brackets set into the stone walls. The light increased dramatically to Vixen's eyes. She realised that she had grown very accustomed to the gloom that must have existed before. Then, strangely, he carried in a table, struggling to manoeuvre it through the cell door. He then left and returned carrying in a simple wooden chair with a red velvet seat, studded with brass fixings. 'Someone important to see me then,' she thought.

The gaoler left and into the room walked a cloaked and hooded figure. Hiding their appearance. The door was shut behind the visitor and again the sound came of the key turning in the lock. Under one arm they carried an extremely large and thick leather bound book, brown with ridges on the spine separating areas of gold lettering. She couldn't make out any of the words but knew who carried the tome from a gait she had seen many times before.

'Hello Campbell,' she thought to herself. 'What's this going to be then. Some gloating or a lecture?'

The Master Thief put the book down heavily on the table and took a seat. The table was between the prisoner and him, she was low down, sitting but he could see her clearly and more importantly she could see him, but not the book. He pulled back his hood, she noticed instantly that he and shaved and she laughed to herself. All the time she had known him his inability to grow a beard had been one of his defining features. Scraggly and like a wash of thin black paint. Yet now she noticed that he had removed his pathetic facial hair, probably not for an audience with her though. 'No, he must have been grovelling in front of that slut princess, Annabella Blaise,' again Vixen laughed, this time the restrictive gag could not hide the intended sound and her body shook a little with the delight.

Campbell remained quiet, he did not respond to her amusement. He opened the book and started to leaf through its large crackling pages. She could see that it obviously had great age but due to the height of the table and her position she could not see what the book was about.

Campbell did not say anything. He did not even look at Vixen, he was looking at the book instead with great intensity, savouring some pages, flicking by others swiftly. From the way his head moved Vixen surmised that the work contained a great many pictures.

'Not one for the written word are you Campbell?' she thought to herself. 'Need the pictures to understand the content of the message!'

He continued his investigation of the volume, his fingers lovingly reached to touch it on some pages but pulled away at the last moment. It looked as if he did not want to damage the paper with any oils from his skin or could not dare to touch what was shown there. He did keep turning back, it appeared, to the same page. It looked as if he was gaining a great deal of pleasure from that particular part of the book. Whatever it contained his breathing deepened and Vixen saw that his eyes would lift to appear only as whites and flicker in a state close to ecstasy.

'Perhaps this is just a perversity of his,' she thought. 'Looks at erotic pictures in front of chained up women.'

Then Campbell looked straight into the eyes of Vixen. She held his gaze, he held hers. It was Campbell who looked down first, back to his book. He kept to the page that so intrigued him and was quiet for a long time before he started to flick through the tome again. Eventually he spoke but in a slower and more considered manner than was usual for him.

"You know, that throughout history, man has always tried to find ways of inflicting more pain on his fellow kind. Or to come up with new and more terrifying ways of killing each other. I also find it interesting how some civilisations were terrified of one form of execution, like beheading, whereas other cultures considered it quick and efficient and designed machines to make the process more, accurate."

"And then, my dear Vixen, I find it astounding that every culture that has ever existed has had jobs for people where they have to kill. Be it soldier or assassin or other titles. You can actually take it up a profession and use innate skills and desires to rise through the ranks of that role. Just take the Guilds. They have departments where it is trained. Just as you were trained. And me to some degree. The Thieves and the Assassins are closely aligned and both instruct their members in the art of murder. And then there are certain divisions, the certain lines of work with peculiar aspects such as information retrieval, the implementation of terror where you learn about intimidation, torture and more frightening ways to kill. To kill others to get what you want. All of which you were well versed in. A star of your generation. Famous for it."

Campbell turned again to his book and turned a few more pages.

"And do you know what really amazes me Vixen? No matter how creative you are, how hard you try to be unique, you find that someone, somewhere has already died from the method you thought you'd just come up with. You thought your imagination had developed a new and terrifying way but it has already been done. Nothing is new. I love this book. It is very large and has many, many pages. I have owned it for years now and I relish reading it on the rare occasions that I actually get home to Rhyell. It has been a big influence on me. This book. These wonderfully crafted pages. On each one of these luscious leaves there is a beautiful print from a wooden engraving. It shows various methods of execution and death that have been used through the ages. It's stunning.

Each picture depicted in minute detail. So varied. So creative. Some quite basic and mundane, it must be said, but they have been well used and maybe we have grown accustomed to their methods. Some, however, are quite unique and it goes to prove my point. You can not easily come up with a method of killing another person which has not already been done."

Campbell picked up a large amount of pages and then let them flick through his fingers in a fast ripple of paper. He stopped at random on one of the falling pages and looked at the picture that confronted him in a sepia tone.

"I mean take this one for instance. A large net is hanging from the bough of a massive tree. It is filled with people, caught together like a haul of mackerel. And there are a group of archers just shooting with arrows, into these people as they are all bunched together and unable to escape. Bizarre. Why not just tie them to posts and shoot them? But it has been done and the reference below indicated that two hundred and three years ago it was performed just outside the city of Ve'Tath upon a family group of sheep rustlers."

Campbell started to turn the pages of the book and listed the forms of execution that appeared on each one.

"Stoned to death. Tortured to death. Head crushed by an elephant. Staked out over fast growing bamboo. Disembowelled by a ship's windlass. Raped to death by specially trained dogs. Garrotted, hanged, burned at the stake. The list goes on and on Vixen. Defenestration, decapitation, excoriation, crushed beneath planks of wood with weights, forced to swallow molten lead, drowned in boats chained with other victims to benches. The boats could then be floated again and used on subsequent occasions for another load of the condemned. Death of a thousand cuts, pulled apart by wild horses, strapped to a metal chair and then heated by white hot coals, forced to take poison, walled up and forgotten."

Campbell fell silent for a while as he reached a certain page. He did not pronounce what the picture portrayed.

"So Vixen. All this brings me to the reason I have come to visit you. As part of the reward package for bringing you to justice, those of us who survived got to select, or be bestowed with, certain titles. Some of those titles have real responsibilities. Important duties. Seton Rax for instance had decided to quit adventuring and has been made the Warden of the Northern Marches. Is-Is required no title, he's a noble enough fellow as it is but he has been made Lord Protector. That role is largely honorary and will mean lots of fine dinners and speaking engagements mostly. Seton however will have to motivate and maintain a body of men to bring back some security to the northwest of Umiat from Noatak to Sitka. Captain Battfin has been made Lord Admiral! Can you believe it? He's done well that boy. He has also been announced as High Captain of the Pirate League now that that post became vacant. Again Admiral is largely honorary. We'll all call him it, but we know High Captain is the role he really wanted. A perfect successor to Percy Fenton. My friend A'Lastor, who you met briefly, has taken no reward. His is to come, it seems. And then there was me. What rank and role in society would I take? Well Vixen I have been made something that I will take very seriously. Very seriously indeed. I have been made Lord High Executioner. It was my personal request to become so. And my first service to my country will be to execute you."

Campbell looked down at the page where his book remained open. He was quiet for some time, gently chewing the inside of his mouth and sucking his teeth.

"Well now you know you have been sentenced. I'm sure you're not surprised by the decision. It was a quick trial but we ensured it was a fair one. The evidence was presented extremely strongly and it took less than a minute for the jury to make their decision and the judge to place his black cap on his head. Pleasantly he only stated the time of the execution and the location. I get to choose the method and as we have been discussing we already know how many choices there are. I have to be right in my choice though. Just like the jury, I have to make the right decision. I will be conducting a solemn ceremony on stage. A scaffold has been specially built for the occasion and we are expecting a large crowd to turn out for the event. Posters are being printed and put up as we speak and the word of mouth advertising is just stunning. Top notch. So I have to make sure it works well for all those who have not only turned up for the entertainment but also as a thank you for everyone who has been involved in the process of your capture. From old Phineas Bunch who first spotted you, right down to the gaoler and his guards and all the judiciary who have made the process so quick. I also have to ensure that it is right for you. Something particularly painful and punishing in respect to the level of your heinous crimes and your betrayal."

Campbell again looked down at the page. Vixen sensed that he had almost lost his temper. Here he was labouring the point and trying to be all threatening by remaining calm and menacing. Trying to be cold and he had almost raised his voice. She knew what she was doing though in response to him. She had been doing it since he had entered the room. When captured one should at all opportunities attempt to belittle your gaolers or interrogators when they were unaware of you doing it. You must not openly antagonise them but the little insidious remarks and belittling comments behind their backs helped you with your own confidence and psychological condition. Being gagged made it easier as the thoughts could run through your head. Campbell began speaking again.

"I've already had many people giving me advice on what to do with you Vixen. Some have suggested crucifixion. It is meant to be extremely painful, but it takes too long. The crowd would get bored. We need the denouement at the ceremony itself. Others think that just placing you in a small metal cage, crunched up and hung out until you rot and start falling through the gaps would be good. Again the pain from the cramps is meant to be excruciating and mentally distressing but we just don't have time for that. Some think something poignant would be appropriate. The ancient punishment for traitors was to flay you alive and then, still breathing and in agony, sew you into a sack containing poisonous snakes and vipers. But that doesn't appeal to me somehow. We want to be able to see your face when you die. Plus I don't think that is scary enough. I want you to be scared Vixen. I want you to be on the verge of madness with the terror of what I am going to do to you in two days time in the main square with a vast and eager crowd looking on."

Campbell was beginning to get heated again. He paused and caught his breath.

"Impaling was a good solution I thought. Frightening. Thoughts running through your head about which way we would insert the sharpened stake. Straight through the stomach or back? Up right through you so that it emerges near your neck? I even have pictures here of people who had it thrust down their throat. I mean it has got to hurt and everyone would get a terrific view as you slowly slid down a thick wooden shaft from high in the air when we raised it to the vertical. But would it truly terrify you? I don't know."

Campbell was now searching her gagged face she realised, looking for any sign, any twitch which would tell him he had his solution. He suspected that she was trying to cut out his comments but he knew that that would be impossible. She would have to hear as she was always looking at him when he looked at her, trying to be defiant to the end.

"Now I know that before you planned to sacrifice Tumbletick you had a little conversation with him. You were trying to scare him as you were not allowed to physically torture him. And you mentioned boiling him alive. Does that perhaps scare you? Wondering whether you would be thrown straight away into boiling liquid or being slowly heated from a cold start. The barbarian horsemen of the east would throw failed generals into boiling water and there were times when our direct ancestors boiled those who committed heresy or sacrilege in large metal cauldrons filled with oil, tar and turpentine. There is a reference here to one gentleman who survived for fifteen minutes, boiling and blistering away. But I don't really think the crowd would get a good enough view again. Most of you would be hidden by the metal of the pot."

Campbell looked again at his book on the page which had remained open, revealing the image he kept looking at.

"No, I have decided. We are going to go for something from our distant barbaric past for you. It is something so simple, so elegant that it surprises me it ever went out of fashion. Yes, the decision is made. We are going to get a wooden frame rigged up in the shape of a square. Set up in the middle of the stage. It will be eight foot by eight foot, made of solid rough hewn timbers. You will be taken and fixed to the frame, upside down and naked. Your legs and arms tied to each corner. You will be very tightly spread out and then myself and another executioner will reveal a large two man saw. We will then proceed to slowly drag the jagged metal teeth of the blade through your body from your foul crack to your traitorous head. If we do it right, slow enough, we might be able to keep you alive for several minutes," Campbell began to get heated. "I reckon that should give you something to think about! You're going to die terrified and in agony you cracking whore!"

He was breathing deeply, his voice had risen to a shouting yell of rage with his last sentence. Campbell picked up the book, left his seat and presented Vixen with the page and the image it contained. A simple woodcut of the wooden frame and the condemned hanging within. The two executioners for ever frozen in the act of their first slicing cut. Vixen started to slowly shake her head, her eyes began to widen and Campbell could clearly see the reflection of the torches and the woodcut image in them as her head rocked in fear but her eyes remained fixed on the picture. Campbell slammed the book in her face with a violent abruptness and went to bang on the cell door to summon the gaoler. The door was unlocked and the fat man removed the table and chair from the small room mined from the rock. When the gaoler had cleared the cell of the furniture Campbell turned to Vixen one last time.

"By the way," he stated. "The other executioner, seeing as this is a two man job, is going to be Admiral Battfin. Thought you'd like to know that as well. It should add a certain piquancy for you that it will be the two of us who conduct your execution."

Campbell put the hood of his cloak back up and left the cell. The gaoler sent the two guards back in and then shoved the door tightly back over the ridges of rock that caught it every time and turned the key.

Vixen waited in the cell, her stomach churning at what was planned for her. She imagined the gut slicing pain of the saw's teeth cutting into her from between her thighs. If she could only get the chance she might be able to transfer her soul and Ahriman's into another body. With a vast crowd she might gain access to a weak minded individual and at least continue to exist in some form. But she was well gagged. They never took the gag off, except when they needed to force feed and water her and that did not give any opportunity to speak as a tube was inserted down her throat. No, she was fated now to suffer a terrifying end and all she could do was wait, chained, until they came to collect her.

The door was opened and shut several more times. She gauged time by the changing of her guards. She estimated they were on intense three hour shifts. Vixen fell asleep, fitfully, nightmares stalking her mind. She awakened in a terrible sweat, pain in her eyes and with a cutting headache due to only minutes of actual rest.

Then the door opened and a soldier entered with a long knife brandished and a bucket of water sloshing by his side. The man put down the bucket and approached with the blade. Vixen guessed at what was to occur. No stabbing in the dark to relieve her of her doom. The guard cut away at her clothes and stripped her. She thought about trying to throw herself against the blade and commit suicide but she still had the hope that she might be able to perform the transference spell plus the man seemed cautious of her doing so as he removed her clothing with care. Perhaps if she had managed to cut herself on the knife and died then he would be the one strung up in the wooden frame. While she had been captured there had been no chance for any of the pleasantries of life and Vixen was very much in need of the wash. The man reached into the pail, produced a sodden sponge and proceeded to clean away at the grime and filth from her body. The water was cold and despite the indignity of the cleansing Vixen did feel good to be clean.

The man left after his duties were performed, sheathing his knife and collecting up her cut and ripped clothes. He left the cell but returned shortly with a white silk gown. The two other guards stood, produced keys and cautiously unlocked the chains at the wall which held her arms up. They held firmly on to the metal links and then lifted Vixen to her feet, which were still manacled together. She felt weak, very weak, and her struggles were futile against three much stronger men as they dressed her in the white silk that represented her status as the condemned.

Two figures came to the door. Dressed all in black and with the executioner's hood already worn. They were slightly pointed with only holes for the eyes so their duties could be performed but their features hidden. Vixen however recognised the bulk and frame of one and could see areas of black skin around the eyes and the other figure walked his peculiar way and she would have known the eyes behind that hood anywhere.

"Everything ready?" asked Campbell to the guards and he received a quick affirmative reply.

Campbell led the way, down a rock passageway, up rough stairs to regular corridors lined with stone and many uniform dungeon doors. Vixen caught the sight of figures clutching at the bars to their cells, catching a glimpse of her as she was paraded up through the dungeons.

They soon came out of the prison and into the lower levels of Rhyell Castle. Vixen could already hear the crowd, the low murmur of many far off voices below the great rock on which the fortification and centre of Umiat power was built. She was then taken to a minor courtyard to one side of the castle, close to the royal stables. It was bright out in the daylight and the sudden searing sun burned away at her eyes. She realised how dark the dungeons had been now. Her days of confinement meant she was blinded by the light of day. She felt herself being dragged and then forced up some small steps and then pushed down to sit on a bench. Her eyesight began to return, she could smell horses. She was sitting in an open cart. A common vehicle used to move peasant labourers around or piles of vegetables and hay at harvest time. She was to be shown off to the crowd during her transportation to the platform, the frame and the saw. Her three guards and two executioners sat with her as the cart began to move off, drawn by two horses, side by side. The driver was a wizened old man who sat on a perch like chair above them. She felt like swooning as the cart rocked its way out of the castle and down the snaking winding approach road towards the city of Rhyell. People were already lining the route from the exit and cheered and booed, shaking their fists and throwing verbal abuse at the well known traitor to the realm. As the cart went by the crowd peeled away from their queues and followed in a broad procession, hemming in the cart in an effort to gain a continued view of the transportation of the prisoner as well a great hoped for vantage point for the execution.

Vixen felt her heart pounding. She could feel her body pulse with each beat. The white gown was light and the day was not warm, despite the sun, but she knew she glistened with hot sweat beneath the silk. The cart slowly rounded another bend of the road down from the castle and Vixen took in the full view of the vast crowd in the main square surrounding a raised wooden platform in its centre.

On the scaffold she could clearly see the structure where she was to be fixed. Exactly as Campbell had said it would be. It was just a rough hewn set of logs, eight feet in length, now in the shape of a square. She could see that some additional stabilisation had been added, little legs at angles coming off both sides of the uprights and nailed to the platform itself. Then she saw how in each corner, the trunk had a hole bored through it. The fixing points.

The sound of the crowd rose to a roar of anticipation, they could clearly see the cart, see the figure in white flanked by guards, see the two executioners travelling with the condemned. The horses plodded on, fast enough so that the following crowd had to occasionally break into a trot but always had to move at a fast walk. The metal bands encircling the wooden wheels struck a different note as the cart reached the flagstones of the piazza at the base of the massive rock of granite upon which the castle brooded. Guards in the crowd raised poleaxes to control the eager throng and pushed back the straining mob to allow the cart clear passage to the platform. There was no delay, the horses skitted a bit but took their passengers with otherwise good grace to the shallow ladder leading up to the scaffold. The cart came to a stop. The crowd was in a whisper now, a quiet before the jeering and cheering would begin. The two executioners jumped down from the cart and were the first to climb up the steps. One was quite small but his immediate assistant was vast, broad and bulky with obvious muscles under his black clothes. The crowd broke into great cheers as both men gave a wave to the audience. They then turned their attention to the frame of wood, pushing on it to check that it was firmly locked in place, they checked some coiled ropes nearby and picked up some thick leather straps that had metal loops attached to them.

Then nine more men climbed onto the platform who had been milling around the base. Four were also all dressed in black, like executioners but with frills and tassels flowing off their clothing. They also carried musical instrument. One held a lute, another a drum and two held small pipes, one a high pitched flute and the other looked so small it must be a piccolo. These were the Jesters of Death that had been advertised on the posters. Musicians and dancers ready to mock Vixen and then play so the crowd had some additional depth to their entertainment.

The other group of four were all executioner's assistants. They were wearing hoods and black leather trousers but were bare from the waist. All were muscular men and had been oiled up for the occasion. They were here to fix and hold the ropes in place.

The remaining man was the town crier. He had on a black cloak with a black fur trim for the event but underneath he was in his traditional blue and red garb. With his famous beard and hat of office he was a well known figure to the people of Rhyell. He started to ring his bell, firstly in huge vertical swings and then in quicker tones as he shook the bell in rapid twitches above his head. The crowd hushed.

"People of Umiat," he bellowed with sonorous authority. "You gather here today to see justice prevail. Raven Hill, the traitor, otherwise know as Vixen, has been captured, tried, found guilty and sentenced to death. You will all bare witness as the traitor is to be severed by the saw. Take heed and hearken to my words. This will now be the sentence to all who would conspire, plot and act against the state."

The crier finished his announcement and left the stage, his plump clumps on the steps a banging drum roll as precursor to the next stage of the act.

Vixen was now grasped by two of her guards, she struggled as she was dragged to the edge of the cart and was passed down to the third of her protectors. She shook her gagged head and tried to fight but she was secured well and the officers who handled her were strong and experienced in grips that caused pain if you resisted and forced movement to be where they desired you to go.

She was half carried up the steps and found her self on the platform hearing insults from some members of the crowd but also calls to hush. The low rumble of indistinct conversation in mumbled tones was a constant noise though. The guards started to remove the metal bindings and chains that had remained on Vixen. As each was removed one of the executioner's assistants replaced the manacle with the leather straps that were ready for her. Her chains at her feet were taken away carefully. Her legs were held firmly in case she tried to kick out. Again Vixen struggled but to no avail or damage to the men. The bands were attached to each ankle and wrist. She was highly aware of every sensation now, the leather felt soft after the hard chains had cut into her but she knew their broad design and tough material was just as restricting as the metal links and would not break but hold her more firmly in place. Next came the ropes, one per limb. The black tarred end of each was inserted through the eye of metal attached to the leather straps and pulled a long way through it. Vixen was screaming in her gagged mouth and tried to pull away to make the threading more difficult but the assistants prevailed and soon all of the bare-chested executioners had a rope each which they pulled and adjusted so that the exact middle was at the metal ring of the bindings. Then in turn they approached the wooden frame and put the two ends of rope that they now held in their hands through the prepared holes. They took the two ends of rope when it emerged and dragged it along to a corner of the stage. They started to pull up the slack and Vixen was dragged closer to the wooden rig. The sense of drama in the crowd rose. Vixen stood still in her white gown. She was now prepared. The ropes led from her to the frame in such a way that the crowd, and she, knew that when they were pulled tight she would be hoist to within the centre, hung, spread eagled, upside down and ready to receive her punishment.

Vixen was breathing very heavily. Her three guards, seeing that she was now secured left the stage. Four men held the ropes at each corner of the platform, four black dressed jesters were bounding about making obscene gestures to the crowd and receiving laughs when they did so. The two executioners stood still for now. The assistants were ready. The victim was ready. The jesters were warming up the crowd. It was all going well. Vixen however was growing desperate, were they going to leave her gagged? Unable to scream properly let alone to perform dark magic.

Then Vixen saw the saw. It lay inconspicuously. Just resting next to the lower horizontal beam of the frame. It was perhaps two yards in length, dull grey with hundreds of double set metal teeth all along it. At either end it had large wooden handles, big enough for two strong hands to grasp through, riveted securely to the long cutting blade. It was just a simple log cutters tool and could cut through a tree, with a little effort. Vixen felt sure she would faint but she must now retain her courage, if nothing else. No-one would have thought her a coward for struggling a little as they had prepared her, would they? Now there was nothing she could do. She must remain defiant and appear strong.

The jesters stopped their routine and took up position standing still in a line. The smaller of the two executioners approached Vixen and pulled a knife from his belt. She recognised it immediately of course. It was the long dagger that Campbell fought with. They had had a brief duel together in Beth Col and Campbell had used this blade to fight then. Campbell took the knife and started to cut away at her gown. He could have just ripped it off, it was so delicate, but using the dagger meant something to him and to Vixen. She knew she was defeated as he stripped her bare but left the gag in place. Campbell turned to the crowd, ripping the gown into smaller shreds and throwing it to the audience who reached and jumped and strained and moved like a thick liquid to try and claim a memento of the day.

Vixen was naked before the crowd. Her stunning body that she had used so often to get what she wanted was now on display to the vast horde of onlookers. She had enough flex in the ropes to move her hands and arms a little to cover herself slightly, but it was not enough to totally hide her voluptuous charms.

Finished with the flinging of the torn garment, Campbell gave a nod to the assistants and Vixen felt the ropes beginning to pull on her. She lost her balance and fell onto her back as her legs were pulled out from under her. Her arms began to be stretched above her head and her legs rise and separate. She felt herself being pulled fully upside down, her head hit the lower bar as she was hauled up into the centre of the frame and then stretched with the tension of the ropes into a cross. The pain in her arms and legs grew as the four assistant pulled the ropes fully taut.

The crowd began to shout again, eager to see the blood letting begin. Vixen looked strangely deformed as her nude body hung upside down. She prayed to Ahrioch to receive her and to prepare her for the pain.

Campbell lifted the saw and displayed it to the crowd. A great roar went up as it flexed and wobbled. The black jester with the drum began to beat it in the classic roll of announcement of execution. Campbell passed the other end of the saw through her legs to Admiral Battfin who grasped the handle firmly.

They lowered the blade, slowly, between her thighs, the easiest part to start the bisection of the traitor. Vixen closed her eyes tight, she was still gagged, she could feel the points of several of the teeth touching her intimately.

Campbell looked too at the teeth lightly dimpling into her soft flesh. Under his hood he had a determined expression to his face. Now he was here, he realised that this was going to be both difficult and welcome. A conclusion for her sins. He let go of the handle, the saw, still held by Admiral Battfin sunk a little deeper into her from its weight, the teeth pressed in hard where they touched. Campbell, bent down and started to reach behind Vixen's head. She was facing him and opened her eyes to look again into his. Campbell was untying her gag, he pulled it out and still bent over flung it into the throng of people nearby.

"Let's play a little game Vixen," he whispered loud enough for her to hear but covered by the beat of the drum and the roar of the crowd. "I reckon I have guessed at your secret. Let's see how good you are. See if you can do what Ahriman did with a couple of arrows in him before Egremont lopped of his head. You can start now if you like. I start when the drum stops."

Campbell stood smartly up and grabbed the handle on his side. He could hear Vixen beneath him start with the strange arcane language Ahriman had used as his final words. A bead of sweat trickled beneath his hood towards his own neck.

The drum roll stopped.

Campbell was first to pull on the saw as Admiral Battfin pushed. Vixen was cut deeply, felt shocking pain but with immense control did not scream out but continued with her swift and precise incantation.

The jesters started to dance and play their instruments.

The second stroke dug deeper still. The executioners wanted to keep the action light to prolong the agony but the teeth were sharp and sank in as they cut. The crowd was roaring in hatred and delight. Still Vixen did not scream. Another bead of sweat formed on Campbell's brow.

The end of the third stroke came and they reached the bone of the pelvis. The handle was close to the chest of Campbell. The teeth had just begun to slice neatly in to the bone. Vixen let forth a massive raging yell of agony. The piecing quality hit notes of pain unknown to most.

At the back of the vast attendance a tall hare turned away and began his two day walk to a castle that he knew of where a little man also brewed some excellent beers. The hare knew the sounds of death throes. He had no desire to see the conclusion of the ceremony. A little hut waited where he could sit with a friend around a campfire, eat roasted meat, drink and tell tales of his recent adventures.

The fourth stroke struggled with an entire length of cutting bone and the two executioners had to adjust their strength and force for the fifth and sixth efforts as well. Beneath them Vixen was convulsing, putting pressure on the ropes in her excruciating distress. The assistants pulled harder to keep her in place as she tugged them in her agonies.

A barbarian also turned away. His gold for the capture was already deposited in the Rhyell branch of his bank. He had to get back to Sitka. This time a carriage would take the newly appointed Warden of the Northern Marches. He had much work to do and he could concentrate better sitting in comfort than walking all the way. He couldn't face a completely mundane existence. As Warden he would get to lead a large group of men in the cleansing of his territory from brigands and other scum. It was a change in direction for the authorities, but who better to lead the new force than a bounty hunter who had succeeded in capturing Vixen?

The seventh and eighth cuts got through the pelvis but the ninth cut too deep as the executioners judged wrongly and pushed too firmly. The saw cut deep, very deep and swiftly, through her lower abdomen and intestines, blood erupted in a gush covering the men in black and many in the front row of the crowd. Happy faces turned to each other displaying the splatterings received from the traitor with pride. Vixen's ordeal was not yet over, her sufferings were worse than many she had inflicted and she cried out so loudly that everyone heard her final screams. The assistants struggled now to keep her tight as the executioners worked on the tenth cut. It was the merciful one, slicing with no effort into her stomach, Vixen lost consciousness. The mess was atrocious, great clumps of innards began to be dragged out with each pull and blood was gushing everywhere. Vixen may still be alive but she wasn't aware of anything now.

Campbell cursed. She was supposed to feel this for far longer. However there was no stopping now. The jesters were dancing frantically, one of them was hungry, the crowd was roaring its approval and the job had to be completed.

"Guide it straight," shouted Campbell and made a small adjustment. They were on the left hand side of the spine and the jagged bone began to jar at the saw. The pelvis had been easy enough to get through but the spine at this angle acted like knots in poor quality tough wood.

Extra effort was again needed as they reached the sternum but here was the prize moment for the activity. Campbell looked down and saw the heart revealed. It no longer beat. He reached into the cavity and ripped out the lump of muscled meat. He raised it in his fist to the crowd. He heard the yells of appreciation from the rabid throng and then he threw it to the floor at the feet of the jester with the piccolo. The black garbed musician danced a little jig and then seemed to play a solo tune just for the organ which lay before him.

The work with the saw increased in effort as they made their way through the chest. Two of the assistants lost their footing a bit when, with their pulling, the corpse began to tear. The extra effort from the work paid off and the saw cut quickly through one side of the neck. The body, now cleaved, instantly sprung to the sides, hitting each upright beam. The halves slopped out contents for a good while, puddles forming on the stage, the crowd roared with satisfaction. They had thought that perhaps it would last longer but she was merely a soft and tender woman who was quite small. Maybe the next traitor would be a tough six footer who would take a couple of minutes.

The executioners dropped the blood sodden saw and then firmly shook hands through the gap of the frame between the halves of Vixen. They then turned and approached the steps that would carry them back to the castle and the room, given over to their preparations, where their day clothes and real identities waited.

Meanwhile the jesters finished their dancing and tunes and the crowd began to disperse to fill the nearby pubs and restaurants of Rhyell.

The assistants lowered the remains and began to butcher up the pieces so that they could be sent to the four corners of the country. The head was for the battlements of Rhyell Castle and a specially prepared, extremely long spike.

The couriers who transported the arms and legs were already waiting nearby with their attaché cases designed for the job. The cases were air tight and held of putrefaction which was needed as the men had long journeys ahead of them. So they would head off immediately as they were handed a limb. Enclosed in the weather beaten leather cases, they rode with pride, swiftly to their destinations so that justice could be seen to have been done by other inhabitants of Umiat.

One of the jesters, instead of packing up with the others, also clambered in to the cart. The one who had played his piccolo to the heart. The horses pulled and the wagon rumbled off for its short trip back to the winding approach road of the castle. Cheers of 'congratulations' and 'well done' were thrown to the executioners and jester as they sat in the cart from those in the crowd who drifted by them.

They themselves did not talk. They just sat, in silence and considered all that had just occurred and how now Umiat was safer than it had been for a long while and that a bounty had been well and truly collected.

Chorus Fourteen

Admiral Battfin had changed out of the soaked executioner's gear quickly. He said his goodbyes to Campbell and A'Lastor and set off for the docks and 'The Peppercorn'. He was not one for long farewells and he suspected that their paths may well cross again. He wanted a decent jaunt at sea with no particular place to go other than where his sails took him. Although he had enjoyed today, being at sea was a much more pleasant proposition.

A'Lastor removed his mask when the large pirate left. The room was small, a little antechamber that had been put aside at the top of the prison for executioners to use before and after their work. Campbell was nearly changed as well, into some anonymous travelling clothes, the pile on the floor between them would be for a servant to dispose of.

Campbell now fully dressed looked down at the demon who was sitting on a low wooden bench, uncharacteristically he had not crossed his legs in his usual repose but leaned forward on his knees, feet firmly on the floor.

"Well?" said Campbell. "Was there a soul for you to eat?"

"No," replied the demon slowly. He looked up into the thief's face.

"What? You're joking! There is no way she talked for as long as Ahriman did with his final words."

"There wasn't a soul," A'Lastor continued. "There were two."

"Excellent," Campbell gave a little whoop as well. "I bested her in the end but gave her a fighting chance."

"Yes two. Another resided within her and it was released as well when you threw me the heart. A dark black and corrupt feast for such as I."

"Ahriman," stated Campbell. "We suspected as much. Correct again. No wonder he didn't do much with the arrows in his legs. Just the arcane mutterings and a leap into Vixen's body before the lopping off of his head."

"Yes Ahriman," said A'Lastor. "It was superb Campbell. Succulent and rich. Extremely fine. I will never taste its likes again. Vixen was immensely pleasant too. Full bodied."

The demon laughed at his own joke, a clear peeling sound of utter joy, almost angelic in its nature. Campbell smiled too. No other mortal had ever heard A'Lastor laugh.

"Well what are you going to do now then? Seton has become Warden of the Northern Marches and is going to close the business. Back to freelance bounty hunting or back to Hell?" asked Campbell.

"Well if I am to stay it must be the bounty hunting," replied the demon. "Although I do fancy a change. What I really do is assassination by any other name, as I only take jobs where death is sanctioned and a payment involved."

"Why don't you come and work with me then?" asked Campbell with a broad smile. "I've got tons to do in that line of work. I like the way you operate. I know your secret and I suspect the ones I've still got to learn will only be beneficial to me if you are on my side."

"An assassin and an executioner," said A'Lastor nodding his head.

"An assassin and a thief," Campbell replied in correction. "I think I'll give up the title of Lord High Executioner to somebody else now. Besides the Guild might think that it is a conflict of interest, or something. What say you then? Come and work with me."

"I say yes. I'd like that Campbell. I'd like that very much indeed."

"Excellent," said Campbell and extended his hand to seal the deal.

With that the two smiled in friendship and respect. They shook hands over the pile of blood soaked garments and formed a bond that would forever be talked about in the continents of Umiat and Kenai.

THE END